Praise for

Cold in Earth

'A quietly chilling account of the destruction of a family. The story unfolds in the journals of some of the people involved . . . It's a difficult technique to employ successfully, but Melissa Jones has brought it off with deceptive ease.' *Sunday Telegraph*

'A near-brilliant first novel . . . The work here is meticulous: bleakness embraced and transmuted into drama by a writer at the top of her craft.' *Kirkus reviews*

'Jones's subject . . . is compelling, and her writing clear and intense.' *Saturday Times*

Sick at Heart

'Grimly compulsive.' *Helen Rumbelow, The Times Metro*

'The language is beautifully chosen to show the damaged mind of Alex as he really is, in a story that will haunt and disturb.' *Birmingham Post*

The Hidden Heart of Emily Hudson

'The psychological tension subtly takes hold of the reader and does not let go. This is a wonderful novel, and it will not disappoint.' *Freya McClelland, The Independent*

'No ordinary piece of Victoriana . . . Jones (sister of the equally talented Sadie) has taken a novelist's liberties with the life of [Henry] James's cousin, Minny Temple, who died at twenty-four . . . She was passionate and ambitious . . . In this novel she is given the life she deserved.' *Kate Saunders, The Times*

'Jones skilfully moves her heroine from freewheeling and childlike to cautious and deceptive and back again, and when the happy ending comes, it feels organic and hard won.' *Publisher's Weekly*

'An elegant, persuasive and engrossing novel.' *Fay Weldon*

'A beguiling erotic read . . . written in the vein of a classic novel and inspired by the life and writing of Henry James.' *Glamour UK*

March 2026

Ben

Gone For A Soldier

with good wishes

Melissa Jones

Melissa Jones

Published by The Authors' Collective.

ISBN 978-1-0685273-1-9

theauthorscollective.com

For my children

Contents

'Civilisation is hooped together, brought
Under a rule, under the semblance of peace
By manifold illusion.'

W B Yeats

Part One

I couldn't breathe after you died – as if by finally squeezing the life out of you I'd killed myself.

And then it came in pants like choking or retching and I couldn't look at you. We had always existed in one another's eyes – impenetrable and yet connected. Inside each other we forgot we were alone. I was terrified to look at you because that light wouldn't be in your eyes any longer and that sombre light which promised oblivion, extinction, even joy. It's not a pretty story. But it's ours.

I didn't leave you there though. After you killed me – you left me for dead without a backward glance. I don't think it was a question of love, although that word was often used. It was a question of ownership.

At that moment I felt like an animal. You know those images of the lion and its kill – they stand casually by – they don't look at it. I always thought it was disdain – the prey didn't merit the predator's attention any longer – but what if it's horror; after the excitement – the intensity of the chase there's a moment of disconnect – when the lion realises it's alone. I felt so alone without you. Except I'm not a lion – if anything that was always you. You had so much courage. And we weren't on some plain in the African wild; we were in a little English wood. I'm sorry this is blurry but whenever I write about you I cry.

There wasn't any blood. I always thought a crime of passion would be bloody. Ours was all holding on tightly and not letting go.

I've never liked woods. Always thought they were creepy. Ever since Hansel and Gretel, ever since Red Riding Hood, even Jemima Puddleduck – who always was a bad sitter. Except for when there are bluebells – or shafts of light in springtime – and when you are with someone you trust. Then they promise something. Then they are about discovery and not fear. So I waited next to you. Your head was at the foot of the tree. I waited on the ground just a few inches from your legs that were always so strong. I wanted to touch you but I was afraid you would be getting cold, and then I would truly know you were no longer there. And I couldn't bear that. I would have talked to you but I was afraid to do that too. I closed my eyes and waited, waited for them to come. You see it on TV, grainy unfocused overhead shots – fast, almost titillating – the roped-off area, the cars parked at an angle, vague figures with no faces discovering all too imaginable things. Or the cop show or thriller – quick victim shot, or sly implied victim and close-up of the anguish of the detective whose inner pain is somehow larger – who sees and comprehends all – in all our steads. And then they solve it, solve the penetrable crime, sacrificing their own peace of mind so we can go to bed.

But in real life, no one came. Real life has always surprised me. Light dwindled through the dark September trees, the sky luminous then fading, the noises from creatures grew. The woodland floor was damp. Through all the heat of that appalling summer, I had been wearing a little red cotton dress. But now it was September – and I could no longer bare myself. So I wore my jeans. You always liked those. You used to stroke them. But still, I was cold. I put my arms around my knees and rested my cheek on my hand and stayed closed. You can stay closed for quite a long time when you know the trick. They might officially call it shock or an altered state but it's simply only hiding.

Your lost face filled the space behind my eyes. The first photograph. The image I always had of you, and cared deeply for, because it was the first – like the one you have of the child in your womb. The heart had said, 'That's a face. That's a beautiful face.' Not in perfection – although there was symmetry – just so much in the eyes – large and dark and with that light; eyes that had seen so much, it looked like suffering, but still were hopeful – a beautiful narrow nose and a mouth quite thin, a little set, a comprehending half smile. That's a face, I both thought and felt to myself. It was moving to look at – it had so much life in it – experiences I wanted to hear about. Most people in selfies look ordinary and clumsy, and most you meet online look like murderers or taxi drivers whose car you wouldn't want to get into, but your face had promise. A decisive, strong, sensitive face. And because you talked so much to me – at least at the beginning – I never had a chance to say these things to you, and now our time is gone. Back then – a little over a year before killing you – I wanted to know your story.

I waited with my eyes closed next to you for a very long time – remembering. Also because you had always told me what to do I was very unsure of the plan. You always had a plan. I'd shifted so my back was to the tree. I don't know how long I waited with my eyes closed. It was like hide and seek when I was little, waiting with eyes closed before you go and look for them, or is it when you're hiding and they are looking for you? We were in a game of hide and seek, I think – I can't be sure. The sounds disappeared. I felt it must be near dark, knew it was cold.

At last, little hunched and broken predator that I was, the frightened murderer of my beloved soldier, trembling with my back to you – and hoping you wouldn't frighten me too much, wouldn't be slumped or a strange colour or stiff or not your beautiful self – I summoned the courage to turn – opened my eyes to the gloaming, lifted and turned my head towards you. But you weren't there. Not where I'd left you. I could see no glimpse, only leaves on the forest floor, vague like feathers. There was an imprint in the leaves but it was very faint. All my body was on fire with sickness and terror and I spun frantic in a three-hundred-and-sixty-degree blur. I remember closing my eyes again like someone going into cold water so I could try to remember what was real and what was in my head. Perhaps I had edited out – deleted – or merely lost – some time. I am a good editor – it's how I erase and correct mistakes. I like things to be perfect on the page. I opened them again. Still only the emptiness of the leaves. I must have wandered from the spot. But no that was wrong. The leaves were flattened. The impression of your body there. You had gone. I was alone in the wood with you, you alive – a trained soldier who could have killed me. I should have felt terror. All I did was howl with loss.

'I killed him. We were in the wood.'

'I think you better start from the beginning.'

This police officer's use of English was shocking. But I decided not to correct her to 'you'd.'

And anyway it was useless to say I don't know how to start and I don't know where the beginning is. It all seemed very shabby – the table and the room, one woman standing, the other sitting; the uniforms, the tape recorder – the sadness. I remember thinking: Is anybody in real authority going to come? Do I have to do this on my own? Did I say it or just think it? I don't remember. But I did try. I tried to be clear.

'I came here in my car from the wood where I killed him.'

I have no memory of the drive. Leaves perhaps and low cold sun.

The woman opposite me was wearing greasy eye make-up. Also green. It had been a green day. She did not have kind eyes. She did not have eyes that glowed like yours. She gave a short sigh as if she'd much rather be talking to someone else. In that we were united. I was suddenly very angry – or was it tired? – and I missed you.

'Which wood?'

I didn't know. I'd merely followed your directions. Or had you followed mine? Again the information could not be retrieved. Memory retrieval compromised, as they say in education. Seek other ways of processing information. Make a referral to Special Needs.

'Who is this person? Was this person threatening you? Were you attacked? Are you hurt?'

These questions were spaced out because I was unable to answer. They were also the most important questions –

the only questions that had ever truly existed – between you and me. When she leaned towards me I flinched – instinct obeyed. 'Why didn't you just call the police? Why turn up here?' This seemed to me to be a very odd thing to say. A strange question even to someone in an altered state. The fact that you were dead was surely the key takeaway from my opening sentence. And here I was, after all, talking to the police.

But then of course you couldn't be dead. I had to be lying.

I found that fixing my eyes on the high louvred windows with their glimpse of the sky helped. 'Because there's no signal on my mobile or perhaps it was in the car', but then I faltered – realising. 'I don't know why.' I had arrived at that little police station car keys clutched in my hand. I could feel the painful indentations in my flesh. They must be back in my bag now – held securely on my lap. Where I had rested your head for such a short time.

The uniformed one stepped forward and whispered in the ear of the one across the black scratched table where we were sitting in that room painted institution green. It was such a subdued room for a place that held so much pain.

'If you killed him, then can you tell me where we can find him?' This time green eye makeup woman did not sigh but glanced away from me. It was clear she did not believe in even a part of me and thought I was a time waster but what confused me was thinking about who would ever waste their time in such a way.

The uniformed one left the room. We were alone.

'Can you please try, please try and tell me?' She sounded quite irritated and bored. Perhaps she didn't believe me and thought I was just mad. I realised I'd just had that thought. That was the trouble with my thoughts. I could have them again and again. I looked at her mouth. It too was smeary.

I did try. I tried again even though my mouth was dry

and I was so weary.

'He's dead. I killed him. He's somewhere in the wood.' And then like a child, eyes wet, eyes dry, 'I'm very sorry about what I did. Very sorry indeed. Because I loved him very much. And of course, what I did was wrong.' The dialogue was stilted I felt – it needed rewriting.

The mouth was moving. Whether to look at the mouth or the eyes wasn't much of a choice. And I was clearly made to have a caged angry voice and weeping eyes at the same time. 'Clearly'. That was another word of yours. You loved it, just as you loved 'seriously'. Oh how you loved that word. If a person invades your mind it is often true you hear their voice as well as think in their words.

She said again, very slowly, 'What is his name?'

Monosyllables provide emphasis. That's what I always teach my students.

'His name is . . .' I couldn't say it. It seemed too great and private a thing. I looked at the cup of water. I hadn't noticed it before. It's extraordinary how one thing can dominate the vision. I worried that although white and therefore pure it was plastic and that its broken ridges would wash up on a beach somewhere where there were turtles and weeds.

'Let's try again. Is he known to you? This man?'

I looked into her eyes – I noticed they were grey and weary if eyes can be weary – this time I looked with conviction – and concentrated very hard, just as you always did. Rob. Your name was Rob.

'Yes. He's known to me. His name is – Robert Fordham.' I held my breath. I think she sighed.

She ducked her head to write it down. 'Can you spell that for me?'

I did.

She looked up, closed the notebook, narrowed her eyes. How must I have looked to her – deranged, disarranged, from nowhere, out of nowhere, crazed. Dark long tangled hair – dark eyes – for I am the dark-eyed monster – stained mouth from the berries that we'd eaten: a witch. Witches lie awake and in wait in the woods. Or was it that they huddled, like me? I closed my eyes again and thought about your name.

Your name had always been a tremendous comfort to me. I say without irony it meant the world to me. Whenever I was confused troubled and alone. Just the thought of it, the sound of it. Robert Fordham. Rob. First Private, then Corporal, then Captain, then Major then Lt. Colonel. It was solid. It was of the greatest substance. It stood for so much in my mind. It had certainty and authority – you had forded danger with the open vowels, closed out weakness with the consonants. It was you.

'What's your middle name?' I'd said.

'Benedict.' Benediction. My deliverance from evil. You'd claimed me.

'Do you have a home address for this individual?' You used to say that. This individual. I always thought it was. Individual to you, that is. But no – it is what the army and the police say as if it marks out the one evildoer from the crowd. But there is no mark. No mark that anyone can see. I was back in the room with my questioner.

'He never gave me one.'

'How long did you know him?'

'A year. Just over a year.'

'And you didn't think that was strange?'

At that point I didn't know how much to tell about you – always there was the fear, or certainty, that you would outwit me and take everything away.

'I have the handkerchief he gave me. That's how you'll know he's real. DNA or something?' Why was I going on about the handkerchief? This wasn't *Othello*.

'Did I suggest to you he wasn't real?'

'No.' But he isn't. Not really. I said this to myself.

Because if they knew I knew that you were lying, it would make me as crazy as you. And, 'It was the only thing he ever gave me. Apart from the seduction presents.'

'What were they?'

I said nothing. I didn't want her to know. Beware Greeks bearing gifts.

'Where are they now?'

'I don't use them. I've kept them though.' Even though I knew they were not freely given; they were marks on my flesh.

I took out the handkerchief from where it was folded in my pocket.

'How did you come by this?'

'He gave it to me, when my – when my –'

At that point I was utterly unable to speak. Or even see. Something happened.

'Have you washed it?'

'Yes. I washed it before he left me. I was going to give it back to him today but I found I – couldn't.' I showed it to the woman, who ignored it. 'So is it useless?' It had been ironed – and was folded, flat, in a square. It was red – the white polka dots telling of a far-off time, the paisley border of another: whole centuries of gentlemen. Gentlemen who rammed themselves into women against trees.

'You say you killed him in the wood. How did you kill him? Or try to? What with?'

'I had a knife. A penknife. In the picnic basket. Richard – my brother – gave it to my son for Christmas – you know – so he could be a real boy.' That was a joke between Pip and I – Pinocchio – but she wouldn't know that. 'He didn't like it though, so I put it in the kitchen drawer.'

She eyed the other woman who had reappeared. 'Your son is how old?'

'Nearly fifteen now.' She didn't say, impressionable age,

or I don't believe you, or boys will be boys, or anything. We weren't having a conversation.

'Where is the knife now?'

'I don't know. Somewhere in Rob I think.' I felt very sick all of a sudden. Very sick.

'Maddie? Do you mind if we call you Maddie?'

'Not at all.'

'Could you take us to this place in the wood?'

'I could. I think I could. But I – he's gone now. That's why I came here.'

'Are you saying he got away? Then how can he be dead?'

'I don't know. I just know I killed him.' I held very tightly to the handkerchief, while trying to preserve its folds. I kept my eyes shut very tight and I began to rock.

'All right I'm going to terminate this interview now. You've given me no choice. You've offered me no real description, no evidence, no name.' She glanced up at the clock. But I had given your name. I was sure of it. I had given your name.

'But you can't stop this. Please. Look there's blood on my hands.' I showed them to her again, spread them out. They were white and clean. 'You must understand though. It was in self-defence.' While I had already begun to feel disgusted with myself and my lying, I also felt it important you be found and held accountable for what you'd done. That was the whole point.

'Self-defence? Why? What did he do to you?'

How could I begin to explain? 'He left me.'

I wanted to scream but I couldn't. I made some sort of noise. When I was quieter one of them said, and her voice was very close beside me, I think she might have been kneeling there, 'Who can we call for you? Is there someone you'd like us to call?'

But that would be you of course. You could take charge

of any situation. That's what the army was for.

It was very quiet outside. Blackest night by then I think. Screech owl and all that. I could see nothing through the louvres. When I was quieter they took swabs, fingerprints – for some reason I was reminded of handprints in kindergarten – Pip's proud face handing out the rough sugar paper towards me when I collected him from nursery – holding my hand. I checked my statement. Stared at it and tried to understand.

Name: Maddie Vane. Date of birth: more than half a century ago, marital status: divorced, domicile: London (rented flat). Occupation: teacher/tutor (former actress and writer) mother to one child (dependent/descendant). Income: pitiful, slender, insecure, terrifying, future defying, haunting, shaking, horrifying. State of soul: wandering and alone. Literary and social status: fallen from grace. Optimism: either unshakeable or destroyed. Dreams: inescapably romantic; belief in a happy ending wavering, hope flickering, sense of humour, almost gone. You get the general idea. I can use many voices. How many voices can you use?

They called Paula. I felt guilty because she lives outside London – the other side – closer to the sea – and she works hard and it was late and far to come and she would have to take time off but still she was the only one I could call. She is the only one who knows it all.

Then they left me in the interview room – thank god they didn't put me in a cell.

While I waited I retreated to my mind, which I share with you.

Back again to the first photograph – the image I always had of you because it was the first – like the first image you have of the baby in your womb – did I say that? – you carry it everywhere – the shadow of possibility – a promise – and it means everything to you. Into the cold cold water I was in when I found it. Into the fear. Only now do I understand how much trouble you must have taken with that picture. I saw it – the image – the picture – you – on a website, just scrolling through. People talk about the curse of internet dating but you never actually think you will be taking your life in your hands. Or putting it in someone else's – particularly if you are intelligent and educated and all the things I'm supposed to be. But I have a fatal flaw. Is it innocence or insanity or both? Are they the same?

I'd tried to take the pseudo historical approach to deal with the loneliness or fear or shame the idea of this marketplace inevitably brought. I'd think how many matches had been made in absentia in all the thousands of years across all the countries and seas and terrains and mountains of the world. All the colours on the hand-painted maps. Your picture was like a painting – an illumination – stained glass. A miniature. In another time that is what it would have been. I'd have held it and studied it and carried it in my hands. Secured it on a chain around my neck.

We messaged on the site. You didn't play any waiting games. I liked that.

'Carrots or peas? you'd asked. 'What's your favourite?' I

was touched and charmed by this. Simple. Not either boring or obscene. Almost childlike. Certainly original. I later found that this questionnaire is an opening online gambit which anyone can Google from anywhere in the world.

'Ooh it depends', I'd replied, feeling flattered. Trust me to weigh the question up and submit an essay.

I'll tell you about it again now, Rob. In case you have forgotten. You liked it when I told you about things. It was late summertime. August overburdened the garden and leaves were already burnt at the edges, flowers drying and preserved for lack of water. I have – am the tenant of – a large garden which I call the field, with a great tree at the end of it. I think of it as Bonnard's tree after the one he painted that was a thick skeleton of black with bright boughs and white blossom that held all the seasons in one, that represented the tree of life knowledge and death and made me cry when I saw it in the Tate Gallery because it was as immediate as an electric shock, lightning illumination or kiss. The reality was that the grass was never cut because uneven weed-ridden turf broke the rented lawnmower and the one I bought to replace it and I was exhausted all the time from teaching, and I never deadheaded or swept the terrace and the tree concealed a large noisy pub with a chip machine that belched sound and fat smells and the nightly bottle emptying made the dog bark and although there was much sky and other most exquisite and gentle trees we were only feet away from a four lane A road. If the flat were not rented, would I look after the garden? If I were married again would my legitimacy in the world be returned?

We had our first conversation while I was looking at the garden, standing out on the terrace, eyes screwed up against the sun. You were very particular about the time of the call. I liked that even though it stirred unease. But I was concentrating very hard on everything I had to conceal. You had just come back from buying a shirt, you messaged. How particular specific and careful of you I thought. I'd have bought three. It was Friday afternoon; you were happy. I had bare feet. Try as I might I could not picture you. Where you were. It was as if you were floating in space. Your voice had no discernible accent – seeming to slip from slight country – you said you were originally a Yorkshire lad – to London, with another edge, maybe Transatlantic even. It was clipped and there was also a naivety, you pronounced anything, 'anythin' – I thought it was charming and wondered why. Online meeting is all looking for clues.

'So you're a writer. How wonderful. You must be so clever.'

'It's not – anyway I mostly teach. But I'll give you a link to my writing website if you like.'

'No – don't. I'd rather hear it from you.'

How quaint, I thought. Was it touching? I didn't know. I wanted it to be.

'Enough about me,' I laughed. 'How about you?'

'I joined the army when I was sixteen,' you said.

'Oh my gosh – a soldier,' I replied. Overwhelmed, overawed. You had been very circumspect on the site. I respected that, I think. I think I respected your privacy. But there was also the sense of control – of information – of information always under control. I could never control my own. And so from the beginning I was – predisposed to admire you for all the things I lacked.

'What's that? Not what you expected?'

'No. It's just—'

'It's been my life,' you said. It sounded so simple. 'I've never known anything else.'

'That must be so strange.' I tried to imagine it. The discipline. I couldn't. I was always restless – longed not to be – longed for peace – saw glimpses – and at the sound of your voice this life's search seemed empty and arrogant and wrong. You seemed to have a better, purer way. Your conviction – soft firm-voiced conviction – had a beauty. And you didn't judge me. Not the way I judged myself.

'And you're still in the army?'

'I am.' Another clear statement. 'Lieutenant Colonel now.'

'Golly.' I laughed I think. I was talking to a Colonel. 'Such gravitas. The army must have so much faith in you.'

'It was just hard work. Still is. But not for much longer. It's nearly time for me to go.' That sounded enigmatic.

But I was still stuck on the vision of the Colonel. 'So you don't have a monocle and a grey beard like in Agatha Christie?' Of course not, I thought to myself. Besides, she was just playing with dolls.

'No. None of that. I'm still pretty fit.' I blushed. On the phone.

'So are you still on parade and things like that?' I knew nothing about the army. Remembrance Day. Horrible wars. Documentaries with young men laughing I was terrified were going to die. The First World War poets who had haunted me. How I'd marched against the bomb. So why was I being pointlessly frivolous and trying to flirt? That's what I do – I flirt. But you didn't seem to understand. About flirting, I mean. Or about me. I'd won the History Prize at school.

'No I haven't been deployed for a while now. I work in Whitehall and in other ways. Best not to go into it on the phone.' In other ways. How mysterious, I thought.

My mind was still actually boggling at the idea of the army. Bravery. I can't stress that to you enough now. 'Ah, OK. Where do you live?'

'I live at the barracks in Camberley – since my divorce. It's just temporary.'

'How long ago was that? Your divorce I mean?'

'Two years.' I didn't like to pry but you had to know these things upfront. In case they were still entangled – in case they were still living with their wives.

'Gosh – that sounds a bit Spartan. Like boarding school. Barracks, I mean.' I couldn't imagine a grown man living in one room. I felt a bit sorry for you and I felt it was a bit odd. But still – so dedicated – so apart.

'I get my own bathroom,' you said. 'Rank has to count for something.' I didn't know whether or not you were joking.

'Indeed.' I was embarrassed and wished I could stop saying Gosh and Golly, which were words I never say, preferring fuck and bugger and blimey.

'Whereabouts are you based?' You asked as if it really mattered. I've never understood that about men. I told you where I was in South West London. This seemed to please you.

'Tell me more about you. What's your favourite novel?'

'Oh I don't know. I think people tend to go for what made an early impression on them – something to do with the science of memory.' God I sounded pretentious. 'Wuthering Heights? I love the nineteenth century.' I wished I didn't have to say anything about myself at all. The book was just one, one world of experience. There were so many – so many thoughts and feelings and states of being and comprehending and beauty and ugliness and wit in every book and there I was with Wuthering Heights, every romantic schoolgirl's clichéd choice. Except that it's about heaven and hell and hate. I wasn't going to give you a theory. 'How about you?'

'For me it's poetry. Rupert Brooke.'

'Really?' I couldn't keep the surprise out of my voice. 'I

loved him when I was a teen!' I thought of the poems in a green hardback book inscribed with my father's name; one of the few things he had given me. Or was it lent? I had never been sure. 'So romantic,' was what I said and smiled into the empty garden, a smile you couldn't see. My mind was moving. Callow and selfish and self-indulgent and adolescent too, I could have said. But I did not. Why do we edit ourselves for others – what good can it possibly serve? 'He wrote beautifully.' *I dreamt I was in love again with the one before the last.* That was him.

'Yes.' So wholehearted – the way you said that word. In all my life, I've never met anyone who could put so much conviction into one word. It was wonderful. 'I'm not your typical soldier, you know. I've educated myself. I read.' I liked that. I truly did. All I wanted was common ground – a secret garden.

'What about you?'

'I acted for a bit after Cambridge. Various things – I was a writer full-time while I was married. I left my husband about six years ago. Now I teach.' It would do. It sounded throwaway, I thought, when in fact it was everything that was wrong. I was not going to tell you about the nights lying awake sweating before I left, wondering how Pip and I were going to survive but knowing I had to go for both our sakes. Going to claim benefits that first time. Proving I had no savings, no job. Applying for jobs I would never get. Working part-time in the solicitor's office and tutoring after work. And at last – finding the college where I was now. Touch and go that they took me with no degree – no teaching qualification. A lifeline that could disintegrate in my hands.

'My goodness – a published writer. I'm still in awe. Would I have heard of you?' The dreaded question.

'I doubt it. I'd love to get back to it. But can't – you need proper time. So . . . I love my teaching.' I didn't say but it takes everything I've got. And foolishly I love them. And then they leave.

'That's amazing. You make a difference. Wonderful.' Again – you put so much energy in to saying that last word. I loved it.

'Not enough.' I laughed – nervous. 'I wanted success.'

'Ah.' A passionate, energetic sound. Then, 'My father used to say something to me when I was young: "Instead of trying to force things", he'd say, "just put your hand gently on the tiller, and the right things will come."' I looked up into the sky, listening to you. And I felt a sense of both comfort and disquiet as if at some insistent parallel influence and I couldn't understand why.

'My worries about success sound so petty compared to war, compared to the army,' was all I remember saying. You didn't deny it.

'And you have children?'

'Just one. A boy. You?'

'Two boys.' The requisite number.

'Lovely. I always wanted more children – but . . .'

We told each other our children's names and where they were at school and I liked that. I imagined yours, sporty and wholesome and keen, running about at boarding school in the open air, uncomplicated and clean. I thought of my boy and his troubles and I wished I hadn't sounded so dissatisfied, so envious – so praising of things I didn't have. But the truth was, I was. This is a story about the seven deadly sins.

The conversation lapsed to silence down the non-existent line.

'Would you like to have coffee with me?' Your voice was soft and a little vulnerable.

Thank god you'd said that. I wouldn't have asked me out.

You named a date nearly two weeks ahead because you had to go away on a course. It seemed for ever. Your time was closely allocated, you explained; you drove to your children's school in the West Country every Saturday to watch them play sports or take them out and on Sundays you worked on your MA or drove on to Yorkshire to visit your widowed mother. 'There will be more time at weekends when the MA is done. But it's very important for the CV. I hope that will be all right with you. And I'm going to be so proud when I achieve it – not bad for a Yorkshire lad with only a handful of O levels to his name.' I thought so too. I had not finished my degree. The date was made; the phone went down. And I was giddy.

After that the deluge. Here is the world of words you made me when we met. Here are the texts. I kept them; I kept everything. I keep everything:

'I am sincere. I am honest.'

'I want you to know the person you are writing to.'

Pictures of your army ID tags laid out on a bed with a pale blue duvet cover – you looking so much younger, very serious with more hair. Selfies. The sweetest picture of you in uniform flanked by four or so men – huge rugged and robust, grinning; you not as tall as they were but clearly charismatic proud and in charge, happy and smiling, your tongue in your cheek, the desert vast behind you.

'That's lovely,' I messaged. 'You look happy.'

'We were. We'd just escaped being blown up.'

You with a tin can making some unidentified thing to eat on a small fire, again in front of a tank, from the side, candid shot, as if taken by a friend. It looked so brave. Your hands were beautiful. More godforsaken desert, more bleached pale hot sky. More recent pictures taken at your desk with your MOD ID tag on, wearing glasses. Smiling.

Respectable. Clean. Polished. A checked shirt and a red knitted tie. A bit goofy. Another terrifying one of you jumping out of a plane, the ground far away below you, crouched in the embryo position and again shot from above. I felt protective and terrified for you and we hadn't even met.

'Cripes,' I messaged, 'How did you do that? Weren't you terrified?'

'Yes, I was. But it was a great career move.' Great career move. I could think of others. 'I'll tell you about that one day. I landed wrong, hurt my back, and couldn't move and I – anyway it's not important now. It's important to do things, even though you are afraid.'

'Yes.' It seemed an innocent dedicated life. It seemed heroic. I felt I had to arm myself to meet you – I wanted to gleam.

Every morning I woke up to a piece of music you sent – usually classical, calming piano, something beautiful but easy to understand.

'How are you?' you asked. 'I can't wait to meet you.'

'Here's some music for your morning walk.'

And I would reply politely but always restrained – defending myself, at least at first – 'I don't know you yet!' My messages would cry.

'I know I like what I see,' you replied. And you sent me jokes and gifs and memes and all the most lighthearted silliness, and nagged me for selfies which I was shy to take and it made me laugh because I was very unhappy, and afraid of the future, something I tried hard to disguise. And you wanted to know what I was cooking for my boy, how my idleness was going, the idleness which preceded another draining passionate term teaching at the college, where the pain of the teenagers would always outweigh my own.

There was a salve in that. And days went by and I dreamed over my books and garden and planning sheet for work and timetable and I looked forward to that moment of sighting and recognition more and more. And now back to looking at your face in my mind. The face on the screen.

How long can a memory take to play out? A dream can be as long as a movie and take only seconds in your sleep, they say.

I was back in the room with my questioner.

'We need to check with you one more time. Robert Benedict Fordham. This is the name you knew?'

'Yes.'

'First you said you left the body in the wood – then that there was no body. Can you see how this is confusing for us?'

'Yes.'

'But you admit there are signs of a struggle on your body although there's no blood. So there may be assault and affray.' No blood. What did she mean by that. How could that be true. 'We will keep looking into this. We aren't going to charge you with anything. Your friend is here. Go home. But we may well call you back.'

What was this – an audition?

I didn't move. 'You won't find him. He can never be found. I've tried for a long time now.'

She looked up. 'Tell me again. Why were you in the wood?'

'We arranged to meet. I had a knife – I don't remember how it got there – I showed you – here in my bag – but it's not here now. Maybe I dropped it in the wood.'

She held her head on one side looking at me like a hideous bird. 'We will look at your DNA. We don't want to hold you. We want you to go home while we look into this.

Can you do that? In the meantime if you are seeking support. . .' That's what they put on the end of TV programmes or on posters on the tube.

'No.'

'We don't think you should be alone.'

'Then call my friend, Paula. She's always the one I call.' We'd met at playgroup when our babies were small. She knows the worst and best. I didn't say anything about Pip. He wasn't there.

They looked at each other. 'Yes – we just told you. Paula is here.' A sort of embarrassment in the room. Like when I'm teaching and I can't remember where we are in the text. 'Is there anything more you'd like to tell us?'

'I can tell you the layby where we met, it's on a lane near here. It's on my phone. I don't know why I chose it – or he agreed.'

'You'd never been there before?'

'No.'

Today had been a beautiful day for it. Golden. Or was it yesterday now?

'Can you tell us what he was wearing?'

'Jeans. Navy polo shirt. He likes navy. Ray-Bans. Trainers. 5'7". Dark close-cut hair. A bit bald on top. Dark brown eyes – hazel, even green sometimes.' My faculties had returned. Like a light being turned on. Like when I had to teach – stumbling in confusion into the room – onto the stage – then taking command. We are all actors.

'How long since you'd seen him last?'

'Three months. I'd thought he was gone. Now he is gone.' I couldn't tell if she was surprised. 'I just wanted to know the truth.'

'But you attacked him. You tried to kill him.'

'He wouldn't answer my questions. I just wanted to know.' And I wanted him dead, I could have said. But there are limits.

She didn't seem to understand how important it was to know – to be able to work things out in your head – the story. When you knew the story then it was all right, then you could rest. The officer's look had none of the pity in it you see on TV. She was just doing her job.

'Which is it Maddie? You stabbed him or you didn't stab him? He got away or he didn't?'

'I don't know.' I remember nothing.

'All right – this interview is terminated.' Finally. I had to sign some things about the statement written in my name. Then I was free to go. Think about those words Rob. Do they mean anything – anythin' at all?

Paula – appearing in the strange police station, that location in the unknown – brought with her all her belief that experience could be managed if never contained or controlled. She made everything real and unreal at the same time. In the doorway, in her outfit, me sitting on a chair in the lobby, in front of the counter, where they greet you and write things down.

'I'm so sorry,' I said. She hugged me, raising me from the chair, the lines on her blonde-skinned pale face cruelly lit in that green police station light – the September night outside us cool and windy and damp. It must have been after one. The feel of her – very clean.

'It's all right. I understand. You couldn't have called your family.' Beyond the first glance, she didn't appraise me. She never looked me up and down the way you did. But it was clear she knew it was an emergency. 'I'm going to take you home with me, Maddie. And then we'll take it from there, OK?' She didn't ask about Pip. But maybe she already knew. Her voice always went up at the end. It was because she taught kindergarten that that was how she talked. 'Is your car here?' I had not thought about my car. I remembered when I wanted so badly to burn it after the things that had happened in it but how still I was driving it around – a tin can full of filth. 'Is it all right if she has a bath? When we get back?' she asked who I later discovered was the Duty Sergeant.

'Did you bring her a change of clothes?' he said, looking vaguely embarrassed and out of his depth, away from me, whose nakedness seemed to astound him. Spiritual nakedness, I mean. 'We'll take hers – if you did – and then, yes.' Of course Paula had thought of it. She thought of everything.

After I'd changed – shivering in the cubicle – into Paula's clothes – neatly folded they were – they put mine apart in a bag – and they were gone, sealed and away. I thought of the body bags in Afghanistan you must have touched and seen.

Inside Paula's tiny snug clean new little car, polished as a toy, she rubbed her hands together before starting the engine. She has eczema on her hands.

A sharp turn of her head. We looked at each other properly. 'So what happened? You found him?'

All disguise gone. 'Yes. I tracked him down.' I thought that was what had happened.

'And you went to meet him – didn't think to tell me – didn't think to let anyone know where you were?'

'It's just between him and me.'

'Really? Do you really think that?' She was angry.

'I don't know.'

'You know he's a properly dangerous person, don't you? You know that?'

'Yes.'

'I'm sorry – I shouldn't be scolding you. But it wasn't safe.' She waited but I said nothing more. 'They said you said you killed him. You know that's not true, don't you? The scratches – the blood – is yours. They'll check your clothes though I think.'

'I met him. I saw him, Paula.' Unbelievable that he was still walking around breathing after all that had happened. 'And we spoke to each other. And I stabbed him with the knife – I think I did. Because I wanted him to die. And I thought he was dead and I don't know where he's gone now and they don't fucking believe me. At all.'

'Do you want them to? Isn't it probably better if they don't?' Then, 'Whatever you did – he won't come after you. He's way too clever. Thank god.' So this really was the end. The one thing I couldn't bear. 'You look awful.' She sighed, started the engine. 'I promised myself I wasn't going to do this – all the way here. Tell you off I mean. I brought a blanket. Put it round you. I'm taking you to mine.'

And we drove away from the wood. At least for a while. And I could close my eyes and remember again and so forget.

I unearthed from my mind this text conversation you and I had Rob before we'd even met.

'What makes you happy?'

'Being by the sea. On the sea. When it's bright and calm. Light reflected.'

'What makes you sad?'

'Unhappiness in someone I love. Loss. Cruelty. Dreams breaking. How about you?'

'Same. Which dream?'

'My marriage. I believed it was safe. I believed in it. I had an image of what I wanted in my head. We both did. House. Holidays. We spent too much money.'

'I've never done that. Always been careful. It makes sense.'

'That's because you value discipline and restraint.'

'True.'

I'd tried to make you laugh. 'This is how I imagine it. You know those beautiful trains like in *Dr Zhivago* or *Murder on the Orient Express*?'

'Yes.'

'I see the train going across the vast Russian Plains – the Steppes. Little lamps with tasselled shades on the walls. And everyone drinking tea.'

'Couples?'

'Yes. They're all in Edwardian dress and there are samovars and petits fours. And you're on the train. Then – you're separated – you're divorced – you're tipped off the train. And suddenly you're in the middle of the plain and the train keeps merrily going and you're not on it anymore. And no one notices. No one even looks behind.'

'What does that mean?'

'It means you cease to exist – no one invites you to dinner anymore. You're erased from the collective memory. With the vast plains around you.'

But you didn't laugh. Merely replied, 'I don't think I've ever been invited to a dinner party in my life.'

'I must sound frivolous to you.'

'No. It's just I don't really have any friends. I have strict moral rules – about behaviour. Not many people get past them.' For you it was all about the work, it seems – protecting sinful people like me. I hadn't told you about my sins.

'What I'm trying to say is that there are two parts of it – one that you don't want to be married to that person anymore – the second is status. You don't have any as a single woman. Not a particle. Worse than that people treat you as if you have a disease. Whereas single men – that's a different story.'

'A disease? Like who?'

'Mothers at the school gates. Other women. Scared you're going to steal their husbands. Which of course you wouldn't do.'

But I was lying again. It had happened. However much I might lie to myself that I was only reclaiming what was already mine. A lie of the mind. Do not build your house on that.

And I know now, knew then, that these were things I should not have told you.

Several hours later you came back with this:

'Can I ask you something?'

'Of course.'

'Do you accept yourself? Love yourself I mean?'

How could someone with holes in their soul love and accept themselves? It seemed distasteful even if they had not been there.

'I don't know.'

'Because you know, don't you – that unless you do, you won't be able to love another person properly.'

'That's what they say.' This made me feel very uncomfortable. I decided not to make my joke about the self-esteem shop and how I wished I could afford to go there.

'I went on a course about it. And I have a book if you're interested. It helped me a lot.'

'Thank you. That would be kind.'

'I'm not saying you're not a gorgeous girl. I'm just saying I think it might help you.'

'Ah.'

'I long to meet you.'

It all seems so obvious now.

What you do is you win trust, don't you Rob: hearts and minds. Then you go in for the kill.

Cheek pressed against the window of the car – the comforting hard coldness of it – the silent journey with Paula – more memory. I wonder if memories can be recorded as a legitimate cause of death.

Our first date – the sting of it – was that unconsciously – even then – I knew it was a duel. We arranged to meet at my favourite bookshop, a little warren of books off the King's Road. I had gone there as a child and watched with wonder how the rows of books slid back to reveal further rows behind and had been young enough to believe that if you kept sliding there might be a secret room or world hidden at the heart where I could hide and go. There would be a fireplace and an armchair and quiet. No one would shout at anyone else. Ever. You said you bought books there regularly for your mother and I was touched by that. You seemed to be such a good son. There is always confidence in men who look out for their mothers. You made the date for coffee although I think it was late lunchtime. I thought your habits were clearly without extravagance but also perhaps that you were hedging your bets in case I didn't merit the investment of time and money. This is the world of dating after all – it's just that it didn't quite mesh with the longing you seemed to have to meet me.

I felt light. Nervous but light. It was a beautiful afternoon – a pretty drive in the car – and I had bought new shoes: shiny pretend snakeskin flats in a showy turquoise and black – not my style at all and I didn't know if I liked them but I couldn't meet you in old shoes – and I wore jeans and a plain dark top. The bookshop is made up of two tiny Chelsea houses interconnected, each with stairs. I proposed that we meet outside. But you said no, you would wait in the fiction section on the first floor. I chose or was it blundered up accidentally one of the staircases on the other side away from the fiction part and so approached you unseen. I saw you look up and scan the rooms without spotting me. It was oddly frightening. I'd eaten almonds in the car so my stomach wouldn't rumble because it was really lunchtime and I remember still the taste of salt and how I'd rubbed my fingers on an old tissue inside the cloth of my bag to take away the grease and feeling somehow sinister for doing it as if it were the greatest subterfuge – I can't explain.

You stood flanked by bookshelves and you were the most immaculate looking person I'd ever seen. Brown slightly bowed head, that military bearing. You wore jeans and brogues and a navy shirt the same colour as mine. We could have been twins. You lifted your head and saw me watching you and you strode towards me with what I took to be bravado – my heart went out to you for seeming so brave under my scrutiny – and you immediately grasped my shoulders and kissed me on both cheeks. I was deeply embarrassed.

'Is this too much?' you said. 'It's just I'm so glad to see you.'

'And I ambushed you,' I said, remembering to smile. 'Took you by surprise.'

I tried to be light with the remark but didn't know why I'd made it. I'd pictured desultory conversation and a look through the books and then coffee. I had pictured glances. But your head was up and your eyes were on me and you were calculating.

'Can I take you to lunch?' you said. 'I know a place?'

I thought about my car parked; I thought about the almonds. 'I didn't . . . it wasn't what we planned.' I am not a weak-willed person, so this was particularly bizarre. I didn't know what I wanted. I was quite literally stunned. 'But . . . yes. Where?'

'It's a surprise. Come with me.'

Everything happened very fast. We were out of the bookshop and you were speeding along and I was trying to catch up with you. You kept changing sides on the pavement – I found out later that this was so I never had to walk on the outside because I was a lady – but I found it confusing with the King's Road traffic and the people and their headphones and the blur of buses and bicycles and cars. You stayed at a distance, assessing me, I felt. You told me how beautiful my new shoes were. We crossed over and were in the quieter streets surrounded by white houses and squares and black railings with their compelling multi-coated gleam. I hadn't known there was a restaurant or anywhere you could eat there.

'This is where they filmed the Alex Rider spy novels,' you said, pointing out a front door of a corner house. 'Did you know?' I wasn't particularly impressed. You cared deeply. I felt mean. We reached a corner. 'Here,' you said. 'Here we are.' A pretty pub with a Gentlemen's club air and leather sofas and a little table close to the door where I sat and waited as you almost ran to the bar.

I was still confused that coffee had turned to lunch and I couldn't remember when my parking had started and now I had a glass of rosé and a menu and your face which was very handsome and – unlike the photograph – entirely unsexy, was in front of mine. Very deep, very dark eyes. I noticed there was a space between the bottom of the iris of your eye and your lower lid – the whites of your eyes were visible there. I looked it up later, in the light of everything that happened between us – it's called yin sanpaku – your lower sclera was visible – and also you looked different without the flat cap of the photograph – your hair was neatly trimmed and thinning at the top. If you'd been fashionable, you'd have probably shaved your head. I didn't care about that, I didn't care about fashion, I didn't know why I was thinking that, I just felt profoundly deeply uncomfortable beneath your stare.

'I usually have a bowl of soup here,' you said. 'On the odd Friday. When I finish early and come from work.' I thought how lonely you sounded. And also how I was not going to order the soup. It was depressing. I ordered a first course salad. We talked about Brexit. I was Remain and you of course wanted freedom and sovereignty and pride and at this point I wanted to go home very badly indeed. Then you said you loved chips. I said I loved them too. We agreed that the thin ones were by far the best but any chips would do. And you got up from the table and disappeared. I thought that maybe this was one of those dating stories where a fast exit through the bathroom window is made but then you returned, no explanation, no words, sat down and continued to eat your soup.

'Where did you go?'

'To order you some chips of course.'

'Why didn't you say?'

'I was just trying to be quick.' This is where I began to question myself. Why was I so jumpy? Why couldn't I sit and have lunch with this man who so clearly wanted to please me? It was only lunch after all. Why was I so unnerved?

'Is this how things are in the army? Speedy?' And I laughed at my own attempt at a joke. You didn't laugh. You didn't laugh once. You didn't even smile.

I decided to steady myself. I asked you about your life. But all I remember is a blur of you telling me how wonderful I was to have gone to Cambridge and written and acted and taught and all the things I'd done. 'You were paid, weren't you? For your books?'

'Yes.'

'That's amazing.' But I consistently rejected all these attempts at praise and said it had been hard and there had been many struggles, all as if insisting on the truth, resisting, insisting that I was not so splendid after all, and the more I did this, the more I felt I was misrepresenting myself, coming over as weak and pessimistic and dark, when I wasn't; I was complicated but the battle wasn't lost – not then – and I wondered why I was trying to do this and then I decided I was a self-involved mess. You were the one who had had a hard life: Northern Ireland, Kosovo, Rwanda, Afghanistan. I was merely frivolous and vain.

So I asked more about you. Only good manners after all. You told me your father had been in the army – a major, how there had never been any choice but that you would follow. Your voice slid over these words. You told me about the men, sending them away on leave, the speech you would make to them to appeal to them to come back.

'"Go away,"' I'd say, '"Go to the pub – see your wives and girlfriends –do whatever you need to do. But come back. Because I need you. I need you to."' I couldn't imagine how it must have been to be so responsible for them – for their lives. Little stories. Vignettes. The army sergeant who wanted to leave to pursue a career in porn. You thought it was funny. I thought it was sad. I concluded you did not know how to talk to women. You were talking at me as if you'd already agreed on the response. I tried to understand what you were trying to say. I'm not a stupid or unperceptive person so this too felt extremely odd.

'How do the army try to help them adapt – when they come back?' I asked. You told a story about a Cyprus air base where men were rehabilitated – how pointless it was – how broken so many of them were. 'I worry about the homeless from the army,' I said. 'We don't value our soldiers when they come home.'

'No,' you said. 'We aren't valued at all.'

'And now?'

'Intelligence. Sometimes in Whitehall, sometimes in the Bunker.' (What was the Bunker? Was this World War Two?) 'And my MA. So I can have a proper job when I leave in the summer. Thesis due end of September. Not much longer.' Such an ordered life. I kept trying to make a conversation – an exchange. You told me a very confusing memory story about applying to work in Intelligence; something to do with a blank PO Box number to write to – an ad in an army newspaper. It was perplexing. I thought they recruited. I thought that part of it was all above board. But then I was naive. Another about a year in Salisbury Plain when you were tired out after active duty. But the planes still screamed overhead, you said. Ferocious noise. 'I tried out for the Paras too,' you said. 'But they didn't want me. They asked me to work in Support instead. So I did.' What was In Support? I was unable to ask.

The chips came. 'Chips and salad. Perfect.' I said.

'Perfect? Good.' And at last your little thin half smile.

The conversation continued a hard struggle. Every truth I tried to establish was hit back at me. And all the time I knew I was lying to you, you this honourable army officer who was buying me lunch in a lovely pub off the King's Road.

And at last you said, 'Ah, I see. You're nervous – often.'

'What makes you say that?'

'I'm a very good judge of character.'

I thought of you judging the men: who to promote and sustain – who to discard and exile. How you governed people. 'And am I of good character?' (I had reasons to believe at that time that I was not.)

You refused to answer.

I was suffused with a most terrible panic. I wanted

to run.

You said, 'Would you like another glass of wine?' and all at once I thought of my car and the parking. Looking at my phone, I knew I must have outrun the time.

'I'm so sorry – I have to go,' I said. 'My car—'

A frank calm stare. 'I had no idea. I assumed you'd come by tube.'

'Yes – I'm sorry – I'm foolishly wedded to my car and I thought you said coffee and I—'

'Well, we must go.' I have never known anybody who thought as fast and decisively as you. You went to the bar and paid the bill double quick – showing no sign of being disconcerted, no sign of annoyance, your rapid step guiding us across the roads, my attempts to joke every time you appeared and disappeared behind me, playing with my field of vision, producing no response. 'You're in my blind spot,' I said. 'I can't see you.'

'Army training. You have to know how to treat a lady,' your reply.

We got to the car. No ticket. I touched the door. You said, 'I can see you're relieved to be reunited with it.' I think you gave another half smile but I avoided looking at you I was so embarrassed.

'Yes, I love my car.'

I didn't want to kiss you, this handsome man – I didn't want to promise anything – I thanked you and I dived into the cover of that untidy little car. I was hasty – desperate to escape. I left you on the pavement, hand up in a gesture of salute.

In the car I shivered – shivered to make you leave my skin. And once safely home I almost ran to the garden, safe and warm in the afternoon. Still neglected, still ramshackle, still not even mine – faded lavender and tired geraniums and the sound of traffic and humming of bees. I trembled and shook. The mess of dust and unswept leaves. Pip was still at school. Time to own up, time to confess and come clean. You who were so direct and I who had obfuscated and run away.

I messaged: 'Thank you for lunch. Sorry to ditch you and run.'

'My pleasure. You seemed in a hurry to get away.'

'I'd like to explain.' But before I could message more the phone was hammering in my hand with your call.

'It's all right. Really.' The same conviction, the same clear clean voice.

I felt confused. 'I'm sorry.'

'I did think – you could have moved the car.'

'I know. It was silly.'

'What are you doing tonight?'

Caught off guard again. 'Oh – nothing.'

'We could have found another place and gone out on the town.' Such an innocent, antiquated expression.

'Look – I've – there's something I have to tell you.' Awful waiting silence. 'It's about me. Something I should have said before. I've been involved . . . I've been involved with – with my very first love – sixth form – can you believe? We bumped into each other after a very long time and we were close friends for a year and I didn't realise – and then – it spilled over. We had a love affair. Just for a few months. It's over now.'

'Why?' The question was spoken as a blank. Why was it over? Why had I done it?

'He's married. Long time. Two children.' Silence as my face burned. 'I'm a bit heartbroken. And I'm in the wrong.' You didn't deny it. Your first advantage. I was shaking in the silence. I didn't say how much I'd hoped he'd leave her.

A little breath from you. 'When did it end? How long ago?'

'A few weeks.' Just a few weeks. God I felt ashamed. Deeply. And you said nothing, nothing at all. How could I say that I'd just wanted a flirtation, that I hadn't realised I would find sincere, serious, well-intentioned you? But was that true? Hadn't I wanted complete escape and remission of my sins and freedom surpassing all understanding? Hadn't I willingly gone into internet dating Hades and found someone new just for my own purposes? And then concealed myself and my past? 'I shouldn't be dating. I should be healing – awful expression.'

'Yes.'

'And now I've met you – and you're so . . .' I didn't say sincere. 'And I realise it's not fair. And I'm sorry.' A very long pause while I watched the vicissitudes of several ants on the terrace beneath.

'I'm not here to judge you, Maddie.' But to me you were. I was sure that you'd made plenty of judgements in your life. 'If you're not ready – I'll say goodbye.'

'It's just I'm not sure how much I could be . . .' Again words trailed off. Again I came up short. And I didn't want to be presumptuous. It was a tightrope calculating what I could be about to throw away. You're so intense, I wanted to say, so direct, you seem to want so much, but only said, 'It might not be fair.' I believed my heart was locked, you see.

Again the soft light almost imperceptible breath. 'Thank you for letting me know. Goodbye.'

A quick message flashed up blue as soon as you were gone, leaving me with the air. 'I loved meeting you. I hope you find what you're looking for. Best wishes, Rob.'

So polite, so formal, so clear.

I was a self-monster and you were a hero. It was black and white.

Hours passed while I smoked cigarettes and drank glasses of wine and felt like a heel.

I paced. Restless. Ungainfully employed. At times like those – after another hollow exchange – another failure to connect – I thought of the houses I'd lost. The one in the country. The one in London. Family homes I'd painted and tended and cooked for friends I thought I had but had never seen since. Where the baby had cuddled down and where he'd lain on the quilt I'd made him and laughed and gurgled with his little toys. The cat curled up next to him in the sun. And I longed and longed for those houses and those days again.

About nine o'clock, on that long summer night, a message: 'Have I told you how beautiful you are?'

'Ha ha, no. Do you think I'm beautiful?' I'd felt plump but pretty.

'VERY.'

'What else did you think?'

'I loved the way you expressed yourself, your mind. How articulate you are.'

'Oh.' A sharp intake of breath, I think it's called.

'The way you hold yourself. It's lovely. Beautiful.' Pause while I wondered. Then, 'And I think you're fragile.'

I didn't know how I felt about that. 'Could you tell?'

'Yes.'

'I am fragile, but also strong.'

'Let me say again – you looked so beautiful today.' I had been beautiful once, I think I knew that, but it came and went like a reflection in water when it was stirred.

I'd felt no sense you'd thought that about me that day – none at all.

'I'm sorry about today,' I wrote again. 'Really.'

'Any chance you might give me another?' you replied. 'Chance, I mean?'

'Umm . . .' I was flattered – jolted out of a sadness I

couldn't control. I had wanted to message my old love and tell him about this strange date I'd had but I couldn't because we'd parted and there was no more laughing together allowed. Those were times. The laughter and the tears and the kisses.

'We could have a proper lunch. What do you think?'

'I'm taking my son on holiday next week.'

'Before then. If you can. 'I'll find somewhere quiet. Near you. Leave it to me.' A perfectly judged pause. 'Please?'

And so it began – the courtship. More music every morning – this time, romantic passionate love songs – you sent them at perhaps five or six o'clock when you yourself had woken. 'How are you?' You wrote. And you sent me pictures of training exercises in the dawn or views of the river from your walk or the cup of coffee you were drinking. 'I can't wait to meet you again.' I would reply, polite and kind, friendly – still trying to maintain some distance. You sent me a picture of yourself with a T-shirt with my name on it. It was image trickery to make me laugh. It wasn't real. It made you seem so naive.

Our second date. The pub garden very near to where I lived. Surrounded by woods and heath.

You strode towards me with the same bravura and kissed me on the mouth. 'Just so you know right from now how much I fancy you,' you said. It was technically a passionate kiss but there was nothing there. Did you love doing that? Were you afraid? I felt a great lack within me. You chose a faraway table from the others. You steered me. We ordered something.

'Do you like the way I'm dressed?' you said.

Curiouser and curiouser. 'Yes. I like blue.'

'But not T-shirts? You preferred the collar the other day?'

'Look – it's really not up to me . . .'

'Yes, but you do – don't you?'

'I do like a collar,' I said and laughed, feeling like a matron in a department store in 1955.

'I will only wear a collar for you.'

'Please,' I said. 'Please don't.' Looking around at the ordinary Friday-afternoon people with their beers and burgers and fish and chips; the woods surrounding us.

'Is it bad to want to please you?'

'No. No – I suppose it isn't.'

'Good.' Again the intent look but this time your eyes had a warmer glow.

'You don't seem to understand what a beautiful girl you are. I'm struck by you.'

'Thank you. It's sweet of you to say.' It wasn't sweet. Not sweet at all.

I felt very hot – the flush spreading up my chest and neck where I'm sure it marked me and was visible. I made a dash for the loo. They were painting the door on the inside of the cubicle and there was a sign saying, 'Do not touch this door. Wet paint'. I read it several times. Then – a creature of habit – I touched the door on the way out, the marks oily and indelible on my hands, uncleaned by water from the taps that I smudged with more paint. A panic of paper towels and rubbing. I put on more lipstick, rubbed it off again with my knuckle: decided I was mad. I didn't want to come out – yet my heart was hammering with excitement – or was it fear? I could not make it out, as if my body was purely animal – desiring flight – while my mind was stunned.

'I was beginning to worry you'd bolted,' you said with a rueful, innocent smile.

'Oh – no. I'm sorry,' I said. I already felt I owed you so many apologies. 'I often spend too much time in the loo. Bad habit.' This was actually true. They were always a place to attempt to suspend time – a good place to think. Not that I'd managed to do any thinking at all in this case.

We drank our drinks. 'Why don't you write anymore?' you said.

'It's been years – just trying to survive. It's month to month.' I felt I could confide this shameful fact, that it wasn't private.

'Why did you leave your husband?'

'I can't explain. Not now. It would be unfair.' That sounded good. We were in debt, I didn't say – and there was drinking – and so much happened that didn't seem to be anyone's fault and was unforeseen and made the wedding photographs look like bright lies.

'It was brave to leave your husband.'

I laughed. 'It was hardly serving in Afghanistan.'

'You shouldn't joke about it – it was.' Eyes, holding my eyes. Quietness in the garden. All the other sounds blocked out. I could have said how I tried and tried and tried so hard to make it work. I'd felt no love at the end – that – that was the worst part. But I said nothing. 'Where is he now?'

'Other side of London. He helps us with money. He sees Pip. He's going away for an extended trip though soon – so. . . We're on better terms than we were.'

'You won't get back together, will you?' You seemed alarmed. Again – I couldn't tell if you were teasing.

'Of course not. What happened with your wife?'

'She was – very cold – and while I was away she found somebody else. I did everything I could to be a good husband but I couldn't make her happy.' You'd tried to be a good husband. What words those were.

'Did you love her very much?'

'I thought I did.'

'Still – it must be hard being an army wife.'

'We moved a lot. She didn't like that. The houses were – the houses were very run down. But compared to where I grew up – Can we not talk about it? I don't want to talk about her.'

'I'm sorry – I . . .'

'It's all right.'

You continued to look at me intently. But it wasn't a sexy look. I can't explain. 'Don't they say all writers . . . If you're a writer you must write?'

'Yes. That's what they say.' How could I describe the wrenching horror – what it was like not to be able to do that anymore. How it was like being shredded. How even in the worst of my marriage, all the loneliness, I would close the big barn door – shut out the world and write. How sometimes I feared I exchanged that for the happiness of my child. And how I feared that that too might be a self-serving lie. I couldn't explain to you properly that since that schism the light had gone out of the world. That I didn't believe in anything any longer except survival and successfully negotiating with pain. That all the years I'd been building my marriage I'd built a cage my child and I learned to suffer in. That all the roses and the jam making and the dinner parties in the world had not made a happy family. Or had we been happy and I'd forgotten? I know we had been at the start. But now the world was tawdry and if the world is tawdry, what then is there to write? And if you slept with sleazy people after you were married and hoped they wouldn't be sleazy and then if you had an affair with your first love who wouldn't, couldn't, leave his wife and he was your best friend – 'What then?' sang Plato's ghost. What then?' I couldn't say that I'd felt dirty and ashamed for a very long time but I felt you understood.

'It's just – you need a routine. Time. I don't have that now. Teaching and being a mother takes it all.' And having stupid affairs, I could have added. But I didn't. It was another thing of darkness and it didn't suit my story.

'There's always time,' you said quite slowly, with exquisite deliberation. 'You need to find the truth about a thing. And then to write it – to write one true sentence. That's what you have to do. That's what Hemingway said.'

'How did you know he said that?' I suppose it was rude to be surprised but I was. How had you read my mind?

'He also said one writes better when one is in love. You think because I'm a soldier, I don't read? *A Moveable Feast* is one of my favourite books.'

Me, rapidly: 'Mine too – I'm always going on to my students about it.' I felt absolute wonder then and joy then – an absolute glow. 'What's your favourite bit?'

You, equally fast: 'The bit about the taste of the oranges . . .'

And more and more, dialogue overlapping, 'I love that bit too – the purity of it.'

'The hunger – the work.'

'Yes.'

'I love working,' you said. 'Early. Pens. Green pens – Coffee—'

'Love green pens – for letters and things. But I write – when I work – with a pencil, always.'

'A clear mind. That feeling.' You left what was a strategic pause. 'I'm not your typical soldier, you know.'

'No. You're not.'

I don't know if I laughed but I was filled with joy. It occurs to me now that I never heard you laugh. Yet there was sunlight in the unremarkable pub garden in the middle of the heath – the ugly grainy pub furniture, the ordinary food that came as interruption instead of relief. There was space around us, and nature became benign. I looked at your hands – small, beautiful, with their bitten nails. I thought of them holding a gun. I thought of all the things they had had to do. That they could be so capable, capable of killing.

'I grew up in books,' you said. It could have been pretentious but I decided it wasn't.

'Me too.'

'My mum was at work—'

'What did she do?'

'It was a bakery for a while and then she was a barmaid. At the Queen's Head. She was a queenly barmaid I thought – I was too little to understand quite the difference between them. But I felt I'd served her in some peculiar way when I served the Queen.'

'Ha – it's like me thinking "Our father who art in heaven" might in fact be mine.'

'It was quite lonely – World War Two comics – then all the books she had on her bookshelf. I felt like an only child – I was the last of three.'

'I was lonely too. But aren't all children lonely in a way?' I said foolishly.

'No,' you said with decision. 'I don't think they are.'

There was nothing more I wanted to reveal at this point so I said nothing.

'Last winter I went to Paris for the New Year,' you said.

'By yourself?'

'Yes. Stayed in the Officers' Mess. Wandered Hemingway's routes. Found

Shakespeare and Company.'

'Ah the bookshop. I don't think it's on the original site now. I haven't been to Paris for years.'

You made a little frown then, as if trying to remember. 'No.'

'Was it lovely?'

'Yes.' You wouldn't stop looking at me. Very intensely. I noticed that you had very long eye lashes, the sort Pip had had as a baby, curled on his cheeks when he was asleep. I should have been embarrassed to examine you so minutely but I wasn't. 'I think you must write again,' you said. 'And I think, if you'll let me, if things work out, we could go to Paris.

'Let's not get ahead of ourselves,' I said but I was happy. The trouble with having very little money is that you rarely go anywhere. Places were memories instead of plans.

'I know. But let me say again – you've had courage. You should be proud.' Were you briefing the men again? 'You deserve to be happy.'

'I'm proud we've survived it – me and Pip. I'm proud I teach young people – I'm proud I can help them.' When you said nothing I had to continue, 'But nothing has turned out the way I expected it to – or ever thought it would.'

'Look around you,' you said. 'How many people here in this garden – sitting around us now – how many people do you think have found their dreams come true? Their lives turned out the way they wanted. Feel proud? Feel contented? None. It's what you do with the wreckage that counts. That's what makes you. You have to be able to look at the truth. You must never be sorry for yourself or give up. That's not the way to look at things. You must always work and be grateful. You must – you have to – work again.' I felt shut out of your belief – tempted, inspired at the same time. I didn't know whether to admire you or reject you. Your vision was narrow, unassailable. You appeared to have no doubt. But you were dedicating yourself to me in that moment and I knew it and was thankful.

'I'm so happy you love books,' I said. I couldn't smile but there was something light between us, like a promise. I made a decision, irrefutable after that moment, and stood up from my side of the bench table and sat next to you. 'Is this all right?'

'Yes.' I looked at you, your eyes. Allowed myself to be open to them. It was conscious.

We looked at each other for a long time. Light brown, the eyes became glowing from within – a gold. 'You have very long eyelashes.' It was true, you did.

'I get them from my mother.' Absurd thing to say I think. But I was touched. We kissed very slowly and I felt nothing. A most peculiar feeling again that nothing was there.

'I have to go,' I said.

'Too bad you're going away tomorrow,' you said. 'Too many obstacles. Too much time for you to forget me.'

'Oh, I won't do that,' I said. 'Have a little faith.'

Driving home I thought of your handsome face, the empty kisses, your rather beautiful military mouth. It won't work I thought. I don't feel anything. It's a mistake. Too soon for a beautiful soldier who looks at you like that! You must be crazy. You're inured. Give him a chance, sang the devil, give him a chance.

'So why is this man always texting you? It's boring and gay.'

'Don't use 'gay' like that, darling,' I replied automatically.

I was on holiday with Pip – do you remember? The one you didn't want me to go on – the one I couldn't afford – the one that came between us because we'd only just met.

'It's just an expression.'

'No. It's not. It's wrong.'

'All right, I won't do it.'

'Now put down your phone.' I glanced up at my tall white-skinned child, his kind eyes. 'Why is he always texting you?'

'I think he likes me.'

'I think it's weird. Even worse than married guy and I hated him.'

'Well – I shouldn't have told you about him.'

'No – you shouldn't. But that's what comes of being mentally ill. Now it's time to swim.'

'Can you not?'

'Well – you've never pretended you weren't, Mum.'

'I know you're trying to be funny but – being bipolar is a condition. My mood goes up and down. I have meds. It doesn't mean I'm mentally ill.'

'What do you think it means then? That you're good at fractions?'

How glib he was. Was he just at that age where you torment your parents or was I simply a complete failure of a mother?

'Will you just shut up?'

'All right. But put down your phone.'

We swam in the sea off the rocks. We had to go down a little ladder holding tight.

The great joy of the sea tempered by negotiating with those rocks, worrying Pip would snag himself, or get caught or dashed because especially in the afternoon with the breeze up, the sea was strong. Pretending I wasn't worried, pretending I was brave myself, leading the way. I was afraid we'd bump into a turtle. We never did. I remember telling you on the phone what a nervous swimmer Pip was – how he needed encouragement. That he was afraid of crowds. That he was frighteningly clever.

I told you how we'd been practising jumping from the raft. How I'd lost my temper a bit at the end because he kept shrieking and you said that nobody was perfect and being a single parent was tough. 'Looks as if you've done a good job encouraging him,' you said. I felt blessed, exonerated by the entire British Army. I imagined you in the water with him, you teaching him things, you with your firmness and kind strength. I lay in the sun and imagined what it would be like to have a man again that was mine.

We drank lime juice and watermelon juice and I had mojitos in the evening and a glass of wine at lunch – the hotel was almost empty and we were at the edge of a peninsula and the peace and beauty of the gardens sloping down to the sea was miraculous. It was all going on my credit card. I'd never put a whole holiday on my credit card before. It was an extravagance I knew was wrong. But as long as I kept well, kept working and making the payments we would be all right. 'To keep well you have to avoid stress, Ma,' Pip said to me. 'I looked it up. Which is impossible, isn't it?'

'I suppose. Let's talk about something else. If you could build your own house which end of the peninsula would it be?'

'I don't want to build my own house,' said Pip. 'That's always been you.'

We read and we dozed in the afternoon in the cool of our room and my peace of mind was only faintly disturbed by the violent book you'd insisted I buy and bring with me to read. You said it had made a huge impression on you. It was about a terrorist plotting against the west, and the ruthless and resourceful hero who was tracking him. I read it to gain insight into you but it was only brutal and black and I felt sorry for the terrorist which I didn't think was the point.

'You should stop reading that stupid book,' said Pip. 'You're meant to be on holiday. You're meant to be resting your mind.'

'I know. You're reading Shirley Jackson so you can talk.'

So many messages all day long. 'He's persecuting you, Mum.'

'No.' Pip – seeing things steady and whole. Isn't that what they said about Giotto? He understood about the colour blue too. 'He says to tell you he's sorry. He says he'll say hello to you if you like.'

'No, Mum. I don't want to talk to him. I mean it,' said Pip. You were reading one of my books. You loved it and told me how beautiful it was which made me cry.

We played Marco Polo in the pool. You have to close your eyes on purpose and give in. That was how you found the other person. One of the waiters tried to pick me up. I just thought he was being nice until Pip explained, 'You have no idea about anything, have you Mum?' he said. 'He told you his wife was away and he'd take you out in his car. Which part of this do you not understand? You have absolutely zero common sense.' We went on a boat and swam off it and the other families were kind and offered to teach Pip to snorkel and I was grateful and proud of him. They could have ignored us because we were on our own, but they didn't. They talked to us about our lives. That was the happiest of an accumulation of very happy days. When we were first divorced I'd always hoped we'd holiday with my brother but we never did. Who'd have paid for it anyway? Pip always dismissed this problem. 'We'd never have enjoyed it, Ma. You just want it because it's the kind of thing other people do – or you've read about it in books. Because you wish we were one of those families and we're not. You fell out with your brother, remember?'

'He fell out with me.'

'Whatever,' Pip would say. 'It's done now so there's no point in right or wrong.' He had very definite opinions about everything. I suspected he was always right.

That night I lay relaxed on the little sofa of the suite we'd magically been upgraded to and we messaged – flirtatious a little – light. Do you remember that time, Rob? I was so happy after the boat – Pip had swum bravely, we had triumphed; it had reminded me of the safe beauty of my own childhood family holidays except that it was just me and him. I was languorous – I was at ease. Then flashed up on my screen: 'Take off your dress.' A command like a blow. My mind told me it wasn't. You were flirting. I was overreacting. A great sense of horror and threat suffused me like dark ink in clear water all while I fought and debated with myself about whether I was being too straitlaced. After all Pip had taken pictures of me folding a towel in my bikini ready for the trip and I had sent them to you. I tried – beginning to pull my dress over my head – but I was drowsy with sun and sea. But it was no good. It made me feel awful. It wasn't as if we knew each other that way at all already.

I'll confess to you now that I had sent messages and pictures to other men in other ways over the last stained years – in my folly – always regretted it – but you were different, you were my soldier. Nothing in the world we were born into, of telephone calls and letters, had prepared for this late-night mobile shadow visit. You sounded so impersonal. It made me afraid. The way a person you want to believe in – you already almost did – can breach your most private world – every physical dream space you could ever retreat to – every mental refuge – that quiet night by the water surrounded by my books and the packet of Pringles for Pip – the day behind us of sun cream and scent – our swimmies drying outside – the sea moving in the bay – I could go to the ends of the earth – pack up all my troubles and someone I'd met twice could command me to take off my dress and I was undone by four electronic words. I was dashed and sorrowful and afraid.

'I'm sorry I can't do this,' I wrote.

'Don't go! I'm so sorry,' you said. 'Let's change the subject. Let's talk about movies instead. You love those.' I was shaking but I allowed you to tell me that John Wayne was your favourite; mine was Cary Grant – my objective mind knew that this too was something terrible. And a cliché. After we said good night I went to sleep troubled and heavy despite the sea outside and the exaggerated brightness of the moon.

In the morning – first thing – you messaged, 'I haven't slept. Couldn't stop worrying I'd upset you last night. I got carried away thinking of you. No excuse. I'm not the man you think I am. I'm deeply sorry. I'll trouble you no more.'

Were you saying goodbye? You thought it was all over? You were going? If someone is troubled, I comfort them. I just do. And I didn't want my dream to die.

'No – don't feel that way.' I messaged hastily. 'Can I call you? Tell you everything's all right?'

A long pause.

'Yes please.'

'All right I'll call later.' And I did. Words exchanged with husky-voiced saddened you about misunderstandings and not being able to forgive yourself and longing for me to get home and late-night passion until I felt I was the one who had intruded on you. That day the wind got up in the bay and we couldn't swim and Pip seemed restless and I was worried he was bored.

Pip and I waking in our little white twin beds and putting the air conditioning on.

'Today's results day, Mum. Your students. You'll find

out.’

‘I know.’

‘You’re awfully quiet about it. Are you going to call the college?’

‘They’ll text me. Let’s have breakfast.’ We loved our breakfasts.

Into my hand on that crazed ill-conceived sun-steeped holiday on that Turkish rock looking on the brutal hot peninsula and its parched trees came a text.

They were the best results we’d ever had. And it was the first year I’d taught whole groups by myself. Unstoppable tears of joy. I spoke to one of my students from the hall – I could picture him by the wrought-iron staircase, the elegant turn of the balustrade. ‘Thank you.’ He said.

‘Now you know you can do it – you can do anything you put your mind to.’

‘Yes.’

‘Does that mean you’ll get more money?’ said Pip.

Your messages pursued me to the airport – in the taxi on the dusty Turkish road, ‘I want to break bread with you, drink wine with you, lie and look up at the sky . . . I’m sorry if I write too much I just can’t think of anything else but you. I can’t believe how lucky I am to know the person who has written the beautiful words I’ve read.’ If you’d looked creepy it would have been creepy but you didn’t and it wasn’t. You looked handsome and decent and clean cut, like those men from old war movies who climbed into fighter planes and brilliantined their hair.

We stopped by the side of the road where they made bread in front of us – stretched and cooked it over an open fire and piled it with yogurt and mezze and we sat at trestle tables with the lorries thundering in front of us and behind the sea blurred in the heat haze and I thought, I'd love this to be only the beginning of a journey. I'd love to travel properly. I'd holidayed which was different. I messaged describing it from the car and you said you'd love to be there and you'd love to tell me of all the sights you'd seen with the army. 'I can't wait to just talk and talk to you', you said and it was so beautiful where I was – saturated with light and heat and water and I was so happy with my brown skin, the one that changes from milky quietness to a golden form of strength, body and mind satisfied – looking at Pip's tiny freckles and pinkish tan, my muscles arms and legs strengthened with swimming and salt. I thought maybe there could be a new day for me and my soldier. All the dirt could be purified with your strength and my tenderness.

Our third date.

'I can't wait to see your tan,' you said. 'I want a whole day with you. Can you give me a whole day? Sunday?'

I laughed, lying in bed with morning tea, looking at my unpacked suitcase.

'What time?' I felt as if the salt was still on my skin.

'I'll come for you after breakfast and keep you till midnight.'

'Don't be silly.'

'I'm serious.'

'How about eleven or twelve?' I felt embarrassed to tell you I wasn't very good at mornings.

'All right. I'll probably come at nine but I'll wait for you outside in the car – in the road.'

'Isn't that a bit creepy?' said Pip.

'No,' I said. It's sweet.'

It was very hot. You came to collect me in a navy blue two-seater sports car which I could not connect to my idea of you. Japanese. It had no belongings in it, not a mark on it. It was like a simulation. Music had been playing very loud and you turned it off when the engine came on – a private glimpse of you you didn't want me to see. The top was down and the wind blew my hair about and we couldn't talk. You were a surprisingly nervous anxious driver and fumbled with the key locking the car after we parked in the quiet suburban road you chose near Kew Gardens – what a sedate date – your hand visibly trembling. 'Darn it,' you said. 'I haven't driven this car for a while and I've forgotten how the mechanism works. It's not the one I use for the boys.' That was an old beige Volvo, sensible and tired. I'd seen that one – an unobtrusive family relic, clean as a bone. In the awkward silence you added, 'This is my fit-of-pique divorce car.'

I wore a very pretty sexy dress. I looked my best. You wore a blue shirt with a collar and white buttons. I thought you looked lovely. We were both blue.

We walked a little. You strode. I tried to keep up with you. We kissed on Kew Green. The kisses had nothing in them still. I'd thought-hoped perhaps it would be different this time. I was becoming used to that – feeling outside myself as if I were posing for a non-existent photograph of love. Could I make a mark on you I thought – was it possible to make an impression? There was no dawdling with you. No strolling, no murmuring. We did not laugh. I put it down to what they say about third dates. It's when you have sex. And you were nervous.

We went for coffee – had an earnest conversation in the back of the café. 'I hate to sit where I'm visible,' you said. 'I like to have my back to the wall. It comes from the army – being alert – unless there's cover.' I thought how terrible it must be for you to have no true peace of mind, ever. There was a drill the army teach you for when you're out in the open. 'I can't get it out of my head since leaving Active Service.' Later you taught it to me but I don't remember it now. Nor do I have any memory of what we talked about, except that I felt very scared and alive. You were nervous – febrile – contained. I told you things; I don't know what they were. Then you said, 'I like the way you listen think and speak equally. It's a great quality.' Or did you message that? I don't know.

We had a glass of wine and something little to eat in a courtyard outside another pub, this one near the station, surrounded by tables and other people, more than a few drunks. You tried to get me to sit inside but I refused. 'Being outside with bare legs is such a joy,' I said. 'Reminds me of holidays.'

'It's a lady's prerogative to choose,' you replied, seeming tense and ill at ease. I don't like it at all when men call women ladies. But this was you. You were old fashioned, that was all – quaint.

I was going to trust you. I was going to take the chance. I'd hoped we'd have a second glass of wine and dawdle and flirt but you were preoccupied. Conversation dried up. Your intense curiosity about me seemed to have gone – replaced by a strange sort of irritation, almost – I can't explain. I tried to ask about your marriage as you had asked about mine. 'She found someone else. I told you. I was away a lot.' Curt, dismissive you. Insensitive me.

'It must be hard being an army wife.' I knew I'd said

that before.

'You don't understand. It's only six-weeks rotation, a tour of duty. Even in the First World War. A lot of rubbish is talked about the army – how hard it is.'

'Oh I—' I was confused.

'I don't want to talk about her,' you said. 'It's in the past.' You seemed deeply hurt.

'I'm sorry,' I replied, chastised. And why did I keep asking, I asked myself.

I'd have hated it if you did the same.

'I should be getting back to barracks,' you said. 'Things to sort out.' It was only twenty past two.

'I thought you said we'd have all day,' I said. 'I thought that's what you said.' I feared sounding petulant but I was disappointed as disappointed could be. What about breaking bread? What about talking of the dust?

You looked hard at me, your eyes opaque – again I could not see where pupil and iris met – it was all dark again like trying to fathom the sea. I offered to pay or split the bill – you had paid the other times – but you wouldn't hear of it. And we left so swiftly and you took my hand as we crossed the bridge over the railway – absentmindedly – the sun beating down – as if I were something you'd forgotten but owned just the same.

Did I ever lay a hand on you? Did you ever show a bruise? What is this vileness? What is in your heart? I can hear you – thinking that. I can hear how much you hate me. When did it start – the hatred? Or was it always there?

Your quietness remained like a punishment in the car on the way home – the feeling of being taken home – collected from school early with a stomach ache – knowing I'd troubled or angered—or was it frightened?—her with my inconvenient pain – the double, triple disappointment of failing both school home and self in a nauseating single blow: below the midriff, the sinking swollen painful gut. This was not so bad. This was merely unease.

You opened the car door for me and I got out. It made me tense that I was not allowed to do anything for myself. You followed me up the garden path to my door.

You were unreadable: I was unsure. I thanked you and tried to give you a kiss. You withdrew. 'I'm sorry. I'm not in the habit of kissing on a doorstep like a teenager in full view of the road.' There was anger in your voice although I didn't identify it at the time. I felt the edge of scorn only.

I would give almost anything I've ever had or claimed to own to have gone alone into the house on that day. All I knew was the day felt unfinished. And I did not know when there would be another one to make my hopes come true.

'Would you like a coffee maybe? A glass of water before you drive back? It's hot.'

'Yes. I would.'

How do I describe what came next? What happened? Before the door was properly closed – your whole body and me against the wall? Not even an embrace. A smothering? A ball of passion and energy.

'Hold on a minute,' I said – I laughed. I wasn't afraid of you. 'Let's go into the kitchen.' Down the hall we went and again you were on me – by the fridge with the water and the glass in my hand not poured. The pounce, we used to call it when I was young. The giant pounce. As if we were Tom and Jerry. As if it were a game. I was not afraid. I was surprised. You – whose manners were perfect. You – who had every grace. I told you to wait. I told you to hold on. You got on your knees in front of me, looking up. You didn't touch me. I think it was meant to be erotic – I was so embarrassed – but your extreme seriousness, your solemnity was like a spell. I think it was because you'd told me how in awe of me you were that I felt in command, that I didn't feel afraid.

'Let's sit on the sofa,' I said. It was as if you were a lad who had never made love before. I thought we could kiss and be close on the sofa. That we could slow down. I love kissing. True kissing – although I have had plenty of the untrue kind.

I don't think there was any kissing. My memory jump cuts to you kneeling over me – I mesmerised, half leaning back. Tilted, looking up at you. Leda and the Swan. You were all muscle and lean and proud. It was alarming. It felt serious and momentous and frightening. And I said, 'Before this happens I have to tell you something.' It was farcical, really.

You remained absolutely still and poised and waited. Expressionless. Those dark fathomless eyes. And I said, 'I have – I have a condition, it's called bipolar. I'm – I'm . . .' what was I trying to say, that I was unclean – that I was not good enough, that somehow if we became lovers, you had to know this so you wouldn't be tricked or traduced into the love you feel or might feel with someone who was in so many ways not whole, who was splintered, often? Who despite all appearances of beauty, was not beautiful at all?

It was as if my words meant nothing. They had no impact on you at all. You remained, kneeling over me. Nothing changed, nothing softened in your eyes or your lean and naked body. Then you moved. It was over quite quickly and then I remember we were on the other sofa. You pulled me above and onto you and I think after a while I asked you to stop. Some of it is in sharp focus and the rest has gone. I was in total detached from myself – you detached from me.

'God, you're beautiful,' you said. I could hear the ticking of your watch. It was one of those flashy ones with time on all the continents that can go to the bottom of the sea.

'We didn't even make it to the bed,' I said, trying to joke – to what audience? It was as if I was trying to summon my desire by pretending it had been there. Hoping you would take me to bed and hold me there, anywhere, legitimise this, wanting to feel something other than a quiet awe for your fitness and strength. And the strange disconnect. The watching.

'You're so feminine,' you said. 'Such a woman.'

And that's when it came to me. Masculine was what you were. It was simply that I had never known such a masculine man.

Now that memory is a carved image – you kneeling over me fixed with such a look of conquering before you entered into me how outside myself I felt. I felt nothing. I was unmoved. And I return to it again and again. You and your sword.

My moment of sudden unforeseen tenderness came after, when you sat on the edge of the sofa and began putting on your clothes, the blue shirt with the white buttons, your handsome brown neck. 'You look lovely in your shirt,' I said, paralysed. You looked at me – I don't remember if you smiled, your strange thin half smile with only one side of your mouth turning up.

'Thank you,' you said. But it's you who are the lovely one.' You went away in a flurry of rush and speed and I was left empty in the doorway, thinking, What just happened? What did I do? Sunlight pouring into the road.

You sent me a gif of fireworks exploding. It made me happy. 'How did you do that?' I messaged.

'My boys taught me.' How innocent. But it made me sad. We messaged. I asked if you'd googled my illness. You said you had. I didn't ask if it made a difference, I didn't ask what you thought. We didn't discuss it. Not in any way at all. Ever again. Back then it didn't matter what I said or what you thought – you had only seen the better part of me. The person I was in the summer. The one before the darkness came.

But – the dirty horror tainting even the most beautiful memories of our so-called courtship – how bloodstained with shame and sadness they are.

My trusting explanation later on the phone that I had not felt part of what we had done, that it was rushed and strange and how crestfallen you were and said, 'I need you to teach me.' And your sad confidences about your life with your wife and how restrained and cold it was, how sad, how the lights were out and pyjamas were on and how straitlaced she was and I pitied you and wanted to make things better.

'And you left so suddenly,' I said. 'I thought we'd have time.' There wasn't enough time. Not ever.

'I have to work now,' you said. 'I'll message later.' And you went away.

I don't remember what happened after that. I think Pip came home from his father's and I made dinner for him. I think that's what I did. 'How was it darling?'

'We had some interesting conversations,' he might have said. And, 'You all right, Mum?'

'Of course.' I smiled and replied.

A week later we went to the Wallace Collection. You – emerging from the crowd at Bond Street station – a city gentleman now – another incarnation. You wore a suit. I knew about your body underneath it, looking at your hand, looking at the watch on your wrist, looking up into the closed off roof of the atrium that was the tea hall, the milky light, the echoes. You were remote. 'This is odd. We're dressed,' I said.

'I know.' I was upset – something to do with money. I wanted you to comfort me and felt bad that I did.

'Is everything all right?' I said. I was worried that you were changing your mind about me because of my illness. I worried that you were unsure.

'Yes.' You were preoccupied and quiet, saying you were pushed for time. 'Either tea or pictures,' you said. 'Not both.' I didn't know what I was doing there. I didn't know what the story was. You didn't seem particularly glad to see me. You were disappointed the Canalettos had been moved to Oxford because you wanted to show them to me – seemed vulnerable that your plan was threatened – bewildered almost. I showed you the Fragonard instead – the girl on the swing. You spotted a detail I'd missed in the painting because I always concentrated on the happiness, the joy of the girl. You showed me the leering look of the man up her skirt as she swung with such gaiety, and the abandoned dog. You spotted all the details everywhere we ever went. You were nervous always, and that day, embarrassed to kiss outside. I wanted to kiss you. I was intrigued to see if I felt anything this time. I thought we would feel closer. I wanted to make it feel the way it should. 'I wish I could take you somewhere private and have my way with you,' you said. It sounded strange.

'First day of term tomorrow,' I said.

'I don't like that at all,' you said. 'I don't want to share you with anyone. Least of all your students.' And then you were gone.

All that worried me was not your strangeness but that I was not the perfect person you felt and believed me to be. That foolish confession I'd made about the wasteland of my twenties and the black dark marks of my illness had meant this new hollow fear. The wrongs I had more recently done. I could not tell you of those things straight out in case I lost you before I could discover you. The pain of the past was lodged inside me – the failures, the disappointments, the balance sheet of life. These are common to all – mine were extreme: the black holes, the leprosy next to the shimmering cut glass of the great and beautiful times when soul is stretched and animated like a swollen drop of dew or an unimpeachable tear. Do you wonder what sort of person you are? – I could have asked you. I wonder about it myself. Intrinsic – imposed – simulated – affected – true. What could these words even mean? What I cleaved to even then was your certainty, the boyish clichés you'd clung to and commanded with. I respected the way you had led your men with these simple convictions. I wanted you to lead me.

Making supper in the September kitchen – thinking on you – the animals dozing outside.

'I don't want to go back to school, Mum.' Pip always said that. Ever since leaving primary school he'd been unhappy.

I tried making light of it. 'I know. Neither do I. But what do I always say, "You'll like it when you get there."'

'That's for parties and friends, Mum – not school. You

know that.'

'True. But we can't have another new school.' There'd been three new blazers in the last year.

'I wish the world would just leave us alone.'

I tried to think of what a man might say. 'Most people hate school, darling. Do you remember that chap we met on the boat? "Never complain and don't be late."'

'He's rich, Mum. Rich people always say things like that.'

There was no point saying it works whoever you are. Pip knew perfectly well he could beat me at any battle of words or wills. It was sport to him, I sometimes thought. 'You have to go. Get through it. Then you can be yourself and do what you want to do.'

That Pip did not reply spoke more of his kindness than my attempt at comfort.

'Good luck on your first day back at college,' you'd messaged at five o'clock. That was what I woke to and comforted, went back to sleep, waking again with a jolt – my suitcase still on the floor from the holiday – in a blur of acute panic. I was late. You were never late of course but I could hear your voice in my head: 'Don't fret, gorgeous girl. It can't be helped now.' Pip had gone already. He started earlier than I did – he knew better than to trust me with time.

On the bus you messaged again.

'Morning again, beautiful. I thought you'd like to see my citation. The one I told you about. For bravery.'

'Ooh, yes, I would.'

You forwarded the picture of it to me. I read the words: all about you, all about your courage and your bravery, your calm, your leadership, your strength. I was so proud. It was a paean. And for some reason I felt all these qualities now belonged to me.

And then the stumble into teaching world. The English Room was – still is – a high-ceilinged third-floor room of a tall nineteenth-century red-brick building in a London square. Once a private house for a well-to-do family. It had two long high sash windows. Tall trees outside. The square allowed for a high sky and light flooded in. Crimson carpet tiles were on the floor. Old-fashioned Formica tables were laid out in an L-shaped formation that sat nine at the most. Mine was a little table facing theirs; the whiteboard behind me. I loved that room. A refuge and a trial of courage and strength and a place of work.

'Let's talk about the love object.' It was *The Duchess of Malfi*. There were just a few in that group. Second year.

'The love object?'

'The creature a character projects their longings – themselves - onto.' Bewildered faces. Silence in the room. 'Have any of you ever been in love?' I asked.

There were squeals of 'No!' and laughter. Theirs was the generation of the self. Or perhaps they were simply too young.

'Why do you think characters fall in love?'

'Because they long for something beyond themselves?' Someone said.

'Very true.'

'There's love and lust though, isn't there?' said one of the boys. 'They're two different things.'

I laughed. 'Who told you that?' No reply. 'There's desire. The two can fuse there. And there can be sexual love only – which can be frivolous, joyous. Or there's love as bravery. When the Duchess of Malfi takes a risk – marrying in secret, keeping Antonio secret – he still longs to protect her, promises to be the "sanctuary of her good name."'

'Those are just words,' said one of the boys. 'What does he do when her brothers come for her? He runs.'

'Yes – but before that – we're doing the courtship. Let's concentrate on that. Her desire fuses the sacred and profane. She calls him "a complete man." Do you know what that means – in the context of the time?' I told them about the Renaissance man. That he strove to be learned, accomplished, brave. 'How does she describe her decision to trust him – to marry him?'

One of the girls, again: 'Like a journey into the wilderness.'

'Yes. So – biblical overtones. Martyrdom. Loneliness.'

'And as if she is a soldier.'

'Exactly. A warrior. It is her act of courage. Does that make her a fool?' There was a critic I loved who called tragic heroes fools of time. But never mind that now, I thought. I often answered my own questions, but I can't remember what happened that day.

'Love gets them both killed, that's all I know.' Said another of the girls. And we laughed again.

A day teaching two-hour lessons back-to-back and afterwards I rushed to meet you.

We walked along the river, the Embankment, looking over at MI5. The water winking at us, me thinking of The Kinks. Like all our meetings, it felt isolated from the ones before and since.

'Tell me about the desert. Were you frightened?'

'Sometimes. That's why I'm not going back there. Ever again. But there were other places – Rwanda was worse. But Afghanistan . . . When we reached the dam in the desert and the men swam in the water – that was marvellous.

Truly. So blue.'

You took my hand. I do like that – sometimes. Holding hands. There was a breeze from the river, surprisingly cool. You grasped me at the waist – pulling me.

'Have you ever killed anyone?' The sharp dry sigh. 'No. No, I haven't. At least not close to. From a distance only.' I tried to understand this.

Letting my body go but continuing to hold my hand firmly you explained as if I were a child, 'There are some bad people out there. We have to – had to – do the dirty work so you can sleep tight, safe and secure in your beds. We have to take these risks all the time. People don't want to know what we have to do. And they shouldn't have to.'

I thought again. 'No. I suppose we don't.'

'What does everyone want? Everyone we pass here tonight Freedom and safety. That's what it's our duty to provide. And we do.' I could have made a joke about thinking I was an individual in charge of my own destiny or George Orwell but I didn't. It seemed the army was in control all the time. Watching us, watching over us – it seemed from the way you talked – that politicians even were only secondary. I'd had no idea.

'Do you know how many wars there are going on in the world – now – that we are part of?'

I shivered and was cold. 'No. No I don't.' I felt a little bit angry to be dictated to. I didn't like it. But I stifled the feeling as if it were the enemy.

'Fifty-three.' We were walking away from the river now in streets I didn't know. 'And we work in all of them – not just the ones it's fashionable to report on at the time. Journalists. So ignorant. And not only men. Women. Doing the most repulsive job – being with men for information. Giving themselves – trading their bodies.' I wondered why you mentioned that, Rob – especially then. I still do.

'Yes – I've heard of it.'

'So don't ask me about killing. Not today.'

Pip was away. You had stayed the night. We lay in bed. You were under me.

'Would you like some coffee? I make good coffee.' Your chiselled nose and dark, dark eyes.

'I should be making it for you.'

'If you'd like it – I won't be long.' You had your phone next to the bed. 'Listen to this song while I'm gone,' I said. 'It reminds me of you.'

Concentrating on the coffee machine – naked in the kitchen. Excitable, happy. Warming the rose-covered cups – September light flooding in. I had bought the whole set of china at auction in the country. Cream and pink roses – soft ones. Not all roses are alike – this I knew. You had to be particular about your chosen flowers. You were listening to the song. I was taut in time, knowing it. And then you were behind me. Surprising me.

'I missed you. I couldn't wait.' Was it weird that you'd missed me or was it lovely?

I smiled but didn't turn. 'No! – wait in bed – I'm bringing you coffee.'

'I'd rather watch you make it.'

'Well don't distract me. What about the song?'

'Yes, I know it.' Your voice was bland. The song had glided off you as if you were safe from it and I was surprised.

I gave you the coffee and thought again. 'Can I show something to you? I've been meaning to ask what you think of this.' I couldn't resist – as if, if I kept trying, I could make a mark on you. Wheeling to find it in my school bag – a poem I'd long loved, a question I was thinking of. You looked splendid and naked standing there, waiting.

'Don't give it to me,' you said as I offered it. 'Read it to me.' Do you remember? The habit of command. And I stood naked in the kitchen before you and read in my best voice, and I did not even feel a fool, *The Sunlight on the Garden*. Loss and beauty and transience and war. I glanced at you – the only audience. You concentrated absolutely. It was a way you had, head tilted up - at attention. When the poem was over you said nothing. Nothing at all – even after the requisite pause. Perhaps I should have tried another one.

'Anyway—' I said vaguely – overcome with the feeling of losing. One more attempt at connecting to you gone. All my feeling, like an offering denied. And I turned away, back to the coffee, muffled, disappointed, alone.

But then you said, 'You mourn so much, don't you? I see it. It is time to put all that away.' And you approached and stood behind me, all our bodies touching and rested there, putting a kiss on the side of my neck in the hollow and said, after a little second, 'I have one for you. Will you listen?' You searched your phone with your blunt fingers, and you read – clear, ringing and proud, standing straight and very beautiful in your nakedness:

Invictus

Out of the night that covers me,
Black as the pit from pole to pole
I thank whatever gods may be
For my unconquerable soul.

In the fell clutch of circumstance
I have not winced nor cried aloud.
Under the bludgeonings of chance
My head is bloody, but unbowed.

Beyond this place of wrath and tears
Looms but the Horror of the shade

And yet the menace of the years
Finds and shall find me unafraid.

It matters not how strait the gate,
How charged with punishments the scroll,
I am the master of my fate,
I am the captain of my soul.

It was beautiful hearing you read that poem. And I could say nothing. My brain knew that the poem was bold and had a broad strokes vulgar beauty and was a soldier's poem about courage. It ignored the incomplete, the muddied and the shameful; it had no interest in the idea of 'mere complexity.' I knew that the two poems articulated the space between us completely, like a scene in a play. I did not know what to do with that knowledge. I had not the least idea – so I embraced you. We went back to my bed and made love in your emphatic way without the gentleness I longed to offer you and the coffee cup was broken and I laughed about it but it made me feel a little sad and numb. Just as I felt that sorrow, you rolled over onto me and I was connected to every ounce of all the energy of a boy-man as lean and fit as a fish, effortlessly rolling in an element so clear and free.

You looked down into my face from above as you joyfully surveyed me – your conquered land – and you said, 'I want to love you, protect you, cherish you.' And I laughed. It was all I had ever wanted to hear. All my life. That was it – the precision strike – the moment.

But I joked. I always joke. 'You're late,' I said.

You had the startle reflex of an animal. 'Late!' And you stiffened as if to climb off me and spring away and run.

'I'm teasing. "Late" means I've been waiting for someone to say that to me for a long time.'

‘Oh, that! I thought for a minute – I had to be somewhere else.’ And you kissed me. And I kissed you back. Properly. I could say nothing. I was moved.

And you said, ‘I thought I’d never get through to you – I nearly gave up. Now you look as though you know how I feel about you. What we can be. How much we can be. We can be everything.’ And there it is – the softness of how I felt – how it revisits me – just for a stranded moment – Oh, my darling Robert Ben. How you could have given that and taken it away I close my eyes and remember the back of your neck. So boyish. And I remember other of our early days – early times in bed when my heart was so close to the surface – always with you and the passionate wild bird like desire for you to understand, and I’d say, ‘Rob Rob Rob,’ an explosion of a call and you’d answer, intensely, intently, ‘Maddie Maddie Maddie,’ and it was all. All my joy.

I gave way – such an unburdening – such a relief. I loved to hear you say ‘yes and ‘no’. We’d be tucked, pretending to be ready to sleep. You fitted around me like a shell. And I’d say, ‘Are you asleep?’ and you’d say, ‘Yes.’ And I’d laugh as I turned to you. I don’t remember you laughing very much. But you smiled at me. Or did I imagine that? And the way you said ‘No.’ Have I said that? I’ll remember it until the day I die. The most passionate tender sound – of disappointment, vehemence and desire or despair. ‘Was there no one you could talk to about it?’ (I’d say that about the wars, about your father’s scorn, about your marriage.) ‘No.’ You gave yourself to the word. ‘No.’ It made me want to kiss you, have to kiss you. To make yes.

I couldn’t sleep. I had had too much excitement. There were light flashes in my head.

'Tell me about a precious memory,' you said. I was touched – I thought you were appreciating me, not eating me alive.

I thought of being young – the first time I went to Florence and walked into the square. I thought of the views of the Ionian from the ferry in Greece or of waking at the Swiss border to have passports checked, sleeping on the floor of the train interrailing at eighteen – the white mountains – the cold.

'I don't know which one to choose.'

'Concentrate on one. Breathe. Tell me tomorrow. Go to sleep now, gorgeous girl,' you said. You were watching over me – so I did.

And that was the bloom of it – the bloom of us – in the autumn with the darkness closing in.

Part Two

You won't remember this:

'Mum – I'm poorly – I can't go to school.' Pip's face like a pale bruise. Poorly. What a Beatrix Potter word. 'My stomach hurts. And my head.' He lay in his bed and I stood in his doorway with my book bag heavy on my arm. Heart pounding – panic rising.

'You can't keep doing this. I can't look after you. I have to go to work.' His white face woebegone. His room a grim cave of sweet wrappers and tangled sheets, cramped and dark. Monsters lurking in the corner. He had no window, just a narrow skylight. 'What's the matter, sweetheart? What are you anxious about?'

'Everything.'

'Who have you got today? Is it your nice English teacher?'

'No. That's tomorrow.'

'Do you have Classics? You like that.' I knew I was speaking to him as if he were a tiny child but I was lost. We had listened to the CDs of the myths – Icarus and Medusa and the Gorgons – in the car on the country lanes back when I was playing the responsible married lady, he the private-school educated boy. 'Is it Maths?'

'Yes. And science. They'll send me to Iso if I get anything wrong again. They'll move me down a set.'

'What are you talking about? Why would they do that?' My voice full of irritation – distress – a thousand things in my head. You.

'Isolation. Iso. I told you, Mum.' My stomach gripped in the same vice knot as Pip's. I would be late.

'Look, darling – I'll call and say you're ill and – we'll talk about it when I get home. Because we can't go on like this. OK?'

'OK.'

'I love you.' The stupidity of words. 'Bye, darling.'

'Bye, Mum.'

Hurrying up the stairs, calling the school in the narrow corridor outside the English room – my students waiting inside, 'This is Maddie Vane, Pip Stuart's mother. I'm afraid he can't come to school today. He's not well.' And so deep in memory now the English room, the trees in the square opposite – the high sky, the waning late September light. The month of my wedding anniversary – golden and sad.

Lessons back-to-back and then the heavy door onto the pavement and the evening square. Then you.

'Don't doubt me.'

We were standing at the train barrier at Waterloo after a brief drink somewhere horrible. Thick, clouded diamond-paned windows – men shouting and patting themselves on the back.

You'd said straightaway, 'What's wrong?'

And I – 'Pip's at home again and I—'

'That boy wants you to make him his whole life.'

'I don't think—' (What didn't I think – that you weren't qualified to say? That it wasn't true? That it had been me and Pip against the world for so long now – it was what I clung to.)

'Listen to me. Listen—' You, grabbing my hand across the table. 'He needs other boys – men – around him.'

You made me hold my breath. 'I—'

'You know I was only a little older than he is when I joined the army?' The army? What were you talking about? 'At first I bottled it, lost my nerve. I liked peace. Silence. I daydreamed all the time. Did you know that?' Such a demanding gaze.

'No.'

'The first day – I hated it. I was terrified – called my mother from the payphone under the stairs and said I wanted to come home. She put my father on. And d'you know what he said?' You gripped my hand more tightly. '"What's the matter?" He made me answer, made me say the words, "I want to leave the army." He said, "Don't want to serve your country, is that it? Don't want to be a soldier? Got something better to do?" I remember putting my fist in my mouth and biting down on it so he wouldn't hear me cry. He told me never to bother my mother with my cowardice again.'

'What did you say?'

'I said – "Yes, Sir".'

Your eyes were burning and shining with pride as you told me of your shame. 'But once I accepted there was no way out – it gives you a reason. The army.'

'That's a story.' Your hand softened.

'Yes.' I loved you so much for telling me that story as I sat there still as a bird. All around us the men were laughing

– slopping beer on the tables – crowding the bar in the Friday rush.

'But you don't think Pip—'

'I'm not saying he should join the army. But don't let him be in love with you. That's my job.'

At the barrier you went through ahead of me in a hurry to catch your train – reaching back – grasping my hand in that familiar gesture – letting it go. 'There will be more time.' Your intent look. Your quick vanishing step.

Giddy dazed unbelieving me. I was very happy. It's difficult reminding myself of that pulse quickening happiness. You on the phone to me all the way home on the train. 'You mustn't let that boy take advantage of you,' you said. 'You must find him something active to occupy his time.' Then abruptly the call was cut off. You'd gone into the night. I didn't call you back. I didn't want to seem needy.

Into the flat. The loud footsteps on the floors upstairs.

Pip emerging from his room – his little face. 'Why are you so late?'

'I messaged you I was meeting Rob.'

'Hmm.' Little disapproving stare.

'Were you asleep?'

'I don't know.'

'How are you feeling?'

He seemed to rouse himself. 'A bit better.'

'Did you take the dog for a walk?'

'No.' The dog looked up at me, silent – wistful.

'Did you eat lunch?'

'No.'

'You know how important eating properly is.' Why was I lecturing him?

There probably wasn't anything in the fridge. And I should have come straight home.

My conscience was screaming at me. 'Supper won't be long.' This wasn't true. Why had I decided on risotto? It takes for ever.

Pip followed me; stood close. Outside it was windy and the night wind beat against the panes. I hurried to cut up the onion and mushrooms – the quick knife trembling and cutting the board. 'It's all about societal change, Mum. I've been doing my research.'

'Sorry, what?' I tried to tease – my heart beating too fast already. 'On your phone again all day? Enlighten me.'

'That you're tired and late and can't afford to buy me a computer.' And sitting in pubs with men from the internet? I say that now. I didn't say that then but tried to concentrate on the risotto – wondering if he could see me shaking. 'In the fifties one income was enough per household.' I didn't tell him that actually it was the seventies – in living memory – trying to slow my speeding thoughts. 'Now it doesn't. Society makes us poor and on benefits. It's called the working poor. Even though Dad gives us money. Even though you teach at an exclusive private college all week, you have to tutor at the weekends because it's zero hours. Think of the markup they're making on you – think of the thousands in profit.'

'It isn't exclusive. There's no exam.' Juggling the stock and the fucking ladle.

But Pip was not to be sidetracked. 'And the worst thing about poverty is it makes you ashamed.' I thought about the lofty, spacious house I grew up in – the private schools.

I wanted to scream. 'Thank you for explaining my life to me.' Why was I so mean?

'Mum – feminism has been hijacked in the service of capitalism.'

'We aren't poor.' I insisted on it. How could he think that? It was just that we had no money. We had lives of the mind. And we were here – we had Bonnard's tree. I held hard to the fact I had been with you so it was all all right.

'We are.'

I could barely concentrate. Trying to pull my mind away from all the things you'd said. 'I like working there. The young remind me of when I was young.' When there was life ahead with no mistakes in it. How beautiful we were. 'And we're not poor. You mustn't say that. There's poverty around us—'

But he interrupted me, 'Don't be such a silly goose.'

Staring at the transparent grains of rice, trying to stop myself from turning and shouting, all I said was, 'Can you not?'

I wanted him to stop talking so I could think my own thoughts.

But he insisted – still looming behind me. 'OK – I've got a survey here on my phone. Remember, we live in one of the richest countries in the world. You have a job. We have no property. Yet there's nothing left at the end of the month. You only get through the summer because your best friend lends you money. You have debts. Can we afford to go and do things we want to do? We've just had a holiday with your credit card and it was lovely – '(he'd swum so bravely). 'I understand we had to use it when the dog was run over. We'd had to mend her bones. But are you still using it? And what if you get sick and you can't afford the payments? What if we really need something? What then?' What then? sang Plato's Ghost – What then?

His fluting questions hammered at me. And my mind was forced to remember and my throat to swallow it. He was right – of course he was. We'd squandered our capital. He would always remind me – there was no coming back from that – it would always be swimming against the current. We had not provided for him properly.

We'd given him so much when he'd been too little to remember. The plums in the market in Castellina the year he'd learned to walk. The pink wicker basket with his things in it on the cobblestones in the dust. Holding him as he went down the slide. I had to pretend that it was all right – didn't I? Wasn't that my job?

Now we had a flagstone terrace and lavender. Those things made the world tilt even more sometimes. I could touch them but they weren't mine. They were simulacra.

All his brittle words told me was that I had put an unbearable burden of worry on his shoulders and he bore it. I was a failure of a mother. 'Every year we get the last Christmas tree because you're still scraping together the money after buying the presents.' He used to watch me fishing the cash out of my coat pocket from the last tutoring hour of the year. Trying to charm the Christmas-tree man for no reason at all.

Please, Pip, please. Don't make this be true. 'You have presence, Pip. Nice use of the rhetorical question. You should be a politician.'

'Not everything is funny, Mum.'

'I know.'

'And then we have to go and be poor relations at your rich brother's house every Christmas and Easter.'

'It's not his fault,' I said – weakened. 'I'm the one who made mistakes and got into debt.'

'He should be looking out for you. You have an illness. You were children together. I hate him.'

'Don't talk about your uncle like that. Nothing is that simple. He has his own family to think of.'

'And his wife's awful. All those discreet diamonds.' I said nothing. 'I'm only telling the truth. Why haven't they helped you? They're supposed to be your family.'

He had worn me down. 'They have. Don't bear a grudge, Pip.' But hadn't I given it to him?

'I'm simply explaining—'

'Will you be quiet? I'm tired.' And now I'd been sharp with him and he was so anxious.

'You wouldn't be so tired if you weren't always worrying about money. And you're too old to find a rich second husband. And you never meet anyone anyway except weirdos on the internet.'

'Rob isn't a weirdo. He's an officer. He's respectable.' How could you not be with a name like Robert Fordham?

'Don't be silly, Mum.'

'Anyway. None of this is the point. You still have to go to school. Promise you'll try to go tomorrow?'

'Yes, I'll try. I'll try for you.'

Did Pip manage one more day after or that or two?

He staggered when he left and when he came home as if his limbs were struggling to obey him.

And then we were together.

'How's school?' You said.

'College.'

'Of course – college. Tell me.'

'They're there because mainstream school hasn't worked out for them. I'm lucky because the classes are tiny. I try to teach them the way I was taught. It's important – to pass things on. Help them become confident. Make a success of their lives.'

'So. You serve. You give them courage.'

I think I laughed. 'I suppose I do.'

'I'd love to see you in action.' I wanted to say, It's not me that matters – it's them. But I feared that was only partly true. The ego of the performer was never far away – the blood seething under the surface of the skin.

You'd been watching me think. 'It's great being admired, isn't it?' That sense again that you were reading my mind. 'Service can be a burden. I understand that. But we're together now. We're going to have such a glorious life.' I tried very hard to imagine it – where we'd live – what our families would think – you turning my hand over – tracing 'I love you' on my palm. Such a peculiar feeling – the sense of having so much to tell you and when we met having nothing to say. You didn't know vast swathes of me. After the beginning, you never asked. Not about my books, not about my family, not even about where I'd grown up. As if I were a diamond being prized out of a rock.

'You're too good for me and I—'

'Less of that,' I said. We held hands in that pub and suddenly everything was so perfect and beautiful and we rode above it all – all the agonies large and small with which we were surrounded.

After that you had flu. We couldn't see each other – we spoke and you were hoarse and strange. The word delirious was used. I was so worried. My head was so full of you. I wanted to come to the barracks with a care parcel – 'No!' you said furiously vehemently. 'You mustn't. Promise. I couldn't bear for you to see me like this.'

Next you had to go away. Something to do with a training course.

Do you remember my colleague? The one I shared some English classes with. Caroline? We'd sit together in our meagre breaks. Sometimes we walked to the station. Sometimes had a drink. She was very analytic – very dry. Pretended not to be kind.

'You're different,' she said, catching me on the stair

between classes. The pale high blue walls with the students' charcoal art on it, the portraits, the bright life they held. 'A strange air about you.' I laughed. 'You've met someone, haven't you?' I told her about you – the army –the other world. I babbled – I blushed. You were a secret I'd been keeping. 'Comes and goes a lot, doesn't he?' she said. 'You seem very up and down.'

'He has a lot of work,' I explained. 'Drives everywhere. Or else he's on a train.'

'Doesn't plan your meetings in advance?' She screwed up her short-sighted pale blue eyes to look at me.

'It'll be different when he leaves the army.'

'Be careful,' – it was all she said. Those pale anxious eyes still on me. She's only trying to spoil you for me, I thought. She's envious. She doesn't understand.

Next time I saw you Rob your arms were full of flowers. And you opened the boot of your sandy-coloured car in the sandy pub car park of what you were beginning to call 'our place' to reveal tins of my favourite coffee. The autumn light – your thin-set firm mouth. The first of your cards with the green writing. They all came from the same shop – glossy nature scenes – no greeting inside – the same size and lamination: shiny phony vulgar badly conceived pointless vile. I knew that. I didn't understand why it mattered so much. Men were always bad at cards.

Dear Maddie

This is just to say how much I have enjoyed getting to know you over the last few weeks.

Best wishes, RB.

I was bewildered – by the formal words – by the presents – supermarket flowers I didn't much like – by your velvet eyes. After that, these cards would come in the post when I least expected them, addressed to Mrs Maddie Vane, always in green pen, always filled with strange formal phrases.

'There's no need,' I said. 'Really.'

'They are a token of my esteem,' you replied, giving me the ugly flowers. Who has ever said that except in nineteenth-century novels and Mills and Boon in the history of the world? I asked you where you'd bought them, while not knowing what I suspected you of. 'At the Sainsbury's on the way here.'

'And the cards?'

'They have a shop at barracks.' I tried to picture the shop. I didn't understand why I couldn't and I didn't know why I'd asked you. But it was as if you'd been backstage preparing. All this fog and mist around you like the special effects in old black and white films.

'Why do I have to go and stay with Richard and Amanda just so you can be with that weird man?'

'He's not weird. And that's not the reason.' This was not true. 'It's so you can have some fun without me.'

'So you can have a break from me, you mean.'

'No. It's because it's a good idea to see your relations occasionally. I really miss you when you're gone.' This was true.

'Me too,' said Pip.

Drop-offs at Richard and Amanda's made me feel sick – standing at the gate, not wanting to go in. Pip – walking away along the path without a backward glance – looking shabby, looking poor.

In bed – that same afternoon I tried to find you with words.

'How did your marriage end?' It was clean lying in bed with you. You held yourself separate, breathing your breaths, thinking your thoughts.

'I told you.'

'No – you didn't.'

'She woke me up early on Christmas morning to tell me she'd been having an

affair.'

'Why? Why would she do that?'

'I don't know.'

I tried to imagine it – staring straight ahead at the wall above the bedroom fireplace with the fresco of the Garden of Eden on it. You, propped up – you used to fold the pillow neatly behind your head the way they taught you in the army.

'What did you say?'

'I was half asleep. I couldn't say anything.'

'God, how awful.' It was outlandish and terrible and you were so calm, telling me. I couldn't look at you. I don't know why – I just listened to your voice.

'She told me she was pregnant. She wanted to keep the baby. She left.' I imagined the whole drama – like a silent film. I imagined it all.

'But why would she do that? On Christmas morning with the children in the house?'

She couldn't keep it a secret another minute I suppose. My thought – not your reply. In all my knowledge of you I never heard you speculate about another human being's heart.

There was silence. Then, 'I told you. She was a very cold person.' (Was? Had she died?). 'She didn't like kissing.'

I loved kissing. But it was true I'd had to teach you how. You moved onto your side and looked at me.

'You know – I never really knew what it was like – until I

met you. Actual, proper passion. Thank you for that.' We had rarely had actual proper passion. Very rarely, I thought. I kept this to myself. Like a terrible disloyalty it was wrong to acknowledge or admit. Like the longing to laugh in bed, like the feeling of being imprisoned away from you even when you were right there. Like the way your words went round and round in my head when I was without you – as if by repeating them to myself I might understand what they meant.

'What happened then?'

'I offered to go to counselling. She said, "No". Said she loved him.'

'No – I mean – who cooked Christmas lunch?' This preoccupied me. I couldn't imagine any woman leaving her children on Christmas Day. Even the honey-coloured blonde you'd told me about. The woman who had no warmth.

'Oh, I can cook – I always cook for my Mum. I can rustle things up.' You were always making rueful remarks about fish fingers and Bisto gravy and overcooked mince but you had a pride in them as well. I who loved cooking had never cooked for you – nor you for me. We had never watched television. We had never been to the movies or the theatre or anywhere at all. Our world was not real. I knew that. But if I waited, perhaps it would become so. If I could only figure you out.

'What's her name – the baby?'

A pause. 'Lula May.'

'Sounds like a country song. What does he do?'

'He's a tree surgeon.' I made a bad joke about tool belts. I didn't know what to say. 'He's a decent man. That's what I keep telling myself. A decent man. I can't object to him at all.' What would happen if you did?

'Do you blame her? Have you forgiven her?'

'No.' Short, sharp breath – vehement little sound. 'I

avoid talking to her. She's a bad person.'

'Do your boys get on with him? Do they ever feel jealous about their sister?'

'I've never asked them,' you said, leaning away from me, eyes veiled.

'Why not?'

'It's just never come up.'

'Did you love her when you got married?' Questions – always questions with me for you. I felt like a dog scratching at a door because there was a ghost behind it.

'I thought I did. I wish I'd met you earlier. There are so many things I wish.' In that we were united. We were good at wishing.

Then at last you turned your head and looked at me and you said, 'You know I never expected to fall in love.' And I was astounded, briefly.

What a thing to say.

I made sausage sandwiches – to make one of the nevers go away.

'Let's not talk about her. I have dreams – and you're in them.'

This made me laugh. 'How so?'

'We could be a power couple,' you said, munching with tidy efficiency. Do you remember, you little dead lost thing? 'You and me against the world. You'll leave the college – become a super tutor – and when I've left the army, I'll have a brilliant career. We'll be in control of everything – we'll do whatever we want.' This made me feel cold. I could not smile or respond. These words took me far away from you – just as at the beginning – far removed – despite the beauty of your slender strong body.

You showered and doused yourself in Floris aftershave but had no smell of your own. 'I've got to get back to the MA,' you said, leaving me with a spooling colour reel of images that did not match actions and words. It was like being wound round with coloured tapestry wool, dazzled by eight glittering eyes.

After you'd gone it was as though you'd never existed at all.

Pick up – Richard in the doorway; Pip putting on his shoes. 'I hear you're seeing someone new.'

'Yes.'

'Army?'

'He's in Intelligence.'

'That sounds likely.'

I felt hot with rage. Richard loved undermining me. It was as if he were pulling my hair.

'Tell Pip I'll wait for him in the car. Thanks for having him.'

He called after me – 'Maddie, don't be like that.'

But I'd left him standing.

We sat in the car.

'What's your MA on?'

'Open-Source Intelligence.'

'What on earth is that?'

'Tracking people – information. Finding things out.'

'Gosh.'

'It's the white elephant'—you actually said things like white elephant—'of intelligence but I advocate it should be more valued.' Tracking people seemed a strange thing to do an MA on but what did I know. I dropped you at the station once – you kissed me passionately – and ran into the road. No one has ever left as quickly as you.

You were nervous – sometimes almost terrified – about places you didn't know, parking; I worried for you that you could be brave in the army but were so frightened at home. I found out later it's called hyper vigilance. When we were together walking along a road – so seldom – you'd look around nervously as if someone were about to approach, as if ambush was threatened. It upset me that the army had done this to you. I didn't know how to reassure you – how to make it all go away.

We met at Westminster tube – you waiting on the corner outside the station – always wanting to blend in with the crowd it seemed – I could never recognise you until I was almost upon you. I didn't know how you did that – it was so odd. We walked across The Mall in the bright autumn day and stood on the bridge in St James's Park looking towards Horse Guards Parade and I told you that view was how I'd imagined Istanbul as a girl.

'But it's not though – it's the seat of power.'

'I know that now.'

'You and your imagination.' I could not discern whether my imagination was a good or a bad thing. You stood apart from me.

'What's it like in the bunker?'

'You know I can't talk about that.'

'Is it a long way down?'

'Yes.'

'Is it like on TV?' Screens?'

'Sort of. We watch. We listen. We understand.' Then a pause. 'I'll take you there one day.' This seemed unlikely. The leaves glittered in the wind as I followed the flight of the breeze over them, remembering kissing boys on those park benches when I was at school. Or on the grass dreaming after summer exams so long ago. I shivered. I would never have guessed I would end up here – a ghost inside my mind.

'Come on let's go. I have to drive to Cambridge tonight.' Cambridge was where there was another military base – and you briefed generals. I tried to imagine these generals but could only think of comedy ones or the famous one who somehow looked louche and attractive on TV complaining about the tanks being ill-equipped in Iraq and our soldiers being blown to bits because we didn't care enough to protect them.

And when I reached the flat – Pip – like a shade.

I knocked on the door of his room. 'Can I come in and talk to you?'

'All right.' He lay in his bed, clutching his phone – looking up at me as if I were a small child bothering him. 'I ate the pizza,' he said.

'What is it about school? Are you being bullied? You know I was bullied when I was your age.'

'We're not all you, Mum. It's not that. I've told you. I'm invisible until they threaten me.'

'Who? Tell me again.'

'If you talk in the corridors, you're sent to Iso. If you forget your ruler, you're sent to Iso.'

'But they wouldn't send you there. You never do anything wrong.' I didn't say, Iso is for prison camps – not schools.

'Yesterday my science teacher said if I forgot my book again, I'd go to Iso. I've looked everywhere.'

'He should know you're dyspraxic – you lose things.'

'If he does, he doesn't care.'

'We'll look again.'

‘He has it. He forgot to give it back after homework. I’m pretty sure that’s it.’ Pip was patient – explaining there was nothing either he or I could do.

‘Are you sure nothing else has happened to upset you?’

‘Apart from existing at the end of history, you mean?’

‘Come on, darling.’

‘A police officer came yesterday. About the knifings. Other schools and us. You know – the turf wars. They’re going to patrol the corridors now – they’ll write to you about how we have to go straight home from school and always in groups – not on our own.’

‘Bloody hell. Sounds like a war zone. I’ll write to the head.’ Take action – that’s what I always tried to do.

‘There’s no point, Mum. She can’t stop gang violence because you send her a strongly worded letter. I just don’t want to go to Iso. It’s frightening in there.’

‘Oh dear.’

‘You don’t understand, Mum.’

‘When we went to look around they said it was modelled on an old-fashioned public school. Do you remember how relieved I was? Music. Latin. Choirs.’

‘Child abuse,’ said Pip. ‘Those places are where you pay to be molested instead of getting it for free.’

I looked vaguely round the room – what there was of it outside the bed. The mess of clothes and food wrappers. ‘Do you know where that Jelly Cat is I gave you for your birthday?’

Pip ignored this question. ‘They should give me a place at your college, Mum. In the GCSE bit. In return for your labour.’

‘I know.’

‘Not just me, Mum. Us all. Everyone should have teachers like you and places that care.’

‘Yes. They should.’ In the silence my little dog pushed her nose against my leg. ‘I’ll speak to Lauren.’

'No – don't. It never does any good. She'll only say no.'

'I'll speak to yours then. I'll make an appointment with the GP. We'll talk about how you're feeling.'

'It's a waste – Ma. A waste of time.' My mind ran over the many appointments since the last summer term. Meetings with the head. Meetings with the team. Meetings with the intervention officer, the welfare worker – unaccountably called Flora. I'd had a feeling she hated her pointless job and wanted to have a baby with someone nice called Crispin or Stephen but that was my trouble, my mind always strayed – imagining, to stop myself screaming and running out of the room. Pip had had counselling from the school counsellor who didn't turn up and he'd waited, trembling outside her door. When I told the headmistress this, she said that Pip was lying. Pip did not lie. This I knew. I had always told him that truth was what we owed to ourselves.

'We have to make the best of it, don't we, Pip? Put our best foot forward,' I think I said. 'That sort of thing.' I thought of Shakespeare – I thought of you. – 'Rainy marching in the painful field.' Perhaps you were right – Rob – the boy needed me to be tough.

'It's so long until my GCSEs and all they do is talk about them and I keep failing Maths and Science. It makes me sad.'

'I know.'

'And I haven't any friends.'

'What about Daria?'

'She left – remember?' Of course. Daria had left. 'You could home school me.'

'And what would we live on? Look – promise me you'll go to school tomorrow?' I could have said, if you don't go to school, you won't pass your exams and you won't go to university and then you won't get a degree which you must do so that you don't end up like me. But we both thought it all the same.

'I promise, Mum.'

'Shall we go to the movies at the weekend? Six o'clock show? We get those free tickets with my bank account.' He said nothing. 'We can smuggle the sweets in.'

'If you like.' Despite his despair Pip was kind – he liked to pretend that would comfort him when really it only comforted me.

'Good morning, Butterfly, I am thinking of you.' You had started calling me Butterfly followed by the bright blue emoji. And off I'd go to college, feeling protected, feeling safe. I'd begun to call you Fox because you were so resourceful. You would not let bad things happen to me. And these were our emojis one to another.

The GP emerged out of our ether.

'We'd like a psychiatric referral,' I said, trying to sound clear and direct like you. The doctor was thin – her demeanour cold. She wore good clothes and had a straight back like the rail of a ship. She spoke in clipped upper-middle-class tones and had an air of weary authority coupled with impatience.

'I think Pip is anxious and depressed,' I said. 'As you know I have a mental health condition and so I'm worried about him. Inheritance.'

She looked at me and I thought – she thinks I have Munchausen syndrome by proxy which would have been very funny indeed except it wasn't at all.

'I understand you haven't been going to school, Pip?' She said, as if Pip were a murderer.

'No.' said Pip.

'Is it all right if I speak to you alone, Pip?' she said. He nodded. I waited outside the door looking at the faded apricot carpet and wondering who this pretty old house had once belonged to and trying not to think about how horrible this was – trying not to cry. If I started to cry, I wouldn't be able to stop. I was very careful not to even try to listen to what was being said until I was summoned back in.

'It's true, Pip is exhibiting signs of anxiety and low mood,' said the doctor. I think she'd made him do a questionnaire. 'But the key is he's not self-harming. He has no severe condition I can see so I can tell you now that any psychiatric CAMHS referral is going to be knocked back. I'm sorry.' She looked at me steadily. 'Even if I were to refer him to cognitive therapy, there's a waiting list of nine months.' She didn't appear to understand that you have to offer a depressed person hope.

'He needs a therapist he can talk to,' I said. 'But first a proper diagnosis. A psychiatrist.' I felt I had to counter quickly, in the presence of this obvious robot. I said nothing about meds. Pip was so young.

The doctor behaved as if I had not spoken. 'You're a reader, aren't you, Pip? There's a very good book about anxiety I can recommend.' Pip just stared at her then nodded again politely. We both did. 'And here is a list of numbers he can call and online services he can access if he is feeling distressed.' There was no point trying to explain to this person that despair and online services were not a match.

'I wonder how much she earns,' said Pip as we took shelter in the car and were reunited with the dog. 'Did you see her jewellery? She knows better than us about us – I hope you understand that, Mum.' At least he could still joke.

'The thing is Pip; there isn't anything she can do.' Why was I trying to make this woman's case now we had gone?

'I know.'

'I'm sorry you had to go through that, I really am,' I said. I tried to sound grown up and not distressed and afraid. 'I'd hoped it would be different.'

'Yes – you're always hopeful,' said Pip in a low voice. 'But I told you, Mum – everyone online says the same. You have to self-harm to be seen.'

'Well don't start.'

'What do you take me for, Mother?' He said. 'And anyway – I'm afraid of knives.'

I started to drive. We couldn't just sit in the car – which needed cleaning – for the rest of our lives. 'We'll have to go private,' I said, making sure I was seeing the traffic coming at me, observing families holding hands on the common and the high concentration of beautifully groomed dogs, trying to avoid being pushed off the road by gleaming four-by-fours.

'No! We can't afford it,' said Pip. I would have to borrow money. That frightened and humiliated me. But I would do it.

'Let's see how it goes.' What worried me was not merely borrowing the money for one doctor's appointment but what about the next one and the one after that? I felt sick and ill. I had to ignore that.

And still I knew he wouldn't go to school. When I wasn't there I knew he stayed in his bed surrounded by a litter of sweet papers and biscuit boxes on his phone. His room gave off a high sweet smell. He stared. He didn't wash. He slept and slept.

I was terrified.

'Dare I ask how Pip is?' Pip – who was asleep only feet away.

'He's worried about Trump.' I said, unwilling to tell you

about the GP, my mind crowded. 'Incessantly. I used to worry about the end of the world when I was little too. Remember – 'Stay Alive in 85?' You didn't reply. 'But we also know it didn't come true.' It felt strange talking about Trump with no clothes on in bed. But I'd brought it up. It was better than saying he is even more withdrawn and I don't know what to do.

'Have you heard of The Great Game?' you said.

'What?'

'Tell him. The Great Game. It's all that these power plays are. Sabre rattling. It won't come to that. Even with the fools we elect. We get the leaders we deserve – but no one wants to blow us to oblivion – that's for sure.' You spoke as if the army could somehow prevent the madness of leaders rather than acting on their wishes. You spoke as if there were secret levels and webs of safety about which I could only dream but you had privileged access to. Your visits to Washington with its secret underground chambers. It was like a dark drug.

The next time it was all changed – the scenery – you. We were in a different smarter pub with dark blue walls beside the river – the table was less sloppy and marked but there were still white rings on it. I examined them, waiting for you. Mortlake river this time – moving and slapping the sides of the shore. More wind – hurrying to meet you. October – nearly the worst month of the year. You were late, which never happened, and I waited quietly.

When you opened the street door and approached me, all of your urgent energy was gone. You looked small and shaken as if in the aftermath of something terrible.

I stood to greet you but you seemed not to notice. 'Let's sit by the fire,' I said.

'No. Here.' You gestured to a cold corner table in sight

of the door. I got the drinks – another first. I didn't like the way the barman looked at me. It was a great shock to me, returning to the table – how helpless you looked. How different you were. Huddled almost. I didn't know what to do. I did not dare do anything – I didn't think. When I was with you, you always wiped my mind.

'What is it?' I said. 'What's the matter? Has something happened?'

'Bad thoughts,' you said. Your eyes looked down. I had no power. You'd given it and now you were taking it away. 'I wish I'd met you sooner.' Bowed you were – and quiet. It's too late for us.'

'No – don't say that. It's all all right. Nothing's ever too late.'

'No. Too much has happened.' When Pip was little he'd said 'no' with just the same determination. It's the closing of the mind of the child.

Where was your confidence – your conviction? I was afraid. And I was so tired – suddenly aware that I was very, very tired. The sudden meetings – the storms – the speed. I wondered if this was what it felt like to be bled in past centuries – leeches pressed against your wrists and along your back. When your humours were out of balance. 'Can you tell me?'

'No.' You shook your head – eyes closed – still like a child, and I wanted to protect you, explain that it wasn't too late and there was no barrier between us. 'Thirty years in the army. Do you think I could even begin to tell you what's wrong?'

'Tell me a little?'

Very quietly, head still down, 'No.'

Deep breath – 'What about – what about counselling – do the army provide—?'

'No. I'd recommend that for the men. Not for me.'

'But . . .'

'There are too many memories. I can't—'

'Tell me.'

Then you looked up. Absolute blaze of pain and horror and anger. 'The severed heads they threw into the camp in Rwanda? The young sergeant I watched being blown up by a suicide bomber – a boy – when he was giving him chewing gum outside our gates in Afghanistan – trying to win hearts and minds? Which one do you want?' Your fury was brief – then it was gone. A sharp sigh, a little painful sound, your eyes full with tears and the little sob – but what was so unexpected was despite these true horrors it felt so unreal, unreal as if we were trapped on stage in a play and you were the only one who knew the words. It was a nightmare play where I was captive to a stranger and I had no willpower. I didn't know you.

You put your face in your hands and when you took them away again the tears were spilling. Real tears. I took your hand and held it very hard so that you knew there was another human being beside you but I didn't feel it – it didn't feel real. I felt disconnected and afraid.

'Please – Rob – don't fret. We will forget – we will forget the past together.

'I'm glad you're leaving the army.'

'Yes it's time. They wanted me to go back. To Afghanistan. They – I've done enough.' The idea of 'them' was so strange.

'Shhhh.' I tried to shield you from the room – embracing you awkwardly – covering your tears.

'I have to go,' you said. I thought you were ashamed – embarrassed – I don't know. You were always in a hurry but this was particularly fast painful and remote. I felt exposed where you did not. I can't explain.

'All right. Yes. I understand.'

A scramble of coats and bags and we held each other tightly again in the corridor close to the back street door, with the dark blue painted walls and the artfully placed black and white photographs conveying precisely nothing. They were all settings – why hadn't I understood?

Again you were a like a ball of energy in my arms – like a little Tigger – breathing heavily with the sobs. 'Shhhh – it's all right. We are together now.'

'Yes. I need to go.'

And the whirl of your departure, the dashing. You always had to go because you had to be up at five. You liked to see the sun rise quite alone. I say this again and again because it's the one thing I think was true. 'It gives me so much strength,' you said. I was drenched in dark colours.

I tried to call you before bed to see if you were all right after that terrible crying. I felt so much for you. I wanted to make it all right. But you didn't pick up. The next morning you messaged, 'Sorry Butterfly – I fell asleep in the bath.'

The days began to dwindle – there was less and less light. They passed. And nights. I was staring at essays.

And you messaged – out of the blue. 'Can I come and see you – meet you at our pub?'

'I have marking.' But my unwilling heart leapt.

'If I could just see you. Please.'

'I know it's late.' It was nine-thirty. 'I'm forty-five minutes away.'

'It's just—'

'Finish your work and I'll meet you at our place.' Entreaty and command – your leadership style.

I did as I was told. I explained to Pip – whispering through his door – and I left.

I felt anxious about leaving Pip with no warning – anxious to see you, pursued by terrifying feelings. Breathless and uncontained. It was a blustery night but not cold. You stood up and greeted me with all your bravest energy: a different man from the one who'd broken and cried in front of me the time before. You wore a blue linen jacket I'd never seen – a perfect fit. All your clothes were – like the grey suit that seemed tailor-made – slightly following your slenderness – not boxy or clumsy like so many men's suits. And you radiated triumph, standing up from the leather armchair as I came into the pub. You were always there first. Always.

'Thank you so much for coming,' you said – embracing me. 'I've just given a lecture about this operation I commanded – years ago now.'

I felt giddy looking at you. What if Pip . . .? 'How did it go?'

'Splendid. It was splendid. And I wanted to tell you. Share it with you.' I felt proud of you. It seems so bizarre now when it had absolutely nothing to do with me.

I stopped thinking about Pip. He was gone and wiped away. 'Where was the lecture?'

'Close to the barracks. For young soldiers and members of the public too.' Members of the public.

'You should have told me. I'd have come.'

'It would have bored you.'

'No. It wouldn't.' I smiled in case you thought I was being defiant, sensing that there was a response you wanted but this was not it – sat down, drank the wine from the glass you had ready on the table. You always had my drink ready. 'Tell me now. Tell me about the op.' I knew what was expected and I wanted to hear.

'It was my mission – my mission to plan. I told you I was in support. We had to deliver precious equipment for the Afghans.'

'Weapons?'

'No. It was equipment – a vital machine part. A long

journey across the desert – I planned a decoy – a misdirect to avoid being tracked. But still – we were exposed – the risk was huge.' Like so many of your stories it didn't quite make logical sense. Too many details omitted or glossed over or gone. Perhaps it was the exhaustion of the day.

Then you came to your best bit. 'The surveillance helicopters above us suspected Taliban moving in the vicinity of our convoy. We couldn't be sure who they were. They radioed – asked whether to fire from above.'

'That must have been a terrible decision to make.'

Your eyes were black and blank. 'You calculate the risk.'

'What order did you give?'

'I said one word: Fire.' You said this without a pause and with tremendous joy.

'How did it feel?'

'Good. It felt good.' A beat.

'But what if—? Women? Children?'

'They aren't people. They're the enemy.'

You reached and held my hand. It was as if the sadness and the mourning by the river had never taken place. 'I'm glad it's over and I don't have to go back there anymore.' I felt nothing. There was something I should be responding to and I couldn't summon it at all. 'What's the matter?'

'Nothing. It's just . . .' I felt manoeuvred into position for this scene and I didn't like it. 'I wish you'd told me about the talk. That I knew your plans. I wish we were . . .' I couldn't continue. What I meant to say was an item, a couple – one of the phrases.

A grim form of fury emanating from you at my disobedience. And a strange tilting sensation – the ground under my feet – your world, Pip's world, the students' worlds and mine, which was shrunken and papery, all rasping together or spinning like discs through light and glinting darkness.

You said, 'Do you have no faith in me at all? No patience? You know I'm leaving the army – doing an MA –

trying to be a good father, a good son, working all hours? If you're not happy with me . . .' There was the threat, hanging in the air – your first – but the one I'd always known was coming.

'You know that's not true.'

'If I'm not what you want . . .' You were very cold. Your eyes the same – dark and empty.

'I didn't say that. And it's not as if I'm expecting we'll get married or anything, it's just –'

I wanted it to be different. I wanted a partnership. I wanted to communicate with you. How did I explain you were either larger than life or a ghost? How every meeting was a separate incident, a new seduction? How did I explain the shifting sands I was on with Pip, with work, with life? And then I felt instantly guilty: why had I ruined your triumphant mood by making a scene – this unexpected treat of seeing you – yet why did I always feel as if my wishes were an imposition? I looked down at my lap. My hands – ringless – telling me I belonged with nobody and nobody belonged with me. I did not know what I was feeling but I knew I was in the wrong. I didn't like the silence between us. It made me afraid. I felt burned.

Then you said, 'Look at me,' in a very gentle voice, putting your finger gently under my chin, against my throat. And I looked up into your dark fathomless eyes.

'I will ask you to marry me one day,' you said. 'Our time will come.'

It was the kind of thing my father might once have said – gnomic, faintly biblical, vague and certain. I believed you.

You messaged the next day: 'Are you free on your day off next week? I can take the day.'

'Really? Can you do that?'

'I'm leaving the army. I've earned it. I can do anything I

want.'

That made me laugh.

'I'll park up on the heath'—you were obsessed with parking—'and you can let me know when the coast is clear and Pip has gone to school.'

'Thursday then?'

'Yes. Thursday it is.'

Wasn't it meant to be Friday I'm in love? Like the song? It was never Friday for us though. Never a weekend. Not since the beginning. But still I counted the days. It's not only reserved for youth.

Early on Thursday morning Pip woke me, white faced and frightened looking.

'I can't go today, Mum. I can't. Please don't make me. I haven't slept.'

I couldn't say – you have to. Rob is coming. And we're going to be—What was it we were going to be . . . ? Together? For a whole day? I couldn't say that – even though it was right that he went to school. Or was it? How could it be the action of a loving parent to deliberately make my child suffer? Pip was so sad.

I looked at him, thinking all those thoughts. 'I don't know what to do.'

'I promise I'll go tomorrow, Mum. I promise.'

And I – protective – sorrowful – was angry that I couldn't see you. Just for a millisecond, but I was. Hauling myself out of bed to make a cup of tea and try to comfort him. 'Is it because of the GP? Has it made you feel worse? Perhaps if we go private you could get some meds?'

'Just because you take meds doesn't mean everyone else has to.'

'Look Pip – I'm not saying—' But wasn't I? I had not had a diagnosis since I was thirty. It was hard with meds – it was impossible without. I did not want to make him another me – but I wanted to spare him suffering.

'Don't you understand, Mum? It's the world that's wrong. Not me.'

I let him be – screaming inside.

Eight o'clock on the dot. You messaged. 'I'm here.'

'I'm so sorry. Pip's not well. I can come and meet you for a little bit – but not long.'

My phone was a wide open space with nothing in it.

Then, strange formal little declaration, 'I'd rather not.'

'Can I call you?' No answer. I did. No answer. I called again. It went straight to silence. I messaged, 'Can we make a new plan? I'm so sorry.'

One word. 'No.' I knew you were near – so near. I called again and the relief when you answered. But all you said was, 'I can't talk now. I have to go.' Your voice strained, terse.

Connection severed. I continued to message even more frantically. No reply. I was absolutely terrified, wild and afraid. Punished.

Pip came into the kitchen while I stared at the tap and the kitchen sink, phone in hand. 'What happened with Rob?'

I had to pull myself away from the screen to look into his eyes. 'Oh – I put him off.'

'Was he upset?'

'Pip, it's nothing to do with you.'

'I'm curious.'

'You're always curious.' I didn't say you know what they say about curiosity. How it killed the cat. 'Would you like hot chocolate? Hot water bottle? Have a nap and then we could go for a walk?'

'No. Rob is angry isn't he?'

'A bit miffed I think. We were both looking forward to a day.'

'You know that's wrong of him, don't you, Mum? To be angry?'

I wasn't sure what I knew. 'Yes.'

'Have you told him?'

'Shhh. Let me take your phone so you can read a nice book. I read children's fiction when I'm low. It's a comfort.'

'That's when it was *The Railway Children* and Narnia, Mum. Now we're meant to read about violence and drugs and children's homes. There's been a cultural revolution since then – in case you haven't noticed. I'm going to lie in my bed.'

'But—'

'What do you think books are there for, Mum?'

'To take us to another world.'

'Wrong. To show us what's wrong with our own.'

And he stalked away.

You were angry with me and Pip was ill. I pleaded with you in my heart – in my mind I said: He's my child. What was I supposed to do? I paced. Then I sat still, which was worse. In this cage of life. It was pathetic.

I knocked on Pip's door. 'It's not good for you to be on your own, sweetheart.' (I avoided the word isolate.) 'You need to go to school. And exercise.

And eat. We need to make a plan and stick to it.'

'I know. I just can't.'

I was standing in my kitchen and you wouldn't talk to me and I didn't have any money and I was alone and my child was sick. Sick unto death, I feared.

I let Pip be. I sat down on the rented sofa and held my little dog on my lap, as I once would have taken Pip. I felt disgraced. I did not know who to message or call. Not my married ex-lover. Because he was gone. I couldn't confide in my friends – recoiling from the burden I would offer of suffering and strife. They had money – they had money to choose. London was cloth ripped down the middle and Pip and I were on the other side.

It was the third school Pip had been to in a year. In the first he had been thrown down the stairs. In the second he had faded as Tinkerbell's light starts to go out in Peter Pan. (Too romantic an idea – again.) 'The system is based on segregation,' he'd informed me. 'They divide the children from different primaries – rich and poor housing – into sets so they don't meet and fight. The building is very ugly. It's cold. They have a computer reading programme with a multiple choice questionnaire at the end. I keep failing the comprehensions because I can't remember the colour of the people's jumpers. The jumpers of the characters in the books, I mean – it's meant to show you've read the books. They don't ask about the ideas. I could answer questions about those.'

'Have you made any friends?' I'd asked.

'No.' Pip had a habit of intense friendships and violent fallouts. I couldn't blame him. He was my child. I'd battled again. This time to get him into a new Free School I'd heard about over the bridge, the other side of the Thames, where there would be Latin and discipline and academic excellence. Remembering my own classical education, I'd longed for it for Pip. I'd agonised about the disruption of yet another move and the expense of another uniform in a year, particularly as school blazers instilled a terrible dread in Pip – in us both – but I had managed to get him in. And here he was unhappy and afraid.

We had arrived at nowhere.

It was a very bad Friday and weekend while I waited and you did not message or call. I felt muffled, mauled – as if pain and exile and love withheld was the inevitable consequence of everything I'd ever tried to do.

Monday. A scramble on bus and tube, thinking of Pip and all the other children going off to school to endure some variation of suffering, walking along the Kensington pavements looking up at the sky and across at the railings and then into college with my special code, up the beautiful nineteenth-century curving wrought-iron balustraded stairs – sweating and afraid – to the English room. A deep breath and into the sanctuary: the long windows, the trees of the square, the faces looking for me.

'Today we're going to start on Gatsby.' I said.

'There was something gorgeous about him,' said a voice. It came from a slight boy I hadn't seen before. He must have started the year late – appearing without warning before me. He had a scholastic air – yellow hair and round glasses – and he wore a maroon cardigan. Donnish, I suppose, used to be the word.

I laughed. 'Yes. There was. But only if 'personality is a series of successful gestures' – that's the first part of the line. Think about that through the novel – not only where it applies to Gatsby. But let's start at the beginning. Who's going to read?

And the boy, whose name was Luke, began to read, gracefully and with understanding, 'In my younger and more impressionable years . . .' We were at the start again. The unerasable start, the past that cannot ever be scrubbed clean. The start where you had not sent me to Coventry because my child was ill – the one where we were going to have a beautiful life and redeem the time. But you'd disappeared.

I didn't want to leave that day. To go home and face Pip. I didn't rush to pack up my things.

A knock on the English Room door. 'I know I've missed

the beginning of the year,' said Luke, approaching. 'What shall I catch up with?'

'Just read the opening of *The Tempest* – if you can. Ask the others – they'll help you. And we can add some extra time here and there. We'll revise it anyway.'

'What about the coursework?' I'd chosen these texts so there was a feeling of a layer of skin being peeled back.

'I'll give you *The End of the Affair*. Don't worry.' Impressive – the diligence. Did I tell him? I don't know.

As I left for the day your message flashed up: 'I'm so sorry, Butterfly. I was disappointed and angry.' Tired in spirit, I replied only with, 'It's all right. I understand.'

'Can I call you?' flashed back.

'Wait a few minutes?'

The pavement was cold and dark.

My days had been long and solitary and sad after your anger. So long.

Now here was your earnest, troubled, intense and intent voice. The same one as in Turkey with the dress – although I didn't connect it. 'It's just I'd been looking forward to it so much. And I was angry.' Why were you angry, Rob?

Why didn't I ask?

'I just don't understand. It wasn't the end of the world. I was disappointed too. But we could have done something nice.'

'I hadn't slept well. I just wanted to be with you. And I was there so early, dozing in the car.' Only my naked body would do, it seemed. My clothed presence was worth nothing – worse than nothing – it made you angry.

'What time were you there from?'

'I can't tell you. You'll laugh at me.'

'Tell me.'

'Five a.m. I was there at five a.m. I'd been waiting.' You'd been waiting for three hours.

'So what did you do after we messaged?'

'I went back to barracks – put on my uniform and went into the bunker.'

'Oh.'

'Discipline. It helps.' I couldn't understand it. I couldn't understand anything. 'Better to be occupied I thought. I'm so sorry I was out of contact. Please – can you forgive me? I love you so much.'

How long had it been? I couldn't remember. I couldn't remember anything. You said you loved me. I was in tears. But I wasn't going to say it back.

'Just don't do that to me again.'

'Never. I promise.'

'You really hurt me.'

'I'm a fool and you're an angel. Never again.'

'It wasn't Pip's fault.'

You sighed – smiled an untrue smile, 'I knew you were going to tell me off. Go on then, get it over.'

We were back in the same place, 'our place' – where I had first left my chair and sat next to you – first surrendered – the pseudo-country pub surrounded by woods. It had an unkempt smell. You liked that you could park in the sandy unmade car park by the hidden tennis courts and chicken wire that marked out the golf course. You were such a practical fox. I'd forgotten by then that I liked glamorous bars, talking about books and movies and theatre and art galleries. And laughing.

'You shouldn't tell me how to deal with my child.'

Intense look. 'Agreed.'

I was surprised. 'He's had a difficult time and . . .'

'He's jealous of me. You can't see it.'

'I don't think Pip not going to school is anything to do with you.'

'Of course it is. Every time we have a date or a plan

there's some problem.' Every time? Was it every time now? 'And check his timetable. He's probably trying to get out of sports. Either that or he's going off somewhere. I mean – you're at work. How on earth do you know what he's actually doing? Could be anything. Could be drugs.'

'He's not like that.'

'All boys are like that. It's how they're wired. You're so trusting.'

'He's depressed. School makes it worse. I just don't want him to be unhappy.'

'Everyone is unhappy – most of the time. You have to live with it. The only way out is through.' It was one of your sayings.

'I know.'

'I'll leave it to you then. Just don't let him take you for a ride.' What sort of a ride might this be, I thought vaguely – or maybe I'm only thinking it now. 'One last thing. Take his phone away. He'll soon sleep again. Lights out means lights out. That's my motto.'

I don't remember what I said then. I don't remember I don't remember I don't remember.

'Now let's change the subject. Forgive and forget.'

It sounds so easy when you put it like that – doesn't it, Rob?

By this time I no longer wanted to look in the mirror. The shadows round my eyes and burns of stubble on my face – it looked like a developing bruise. I'd never gazed at my own reflection for hours on end but it was important – necessary –to check I didn't have makeup smudges when I had to teach. But now I couldn't bear it any longer – even reflections in shop windows or houses or the windows on the tube. I'd look at the other women opposite and imagine their confident lives. I couldn't bear to see myself and I didn't know why.

'I haven't seen an essay from you, Luke.'

'Oh—' He scratched the side of his head – looked a bit sheepish.

'I know you started the year late. It doesn't have to be perfect – just get some thoughts on paper. It's your first attempt.'

'It's just I . . . there's so much other work.'

'Yes, I know.' I was collecting my things together into an untidy bundle at the end of the day. Because he didn't have the look of a shirker but someone dedicated and mature I didn't worry. No that's not right. I did worry. But it slipped my mind. I had to rush to photocopy Shakespeare crits in my half-hour lunch break so there wasn't time – or to do so many other things. Concentration was a feat of will – I felt powerless and vague – strained – a weakness I couldn't trace or understand. I was used to feeling low in the winter – feeling bad – but when I was working, I could always summon strength and passion. This was different. Now – unless absolutely required to speak – I wanted to disappear.

'I'm sorry. I'll get it to you. I'll get it to you soon.'

I'd forgotten he was there, lifting my head to look at him, avoiding his eyes. 'I'm sure you will.'

Another evening at the stinking wooden shed-pub in the woods. There was no straw being gathered for Jemima Puddleduck but you knew your nickname was Fox.

You – jumping to your feet when you saw me. Enthusiasm and manners and charm. Alert to you – I could see it would be that kind – that kind of happy floating piece of time.

'How was your day?' You were so interested. Holding

my eyes. It felt lovely. I needed it to feel lovely again because I was so tired. I was so tired of not knowing how it would be. 'Tell me. Speak. I love it when you speak.'

What could I tell you? I couldn't say what was wrong. The world was wrong. It's only a wrong in the world – *Othello* was it? I floundered for a part of me to hand to you.

'I'm afraid of my boss – the head – Lauren.' I told you she didn't like me.

'She must be jealous,' you said. 'I feel like going in there and giving her a piece of my mind. I can't bear bullying,' you said. 'Especially for you, Butterfly. Leadership should be fair.' I imagined you striding into her sanctum. Briefly I was comforted in my pathetic wine-filled blur – trying to imagine your life, even though you were right in front of me, even though you were visible tangible and real.

'The army would never lead like that – they look after their own.' You said it so surely – a proudful boast – a certainty. Their own. The men. Their own.

'I've been researching Fitzgerald,' said Luke the next morning. 'Show me a hero and I'll show you a tragedy.' Clear, light, clever eyes.

'Mmm – I didn't know that one. That's good.' He smiled I think. But he didn't blush. I worried when students blushed. 'Today, we're going to do close reading.' An echo in my mind. What was that poem? 'Today, we have naming of parts.' I must tell Rob, I thought, he would like that poem. Or know it even. It was about the army. But I didn't know when I was going to see you again. I never did.

'Right. Let's get started.'

And we concentrated on the text.

In the English room I could forget about real life again. Tell my students about the clever and droll things Pip said – I made it sound joyous – so they would be inspired by him. I don't know how to interpret this – but I think it helped them. Forgetting the reality was very important – or rather knowing it was there but inventing a new one. I created a different Pip – or rather – the essential Pip. Not Pip lying in his preternatural premature tomb. I do not know if this was right or wrong. I write this to you now in the urgent desire to work it out and to understand what happened. It's always been that way for me. It all had to go away until it crowded in on me again. Like my bank balance, like the unkempt garden, like Pip's shoes. Pip's shoes were scuffed and broken. He wouldn't let me buy new ones. It sounds weak, doesn't it to say now – and I never told you then how I let him have his way but the truth was I was relieved I didn't have to spend the money. Relieved and simultaneously ashamed that I bought a new dress for college – and not shoes for my son. Or anything for him really – anything at all. I exaggerate – he had books – he had chocolate – I took him for treats – but I dreaded it when he grew. Once there was a bailiff who called me from outside the door. His name was Mr Love. But there was nothing for him to take. And somehow I became convinced that with you here all these things would have less power to hurt me.

It repeats and repeats.

You looking up at me, looking up at me deeply, another of those glorious squalid evenings in the pub – I don't even like pubs – and you said, 'I've never felt about anybody the way I do about you. Not even my children.'

'Don't say that. Children are – they're different.'

'You just don't understand how beautiful you are. Your spirit. How lucky I am to have found you.' When you are little you are taught to say magic words. Why did I feel so transparent, so disconnected and dreaming?

You looking down, until we were both intent on our

hands wrapped and tied together.

Memories rise up unbidden. That's what they'd say in the nineteenth century.

In this: Memory assaults me. Memories come. You: 'You must believe. Tell me you believe.' 'You just don't get it, do you? I love you.'

Or did you believe it?

Every. Single. Word.

I told my students all literature was about sex and death. Yet how could death come anywhere near you? I knew you had not died after thirty years surrounded by weapons and explosions and guns. The little hollow under your hip and the seamless soft firmness of your balls that I could hold in my hand as you sprang to life. That did not signify death. Nor the groans I could bring from your throat with my tongue or the deepest of the moaning shout and cry when you made that moment of our lovemaking the hardest and sweetest and softest.

I cannot describe to you – to anyone – how you possessed me – because the urgency of your desire obliterated mine – especially at the beginning when we were first lovers. The sense of my watching eye as you took me (your words), the distance, was profound. It was strange as I am a passionate woman that I was so frightened in bed with you. And yet I could be exultant too – my power over you. When I began to want you back, I was afraid. I tried to tell you things, to share things with you, but you took me over with the blindness of your desire – your hard fingers and your fierce tawdry words. It was clear – and yet shaded – that I was an adjunct to your desire as your newly shaven cheek nonetheless cut me and your shuddering filled me.

Yet still I felt as if your desire were impersonal to me. But you told me it wasn't. So I didn't know how to think or feel about it. It's taken all this time for me to work that out. And your speed in recovery and leaving – or wanting it again to 'take you' – you kept saying it – your rapid way of dressing, your unfocused eyes – as if what happened between us was as perfunctory as your goodbye. There was one time – we were both there – you were present – and we both cried. One time of tenderness. I hoped there would be more. There were not.

Then more – when we were together sharing our little dish of chips and glasses of wine. 'I have never felt about anyone the way I do about you.' The repeating. Like a spell, like a charm. The hunger. Narcissus. Dracula. Frankenstein's monster, clumsily blindly strangling the thing whose purity he pursued. 'The way you dress, your eyes, the colour of your hair. I hear your voice and I am hard. I see you and I am hard.' And I couldn't understand why that didn't make me happy. If I loved and desired you, why didn't it make me happy to hear you say that. Why did it make me feel so horribly paralysed and afraid? 'I look around every place we meet and think, "Everyone here knows that I'm the one who gets to fuck you."' These words hurt me when they were meant to make me glad. And yet I could see no way out. You had chosen me.

Nearly every day – Halloween – Guy Fawkes – Remembrance Day – proudly I wore the poppy thinking of you – Pip stayed at home. My class were used to my phoning the school from outside the door. They made a joke of it and I pretended to be light and smile even though it was horrible. But there was still the work.

A little pile of essays to take home. All the students were improving – and still I could find nothing from Luke – until a scrappy page with half scribbled out unfamiliar writing – and a few clear lines: '*An anxious fascination around control exists in both these texts. A historicist reading might indicate a sense of the orphaned generation of both forties Europe and fifties America – and its rage – but a Freudian critic might argue differently.*' 'Well put,' I wrote – relieved. But the rest was vague – incoherent – illegible. I was afraid looking at it. But then I was afraid nearly all the time. It was the way his mind was so sharp but flaring and guttering so fast.

'It was excellent – you just need more,' I said to Luke the next day – giving it back.

'I know. But I couldn't write any more. I just couldn't,' he said. 'I just sat there staring.'

'Have you tried saying the words out loud and writing them down that way? Or maybe try a computer.'

'I can't organise my thoughts. I can only think them.'

'It might be dyslexia – that's manageable. Don't worry.'

'Yes.' There was no specific anxiety or other diagnosis in his notes and he looked so at ease in lessons. It was confusing but I didn't want him to see that I was confused. 'We will sort this out.' He was deeply embarrassed – shifting – uneasy. 'Let's have a meet when you have a free period and we can practice together.' His face brightened. 'That would be good,' he said.

But I couldn't think too much about Luke. I put him to

the back of my mind.

And every time I came home from college, from you, there was Pip like a tall reproach. I'd been so determined that he would not have the travails I had had. He was listened to, loved and nurtured and yet here still was his lethargy and despair. Like a bundle put into my lap. I had tried to give him all that I had not had and not only had I failed – leaving his father had only subjected him to uncertainty confusion and fear – I had actively harmed him with my love affairs and unhappiness. I knew too much. I did not want to know any more. I had tried to make his childhood home as perfect as I could make it. But it had a crack all down it and the façade could be smashed like an egg.

You have to go to the original site of the trauma one of my therapists had said.

Or was it a self-help book? I don't know. And heal. How did you heal. There's no healing my past. No healing my illness. It wasn't fucking *Harry Potter* and good versus evil and magic wands was it. I was marked for life and there was absolutely nothing I could do about it. I could be angry. Or acceptant. Or pretend it hadn't happened. Or concentrate on the joy. Ride it out and endure. Endeavour. Pip got a prize for Endeavour once. I was very proud. But there was my unconscious – catching me out – sending me towards alcoholics and troubled married men and cruel lovers. But you Rob – you were different. Clean and whole and unshackled by any hint of doubt. You looked at me and told me I was beautiful and I was.

'I've been thinking more about Gatsby,' said Luke – by the door as I was leaving. Looking at him I remembered we hadn't made that plan for me to help him write. 'We never see him. We never see him from his own point of view. We never know him.'

'No. We don't. But we know how he wants to be seen. From the beginning – making those lists in his room as a boy. Watching the moon spilling its light. Inventing his name on the lake shore.'

'Creating himself.'

'That takes courage.'

'And vulnerability,' said Luke. 'The essence of tragedy.'

'We're so clever, aren't we?' I said.

And home.

'The odds are stacked against us – don't you see, Mum?'

'What can that possibly mean?' I was making chocolate cake for the students and for Pip.

'We won't get out of this alive – you and I.'

'Pip – these aren't good thoughts to be having. Why don't you help me measure the sugar?'

'I can't. I'm too clumsy. Cognitive therapy is just the thought police in disguise you know, Mum.'

'For fuck's sake! It's Sunday. I have to tutor soon.' It wasn't real anger – it was comedy anger – but oh no Pip – what if it was?

'I'm sorry, Mum – really I am.' And Pip went away.

I messaged you. You didn't reply.

I had a new private student online. We were doing '*Tess of the D'Urbervilles*.'

'I loved Tess when I was little. All that beauty. The landscape. Poor Tess.' I'd written an essay about it that won a prize at school.

'We do the male gaze now,' she said. She had long hair

and a bored expression.

'Ah. Well – that's part of it, I suppose.' I was too tired to argue about feminism.

'Shall we read some of the words and see what we think?' I said.

'Mmm.' She looked distracted – down to the side. I could tell she was hoping I'd just tell her what to write. I probably should.

'Would you mind putting away your phone? Things will work better that way.'

'Oh – yes – sorry,' she said.

'How did it go?' asked Pip. He was very caring – always – such a kind lad. 'All right. The essence of tragedy was slightly beyond her. But I shouldn't be mean. Let's take the dog for a walk.'

'What's Tess's tragedy?' Pip asked as I fumbled for my keys.

'Stuff. Hardy called it the ache of modernism. I can't be articulate now. I'm exhausted.' Beaten down I was. Beaten. But you never hit me.

'You're always exhausted,' said Pip.

'All right – I'll tell you quickly.' I was anxious to get to the park, Puppy looking up at me beseeching. 'His tragedies are about society. Those who are left behind. The most terrible is *Jude the Obscure*.'

'What happens?'

How had I started this? Why? 'I can't tell you.'

'You might as well. I'll only google it.'

'The children – kill themselves because they don't want to be a burden. "Done because we are too menny", their note says.'

'How. How do they do it?' Asked Pip.

'I don't remember,' I said. But I did. 'Let's not talk about it.'

'You started it, Mum.' And it was true. I had.

We walked down to the water – the river or stream at the edge of the park. The deer forded it sometimes and we'd look at them – astonished – as they attempted the banks with delicate legs that looked as if they would snap. We watched the fish and birds and the dog played. I was comforted. But Pip's head was down.

There were still the students. There was still Luke.

'I thought it might be interesting to look at all the texts we are studying in terms of tragedy. Just quickly. It is easy to concentrate on hubris – the tragic flaw. But what is the beauty of tragedy – the tragic energy? Is it that the hero has some belief or understanding or insight or desire or longing that it is beyond the world to provide? Is that their charisma?'

'I think so,' said Luke. 'In Gatsby's case it's romantic. He wants to escape himself.'

One of the girls: 'By having people murdered?'

'Tragic heroes are often murderers though, aren't they – if you think about it,' I said.

'Either that or they're sacrificed.' Luke was looking directly at me. 'I read that tragic energy is essentially sacrificial. The hero cannot exist in reality – not in the real world – and so he dies.'

'Or she,' I said. 'But it's whether they die defiant or defeated. "I am Duchess of Malfi still."'

'Those are just words,' said one of the girls. 'They put a rope around her neck.' Just words. And she says '*Pull and pull strongly*', I thought.

'At the time those words were written – death was the supreme end of life. Almost an accomplishment. Now it's seen as some sort of failure – some sort of shameful collapse. Anyway – let's forget about tragedy and do *The Tempest*. Much more fun.'

At the end of the lesson Luke appeared again by my desk as the others trooped out.

'My dad wants to have a meeting with you.'

'Of course. Ask him to email your personal tutor and we'll arrange.'

'He wants me there too.'

I was surprised. 'All right.'

We were in the place. You'd started having jovial conversations with the barmen.

'It's so good to see you,' you said. 'Really. It's been so long.'

'Shall we try and do something next week? I said. 'It's half term. We could go somewhere.'

'I can't. I have to take the boys to Mum in Yorkshire. Make her endless cups of tea and listen to the village news. But at least I can go swimming with the boys – we can play some football with them.' You looked pale and thin, soured. Dark shadows.

'Ah.' I looked down – trying to disguise any feelings I might be having in case they were the wrong ones.

I could feel you examining me. 'Look at me. I know you're disappointed. I'm disappointed too. But remember – it was Pip who messed up our last day. If I didn't trust you – I might say he'd done it on purpose. I know you don't like me saying it but he's so jealous of you. Having your own life. Me.'

'Pip's not like that at all.' Pip was such an honest and truthful child.

'You're too soft on him. You are. You know what I'm saying is true. I'd never let my boys get away with lounging around in bed.'

'He needs a father. That's all.' You had promised to mend Pip's bike when we first met. You'd whizzed over on a

Sunday morning just for half an hour to see it – taking the time away from your desk and MA research for a glimpse of me. I had not been properly dressed – taken by surprise – and Pip had stayed in his room. I had felt giddy. You'd told me how sexy I looked. I didn't much care. It was the bike I cared about. It was still upside down on the terrace where you had spun the wheels. Exposed to the weather. I didn't remind you that you hadn't remembered and it had never been mentioned between us again.

'He needs a mother to stand up to him and say no.' I was angry. At that time I still had the confidence to be angry with you – defend myself.

'That's not how it is at all. I know what's best for my child.' (I feared I did not.) 'We have different ideas. Our children are different.'

Then you began to cry. It was horrifying. Horrified I felt. 'I'm so sorry. I've been ill and having bad thoughts. Flashbacks. Memories. I'm so sorry.' There were actual tears coursing down your cheeks and you brushed at them blindly with the backs of your hands.

'Rob. Your handkerchief,' I said gently. 'You've forgotten.' And you pulled it out of your pocket and blew your nose like a little boy.

'I'm so sorry. So sorry.'

Putting my arms around your neck – straining to connect to you. 'No. I'm sorry. I'm sorry too.'

You had been the commander of the landmine hero whose death had splashed itself over all the front pages back home. You had written to his widow when he had died. I knew these things. And while I felt powerless to console – how I tried. These were the sins of the world you lived with and tried to make sense of and give meaning to. Every day.

I said – conceding, 'I'm sorry I'm so defensive – so inflexible. It's just I'm so scared.'

'I tell you what,' you said. 'Why don't I have a word with

Pip? A different approach.' I thought of how your men loved you. How charismatic you were.

I laughed – close to hysteria. 'What are you going to do? Teach him press ups?' Your eyes warned me – you could not be laughed at or teased ever. 'The trouble is I don't think he'd agree.'

'That's easily solved,' you said. 'We just won't tell him.' Did that mean you planned an ambush? I was too stunned to ask.

'It's simply that he's lazy,' said Luke's father – a small man dressed in brown. I could see no trace of Luke in him at all. For parent meetings we used the large ground-floor room with sofas and blue damask at the windows with the old dark shining dining table and sometimes a vase of flowers. Luke – blushing – shrinking – beside him. 'We had this at the last school – no essays – no writing.'

'I'm sure he'll get there,' I said.

'I don't think you understand me. He has to be made to do it,' said the man – whose hand I'd shaken – whose child I was teaching.

'He's very good in class – full of ideas – ahead on the reading,' I said. 'And he has started the year late.'

'It's no excuse. In fact, it's pointless,' said the man as if I were stupid. 'If he won't write anything down.'

'It's a process. I'm confident that—'

'Well at least you're confident. No one else is.' My head swimming in the miasma, Luke blushing – blinking – almost in approval and agreement with his father – saying nothing. 'I want to know what your strategy is.'

What the strategy was. You'd planned the operation a certain way – hadn't you Rob but it doesn't always turn out for the best. It wasn't your fault if the innocent lost their lives.

'The one year course is very intensive but when we've finished each text we write essays and plans together on the board. Plus I mark all the work very carefully so they can see what needs to be done. Anything he can come up with we can work with. I can give him extra time here and there too. He can also write in the library – we can schedule it in – if it's difficult at home. What do you think, Luke? Will that help?'

'Yes,' said Luke. 'I do try. But the words won't come.'

I continued to look at Luke and not at his father. 'And remember – we're going to grab that half an hour together and practice how to start. How to write. It's stage fright – perfectionism. I was like that when I started proper essays. Lots of people are.'

'What I fail to understand—' said his father. He sniffed.

'I've referred him to the special needs coordinator. We'll see what comes of that. She has loads of strategies.' There was that stupid word again. 'There's plenty of time for him to build his confidence.'

'I'm not interested in his confidence,' said his father. 'I'm interested in results.'

'I'm going to take you for a walk in Richmond Park,' you said. 'You like it there.' It was a shadow of light.

We took two cars because you had to go on somewhere – Cambridge I think it was. Looking behind me in the rear-view mirror as you followed my car I saw your eyes – watchful – darting from side to side at the people on the pavements – the people in traffic. I wondered how they looked to you – sloppy – lazy? At that crossroads of fast-food outlets and newsagents and laundromats, I thought – is this the England you kept in your mind – that you were fighting for? Were these the people for whom you keep so vigilant and sharp.

In the park's car park you made a great to-do about helping a young mother with her pram and a gate.

'Which way would you like to go?' I asked. 'River and hill or woods along the boundary wall?'

'Woods please,' you said.

Why had I asked? – I was longing for the open air – to show you the water creatures Pip and I watched for and the deer – before the light faded completely against the black of the far trees.

We trudged through the woods – you ahead of me. 'I'm hardly in the shoes for it,' you said. 'This is usually the terrain for a run. Clear my head.'

'Well I'm glad I'm walking with you,' I said – even though I was unhappy and felt afraid.

You broke off a stick, finding exactly the right one to give you the impression of a gentleman out of a nineteenth-century etching carrying a cane. 'Stop a second,' you said. 'I want to tell you something. It's about a mission.'

'The desert one?'

'No. This was different. It was a retreat. I can show you exactly what happened right here.' And you traced on the sandy path and through the puddles the terrain – the bridge – the exit point – the plan. 'It was perfect,' you said. 'The perfect plan.'

'What happened?' I waited for tales of glory.

'When they approached the bridge the fools shouted with triumph – thought they were home free – gave themselves away. Taliban opened fire. Two killed – one lost a leg,' you said, still looking at your tracings on the ground.

'Oh my god.'

You looked up at me without seeing me, back down – pointing. 'You see,' you said – stern. 'You see how it wasn't my fault. There was nothing I could have done.'

'Yes. Yes – I absolutely see,' I said – having no idea what you meant at all.

You still didn't look at me. Still you were staring down at the marks you'd made on the ground. 'There was an enquiry – it was in open court – do you understand what that means? *Open court.* The families were there. The verdict was there had been no negligence but after it was over they – the parents – they wanted to meet with me. But I said no. I wouldn't speak to them.'

I was too shocked by this even to ask why – looking at the marks you had made on the ground. 'I was so alone. One of the worst days of my life. And my wife didn't come with me. I cried and shook in the car.'

What was I meant to feel?

'Did I tell you that when I was a boy I kicked a football through the window of the house by mistake and my father came outside and hit and kicked me to the ground? He called me a disgusting little rat.'

Something rose in my throat. 'No. I didn't know that happened. You've never said.'

'He said I was no son of his. How he wished he could keep me away from my mother. I don't belong anywhere – not to anyone. You understand?' You continued to contemplate the marks and lines. 'That's why I never ever punish people – blame people – unless it's their fault. Do you understand that? My boys do. It must be fair. Everything must be fair.'

'Yes – I know.'

At last you looked up and into my face. 'When I come back we'll deal with Pip.'

'All right.'

You kicked the loose sand and earth back into the marks you'd made and stamped them down.

'The light's fading. We should turn for home now,' you said. 'Before they shut the park gates.'

'Where were you, Mum?'

'What do you mean?'

'We planned to go to the new hot chocolate place – don't you remember? In Wimbledon Village. And we were going to look at the ducks.'

'Was that today?'

'Yes. Your day off. Today.'

All the anger flared. 'Bloody fucking hell! Why are you always accusing me? Why are you always putting me in the wrong? It wasn't a definite plan.'

Pip looked as if I'd hit him. 'It was. A definite plan is when one person says to another, "Let's go to the hot-chocolate shop on Thursday," and the other person says yes.'

'I'm glad I know who the other person is.'

'You were with him again, weren't you?'

'He's right about you. You try to control my every move.'

I was sick with rage and Pip flinched. 'Thank you for letting me know what you really think,' he said.

He went into his room. 'Pip! I didn't mean it. Let me explain.' I tried to follow – open the door – but he'd wedged his chair in front of it.

'I'm not coming out and I don't want a scene,' he said. 'Just leave me alone. You are not my friend.'

Outside the English room. The others had trooped out. They all liked Luke – in class – but didn't talk to him outside of it.

'Miss?'

'You know to call me Maddie – please.'

Four o'clock. An early day. Time to go home. 'I'm sorry about my dad. I'll try and write some more paragraphs over half term. I've been reading more about Fitzgerald. His life. Zelda. He didn't have to make very much up.'

Trust me – I wanted to say. You always have to make it up.

'Walk down together?' he said and waited while I put my books in the cupboard and looked around for my things.

'I'm ahead in *The End of the Affair*,' he said babbling like Pip used to when he was carried away. 'I'm interested in the common as a purgatorial space. The way Greene uses London. The religious and the Freudian reading combined.'

'I'll have nothing to teach you,' I said vaguely, smiling – not looking at him.

'And I'll read *The Age of Innocence* at half term – and get started on *A Farewell to Arms* if there's time.' Female heroism, I thought with a blurred mind that once was sharp as a scalpel. Catherine – Hemingway's heroine whose mind is a wound. That's what Lionel Trilling said. I wondered if he trilled. I wanted to watch rubbish on TV and never think again. I wanted to be warm. I wanted to rest. I wanted someone to bring me toasted teacakes and tea and be in a bath in a cold empty country house with a fire in the grate and soft darkness outside and a moon.

'Yes, do. If there's time. But don't worry – we'll read it in class anyway. Have a bit of a break. It's a long stretch to summer.' We left the English room and descended the well-worn stairs, past the Art room and the library – a long way turning and watching you didn't slip – all the way down. 'Hemingway's very romantic,' I said.

'Really? I thought he was macho. That's what everyone says.'

'Everyone isn't always right you know. See what you think.'

Such a long way down.

'Can I ask you something? Before you go?'

'Of course.'

'Do you think it matters I don't know what I want to be when I graduate?'

'I don't think it matters at all. Loads of people don't. I was always getting fired from jobs. Never had any idea.' You shouldn't be telling him that a small voice said. It was probably Pip's. 'Things will become clearer – as you go along. I promise.' Luke did not reply.

'Have a lovely half-term break,' I said in the hall in front of the huge carved mirror which I tried not to look into, giving eye contact, being calm, being resolute, being friendly. It was all acting, or all real. 'Don't forget the clocks go back. See you in November.' I smiled. He smiled back.

And I walked out into the sharp October sunlight of the square, the wrought-iron railings with our teen smokers standing by them – thinking of all the glorious and beautiful books.

Half term was sad and blue and grey. I was afraid because of the clocks and the beginning of the darkness. And I didn't see you. You barely messaged. I wondered why you had gone – taking the colours with you. I tried to apologise to Pip and he said, 'I understand, Mum. Don't be sorry. It's my fault.'

'No it really isn't.'

'What's the opposite of the Midas touch? That's what I've got. Everything I touch is tarnished,' he said.

'It will come right. Things will come right. I promise.' After that he kept to himself – his thoughts concealed. I felt very guilty. We went for walks and played with the dog and I tried to offer hope but I knew it was missing – our trust.

When term began again I looked at the five faces of my little class and Luke's was blurred. The bottom half of it had crumpled and fallen in – his glasses and his forehead and hair were the same but he looked like someone who had been shot – and was bent over the wound. When he looked at me – he looked straight up at me but his eyes were full of shell-shocked wonder as if he didn't fully understand. When he read out loud he stumbled over the lines and could not make sense of them. The others were embarrassed and seemed to shrink from him. I didn't know what to do. I had never seen so complete a change in any human being in so short a time, as if there had been some sort of accident or violent event or he had witnessed an appalling crime or act of war. At the end of the lesson the others trooped out and he stayed behind – not looking at me – gathering his things slowly as if he couldn't see them. He was hunched over his belongings and I wanted to help him and knew I couldn't – bound by my role in the drama not to approach too closely. It was safeguarding training. You were not allowed to encroach. But I couldn't help watching him before turning away to wipe my writing from the board. When I turned back he was closer.

'I just wanted to say . . .' he said. 'I just wanted to say I feel very bad.' He cleared his throat. 'And so I can't write anything – I couldn't write your essay.'

You have to look calmly at it – don't you, Rob? – look steadily. It felt as if you were with me in the room. 'That's all right,' I said, concentrating on his eyes, embarrassed at their suffering. 'Quite all right. I know you will when you can.' A faint nod. Then again the memory of our training. You can't lead the way in a confidence and you cannot keep a secret. 'Have you told anyone else here at college?'

'No.' Blinking in the overhead light. Thank god we didn't have strip lights in the English room.

'I hope you understand that I can't keep this to myself. It's part of safeguarding. I have to let the head know and your personal tutor.'

'That's all right. Thank you. I wasn't sure how it worked.' I think he was relieved. Did that ever happen to you, Rob? Responsibility gratefully passed on. Still you felt next to me – even though I hadn't seen you in the flesh for so long.

'Have you spoken to anyone about how you're feeling yet?' 'Anyone' – the go-to mental-health euphemism.

'No. Well – my parents know. They think I should make an appointment to see the GP.' The fucking GP. Good luck with that, another voice could have said. If you can persuade them to prescribe anything they won't know what they're doing.

You'll never get a psych referral, you'll have to go private, you'll be on a waiting list – you'll . . . But I said nothing.

'Yes. That's a good idea. It's very brave of you to come to college.' I have no idea why being called brave is meant to be some sort of wondrous consolation prize. I was given the red shield badge at school for courage when nobody spoke to me for a term. I was eleven years old.

'I might have to go home now though,' he said mildly as if it were nothing to do with him. 'Instead of going to my next lesson. I just wanted to tell you. So you wouldn't think I was lazy.'

'I wouldn't think that,' I said.

'I don't know what . . . I was so looking forward to everything,' he said.

'I will let the head know. And – don't forget – you'll need to make that appointment. With the doctor.'

'Yes. I think—' he frowned. 'I think maybe my parents tried and – he's booked up. I'll try to go to my lesson. It's just I can't do anything.

'Or see very well.' When you are very depressed you can't see, did I tell you that, Rob?

'You know we have nice Laura here – downstairs – she can offer counselling – I can go with you to speak to her if you like. Or I can just tell her you'll be in touch.'

'Will you?' he said – pathetic, grateful.

I nodded. Then, 'I'm so sorry,' I said. 'It's the worst kind of suffering.' To impose myself further would have been wrong. He was slipping into the dark right next to me – onto the pavement of the street – not into the trees like Pip. But nothing could be done. The trees in the square outside remained impartial. The only thing I could do for the boy was to be in the same room with him and stand still and not be afraid. Not show him I was afraid. Outside it was suddenly black.

'You might need some meds. They can help.' I wasn't even meant to say that – recommend any sort of remedy. I wasn't meant to share but I said anyway, 'You'll find there are ways to deal with it.' I felt sick looking at him and angry with myself because my eyes were stinging. 'You just need to find the right doctor – the right help.'

'Yes.'

'Off you go. I'll see you soon.'

He went away and I turned towards the black windows and looked outside into the square I couldn't see and cried. The English room could hold pain and joy but not abandon. I had to pull it back inside myself before going downstairs. I had another lesson in another room from four to six. I went to my chair and sat full of pain. Pulled out my phone as if it would remind me who I was and what I was meant to be doing. Three missed calls from Pip's school. Two emails. Pip had not arrived that day and 'In the absence of an email or call from me they were very concerned.' Fuck.

I had forgotten about Pip. I had forgotten about my child. I called his phone. Nothing. I called the school. Nothing. They'd closed. I had ten minutes changeover and in that time I had to find the head, find and talk to Luke's personal tutor and the counsellor, and somehow get hold of Pip. He had left for school before me in the morning – dispirited with his bag and his unbrushed hair – panicking about a lost text book and Iso; after my words of irritated patient hurried reassurance he had gone to school.

I sat down at my table facing the empty chairs. 'Bloody fucking hell,' I said. Paralysed. I kept ringing Pip. It went to voicemail. I emailed the school and because I had so little time rushed to find Lauren. She was coming out of her office into the delicate hall carrying her notes – ready to teach. She could see from my expression that I was upset – that it was important.

Far too fast – afraid she would escape me – I said, 'I have to report something – something about a student,' trying to keep my voice low. I couldn't be specific that it was Luke because we could have been overheard. 'Can we go somewhere quiet – for a minute?' I couldn't invite myself into her domain but I stood between her and the stairs.

'This isn't the time. I'm about to teach.' She was irritated – lifting her chin to imply I was standing in her way. 'Put it in an email – mark it confidential.' The wording of the safeguarding training repeated itself in my head: If you have cause to be concerned about a student's safety do not keep it to yourself. Report it immediately to the head of safeguarding so they can take the appropriate action. Do not delay. She knew the words better than I did. She did not flinch. I moved aside and she was gone to take my place in the English room. I wrote and sent the email in the hall copying in the others before my next lesson. I don't know why I didn't leave – just leave – and go and look for Pip. But I went back to work.

I was home.

'Pip? Pip? Are you here?'

Pip emerged from his room, moving out of his doorway to the sofa to avoid my eyes.

'I'm a failure, Mum. That's the truth.'

'Bloody hell, Pip, you terrified me – where've you been?'

But Pip was not focusing on these things. 'I'm a failure,' he said again.

'What are you talking about? How can you be a failure? You're fourteen.'

'I can't do anything. I ran away from school today. I got there – saw the gates – and ran.'

'Oh my god, Pip – why didn't you call me? I've been so worried.'

'You couldn't have come.'

'Of course I could.' He said nothing. 'What did you do?'

'I walked around the park.'

'The one you used to go to with your friend?'

'Yes. But I was afraid of the gangs because sometimes they hang out there and chase me so I went around on the bus for a while. I felt confused. I didn't have enough money for a coke in McDonald's. I just stood there and cried. Everyone saw me and no one helped.'

'No one asked you what was wrong?' I wanted to kill every last one of them. 'Please, please always let me know where you are. The school were – please message me.'

He said again, 'You were teaching. Your phone's on silent. You couldn't have come. You wouldn't have.'

'Of course I would – if it were an emergency.' I was lying. I had known he was missing and I had stayed at college where I felt safe.

This he ignored. Then, 'I'm going to fail. I'm going to fail my—'

'That's not true. Of course you're not. And you're so clever and wise and funny – so clever.'

'It doesn't do me any good.'

'Look at me. You are not going to fail. Stop thinking that. Things will get better.'

'How?' He foiled me again. I tried to keep looking into his eyes but they didn't take me in. 'I try so hard.'

He lay down on the ugly sofa and pulled the pink blanket around him; the dog looking at him with concern and the cat prowling affectionate and clumsy above him, carefully licking his hair. He started to cry. His whole tall body shook. It wasn't the crying of sorrow or pain. It was desperate weak dry sobs with no emotion in them but defeat.

I sat next to him and stroked him – he hated being stroked but he allowed it – and told him it would be all right. I had no idea if it would.

Love is blind and so is faith.

We were in the dark and we were alone.

He begged me not to make him go to school.

'How about if I take you in tomorrow?'

'You'll be late for your first lesson.' It was true I was already in trouble for lateness. 'I can't go, Mum. Please don't make me.'

'I won't make you.' I promised he could remain behind.

That night we talked about waiting for his CAMHS referral, we talked about changing schools, we talked about endurance, we talked about the future, we talked about the past. I tried to offer comfort and hope. I tried to remind him of joy.

He went to bed without a word – retreating – and I felt too ill to impose.

Even before what happened it was important to have particular memories I could go to. A mile or so from our village there was a farm and it had a stall where they put eggs and vegetables and fruit and sometimes there were people to pay and at others you left money in the box. There was a dip in the road and you had to be careful not to miss the turning. The summers in the country were bright and hot. I remember sometimes windy – straight from the sea it came I think. We had the first asparagus there – we used to pull over and leave the money in the box. There was a stream and they grew strawberries on the hillside above it. One day after school I took Pip there and we picked raspberries in the softening afternoon light. We parked in the unmade gravel yard next to the barn. Pip liked the scrunching of the tyres. 'Make sure, Pip, that they're not green at the top – that they come firmly from the stalk and are not too mushy. Leave the green ones to ripen more and then other people can have them later.' I can't remember what we gathered them in – little grey cardboard panniers I think with handles. The light on the raspberries piled, and on their canes and on the earth at my feet was very beautiful and Pip was purposeful and happy. Children exist and are absorbed in real time. It's a blessing. And so much responsibility for those who make those times. We made raspberry jam as soon as we got home – sterilising the jars and doing the saucer test. Pip stood on a chair. I don't think it set very well. But we loved that jam. The flavour of it – the colour. We were so proud. You make a bank of memories for them – for your child – for the young – and then at fourteen they all grow grey – their faces – like litmus paper.

In the morning he left before me – too anxious even to say goodbye. So we didn't see each other with our eyes – only hurried outlines – only shapes. I think I said good luck, I think I said I hope it goes well. I forgot to say, spaghetti bolognese tonight. It was his favourite. I was confused about what dress I was going to wear. I wanted you. It had been so long.

These were our messages that day – yours and mine:

'How are you today, my butterfly? I'm back.'

'Feeling afraid. I have a bad feeling about Pip.' I had woken from a vague and terrible dream.

'What's happened? Did he go to school?'

'Yes. I called and checked.' This was a miracle. I had

been determined not to forget everything else – not to let the world outside the English room feel remote and nothing to do with me.

'And you're at college now?'

'Yes. But I'm going back to the flat – I'm not well.' My stomach was swollen like a bloated painful ugly pregnancy. I could barely climb the stairs. Deciding to leave only ever took place when all other avenues were exhausted.

'What time will you be there?'

I didn't know what you were talking about. Had I forgotten something? Were we meant to meet? 'Where?'

'At the flat?'

'By three. I'll be there by three.' I'd never been able to call it home.

'I'll come over.' This was deeply shocking to me – the intercept. You were always so hard to see. I never contacted you first. You had the keys to the kingdom.

'Don't you have to work?' I messaged. I was on the turning of the slippery stair outside the art room – I feared falling – usually I never used my phone except somewhere private and hidden.

'No, it's fine. I'll leave early too. I don't like you feeling this bad.' Perhaps this was just what being in a close relationship was like but it felt so strange. You were always so busy – always.

I could barely open the door to let you in because of the stomach pain. I was hunched over it holding a hot water bottle.

'I'm not at my best,' I said. You just looked worried and concerned. Soldier with a furrowed brow. 'I get these stomach aches sometimes.' I'd run out of the pills I took for it and forgotten to get more on the way home.

'You look beautiful,' you said.

I knew this was not true but I was blurry. 'I've been lying down.'

'Go back to bed.'

'Do you want tea or anything?'

'No. Go back to bed. Our bed,' you said.

I lay down on my side in the same place I had been lying in the bed – where the imprint was.

You came around to the other side and lay behind me – holding me – your arms around my diaphragm, your head against my neck. I imagined us shot from above, the camera on the ceiling. 'Bad thoughts?'

'Mmm.' It was not a premonition – it was certain knowledge – something thick from my dreams.

'Shhh – it's all right,' you said. 'Don't worry.'

I felt drowsy and calm. All the whirling in my brain subsiding. You were firm and clean behind me. You held on to me in just the right way and I was truly thankful. I thought about answered prayers. For what we are about to receive may the Lord make us . . . 'I won't stay long. I'll be gone before Pip gets back.'

'All right,' I said. And it was.

But oh the space and gulf after you had left – aching and open and yawning and wide. And Pip home white and barely speaking and the sleepy spacey cooking of the supper he pushed away.

I woke at six. The stomach pain was gone but there was an empty gnawing feeling and no sound. My door was ajar which was odd because I usually closed it at night. I couldn't hear the breathing of my dog who always crept up the bed in the night and glancing round I saw she was not there.

Pip was a restless sleeper and I often heard him twisting in his sleep or swinging on his long legs down the corridor to the bathroom opposite my room in the night – I used to shout out of my sleep and complain: 'You woke me.' 'Sorry, Mum – try earplugs.' 'Sod off.'

Today there was silence – my mind racing – the rooms around me still. I felt alone. 'Puppy, where are you?' A scratching noise and a whine. Perhaps she had got shut in somewhere and why couldn't I move.

I remember my feet in the corridor looking down at them and the dog scratching at Pip's door and whining and calling 'Pip darling can I come in?' and knocking, believing because of the stillness he was not there – if he had gone out – and opening his door. I had not heard the front door go and I didn't understand why his bed was wrinkled and empty and then our little dog was whisking about and sniffing and I called gently, 'Pip,' back in the corridor and the door to the tiny laundry room was ajar and I couldn't push it open because it was wedged and I tried again and it was Pip's foot on the ground. He lay on the piles of laundry on the floor. He was as long as the room and his eyes were closed. His skin was like marble with tiny blue veins. I said 'Pip? Pip?' and the little dog walked on him and his eyelashes moved and he opened his eyes and looked gently and wonderingly up and then towards me and focusing said, 'Mum?' He came back from that faraway place babies go to when they sleep.

'Pip – what happened?'

'I don't know. I was frightened all night and couldn't sleep and I didn't want to go to school and then I tried – I made myself – I was just – I must have fallen asleep.'

'You're in your uniform ready.' This was a very stupid thing to say.

'I know.'

'Did you sit down to rest? Or did you fall?'

'I don't remember.' He was blinking and looking not at all of this world.

'Darling.'

'Ma?'

'You gave me such a fright.' I wanted to tell him I didn't know what to do – but I couldn't.

'Can you get up?' I extended my hand but he didn't take it.

'Yes.' And he did – pushing himself up on his hands – wobbling a little. He was so tall that it was a very bizarre thing to see.

We looked at each other either in full or partial knowledge – it's hard to say. 'I think we should try to soldier on,' I said. 'I'll get you a glass of water. Have you eaten your cereal?'

'No.'

I should have been up, making it – of course I should.

'Let's go to the bus stop together when you've had something to eat.'

'No, Mum. Go and have your shower. Otherwise we'll be late. I'm not hungry now. I'll get a bun on the way in and you can too.'

'All right.'

We locked the dog in the house and we walked together to the bus stop which was very windy and filled with so many sounds and swirling dirt and the cars on the four lanes were as immune to us as ever and the other people at the bus stop looked distressed or angry or tired and I said good morning to the bus driver because that was how I was brought up and we sat together and said nothing for a very long time.

At college the little class was waiting for me. They were kindly chatting but it was horrible horrible horrible and Luke was not there.

At lunchtime I was walking slowly down the long staircase carefully thinking of nothing when Lauren came out from her office into the hall. Before I had lifted my eyes and looked at her I knew that something terrible had happened.

'Luke.' She said. 'Luke's killed himself.'

There was just stillness. We were in the hall but there was no one there. She was white. 'What do we say to the students?' was the first thing I said. God help me.

'We have to keep it from them – at least for another few hours.'

My mind began to run and leap and vault. 'I saw him yesterday,' I said. 'He didn't come in today.'

'I know.' The hall was empty – hushed and quiet – the walls were still there. 'Come into my office,' she said. Her room was small and private with an oak door with her name and title on it and a large window but it had no view. I sat down. 'I'll make you a cup of tea,' she said, leaving me on my own. She did not know Luke. She did not teach him. I taught him five hours a week. He couldn't be dead because I had seen him yesterday and I was going to help him pass his A levels and have a new life. I looked down at my book bag and the carpet which I had never noticed was blue before. She came back – handing me the tea. 'Maddie,' she said. 'We have to be strong. You were the last person to teach him before he went home and I know you came to talk to me and emailed he'd told you he was very low. You need to write a careful report of the conversation you and he had in the English room –it all has to be noted for safeguarding.' She talked on and on. 'The police might not even have to be involved.'

'The police? Why?'

'Can you do that today? Write the report? Do you have any more lessons to teach? You could go into the library now and do it.' I couldn't understand what she meant. 'We have to be strong for the students. And everything has to be in order.'

'I know.' She was better than me – she was calmer – she was stronger. Why would Luke do that – I'd told him it would be all right – hadn't I? Hadn't I said that. Hadn't I told him not to worry? But maybe I hadn't maybe I'd been too weak and had forgotten. 'When did it happen?'

'They found him this morning. I've just come off the phone to his parents. I'm sorry for the shock – I'm just – we need to act.' Leadership. Fucking leadership again.

'I'll write the report but I need to go home. Is that all right? Please.' I needed to go home and see Pip.

I don't think she thought it was all right at all.

It took a sickly grainy age to get back and of course Pip was not there. I had not remembered. We had gone to school together. I couldn't even remember my own child's movements. He had actually gone to school. That morning it had seemed all important that we go as quickly as possible to the places we had gone to. The big transparent room looked dirty. I could see the dust motes in the air. I sat with the animals and stared down the garden and my mind was filled with Luke. I had a strange vision of him falling off the edge of a cliff and my hand outstretched and not being able to reach him and catch hold of his hand. I had a feeling of flying – flying above all that had ever happened in the world. Looking down. I had a feeling of guilt and horror that I should think it was anything to do with me and another that it was absolutely my own failing. There was a great deal of gold in the air. I remembered talking to him about transcendence and tragic energy and I felt sick. He had confided in me and I had done nothing. Not one fucking thing. All my egotism about helping young people do their best and pass their exams and live fulfilled lives – that was all it was. The unbelievable idiocy of any attempt. But I mustn't think like that. His life. His life was his own and nothing to do with me. But he'd gone. I couldn't understand that when I saw him so clearly before me with his glasses and his cardigan and his talk of cultural malaise and twentieth-century sorrow. But it was nothing to do with me. Why couldn't I get that into my head? I mustn't swamp Pip. I mustn't scare Pip when he came home – that was all I thought.

And you. You would know what to do. I messaged. 'Can you call me. Please. It's urgent.'

Miraculously you answered. 'I'll call you in five.' We hardly ever spoke on the phone because you had to be in the bunker and all the other things you had to do.

Pulling the heavy sliding doors open I went and stood outside on the terrace. The leaves were leaving the smaller trees. I looked at them and up at the sky. Not at Bonnard's tree. I couldn't. I don't know why.

'It's me.' I knew it was you. I'd never been so relieved to hear another person's voice. 'Oh god Rob,' I said. 'Thank you for calling me.'

'What is it? You sound bad.'

'It's Luke – my student – he's killed himself.'

You made a terrible sound. Such a terrible sound. As if you had been punched – a groan cry – a shout – a moan. I can't do it justice – I can't do you justice in describing it and I am still so appalled that now I even try.

'Oh no – I'm so sorry,' I said. 'I shouldn't have told you like that – I should have warned you—' What had I thought? That you would be calm and all right that you would know how to feel and what to do. 'I'm so sorry.'

There was a little pause and then you said, husky, 'Not another boy.'

'I'm so sorry.'

'So am I.' I was crying without realizing – I didn't know what you were doing. I couldn't see you. 'It's just I—'

You said, 'You had a premonition, didn't you?' I had forgotten. Was that what it was. Another pause. 'I don't know what to say. Call your family – call a friend. Don't be alone. Look – Butterfly – I have to go back now. We are in the middle of something. I love you. I'm so sorry. I'll message you soon.' And you were gone.

I stood and held on to the phone and saw nothing – hearing the front door bang. Pip was home. He was calling to me, 'I managed it, Mum. I managed a whole day.' I turned from the phone call back into the room thinking I must must answer.

'That's wonderful, darling.'

'What is it, Mum? – What's happened? Your face—'

'Nothing. Something. I'll tell you in a bit.'

'Your face looks weird. You're not making sense. You're scaring me. Who was that on the phone? Is Dad all right?'

'Yes. Of course. Everyone is all right.'

'Then what?'

I tried to move past him – not looking at him – looking vaguely at the objects in the kitchen. 'I'm going to make some tea. Would you like some chocolate milk?'

'Mum – this is weird. Just tell me.'

And so I did – turning and looking at him. 'It's one of my students – I'm sure I told you about him. Luke. Something's happened—'

'He's died hasn't he?

'Yes.' Pip blinked. 'I'm so sorry to upset you. It's – it's difficult for Mummy –' Oh god I was pretending he was tiny again. 'And it will be hard for everyone who had anything to do with him to understand. To come to terms with. Even you who never met him.'

Pip stared at me. 'What are you talking about? Why did you tell me?' He said. 'You should have lied. But you've never been any good at lying, have you?'

He went into his room and closed the door.

Luke had been suffering from depressive illness.

Luke's soul rebelled against the world.

Luke's parents failed him.

Luke's society failed him.

Luke's teacher failed him.

Which of these statements were true?

Press One for connection to an appropriate psychological service, two for a philosophical and religious treatise, three for Freud and Jung and four for the anthropology department. If none of these options apply hold the line.

Pip stayed in his room much of the time that weekend and I walked in the park. It was grey and misty and rainy and I couldn't cry. All my mind was memories and terror. *You make the necessary judgements – it's not your fault they lost their lives.* There were families and lovers in the park: couples teaching their children to ride bikes and laughing, patient ponies on lead reins with toddlers on their backs, walkers with rucksacks and me and my polite enthusiastic little dog. She deserved a better owner. I messaged you and you didn't answer. I think it was only a couple of times. I was very good and very restrained. Maybe the last one wasn't. Something about not understanding why you were ignoring me. As night fell I messaged again, 'Where are you? Why haven't you answered?' I forgot to say please, forgot to say please call. The message fell into the darkness.

I slept. And I woke – I don't know what time it was.

'Selfish.'

Just one word bright on my screen. Out of nowhere. Stab in my heart. It was you.

'I'm sorry.' No reply. Racing heart. 'I'm sorry – I felt let down.'

Silence. Then:

'You think only of yourself. I have an elderly mother and two children to look after and you are unwilling to share me.' It was so well phrased. A fully formed grievance I'd had no idea of.

Share you? I didn't understand but it was clear I'd asked too much. I was too greedy, too needy, too—

'I'm sorry – please – you know what happened.'

Silence and an empty screen – the flat – the animals – Pip – the city breathing around me.

'I'm terrified.' That's all I could say. I was terrified that you were speaking to me this way. Another very long silence.

'Don't be.' Those words I could hear in my head – the little vehement way you said them. They sounded like you. But the other words not at all. They were like a demon had got hold of your phone. And then an altogether different tone, a different message, equally spaced out in time, like a metronome. 'We just need to be careful how we speak to each other, don't we?' Such a cool threat. So deliberate. I really didn't understand.

I held the phone in my hand and felt eyes hurting with tears. I hadn't cried so violently over Luke but I was going to cry over you alone in this grey light. Involuntarily – in an involuntary fashion. Why was I saying that when I hated adverbs. I felt very cold and I didn't know how to plead – how to explain that I just missed you over this long terrible weekend – that I'd needed – but there it was. Needed. I needed love, support, kindness, holding, talking. I needed to hear your voice. But it wasn't allowed. I felt this strongly. It was not part of your plan. I felt sick and didn't want to say any more and I archived your message, slid it away, trembling in my soul, sat on the side of the bed, turned the light on, put my head between my knees and breathed. I just needed to breathe. Then another black sleep.

I woke a few hours later – it was Monday I knew – I was afraid to look at my phone. 'Butterfly – I'm sorry. I should have been there for you.' And then your call. 'My mother was – it was a difficult weekend. What's the matter? What can I do?'

I forgave you instantly, unthinkingly, completely. 'I'm so sorry – you were busy – I didn't think.'

I was so relieved that the hard judgement in your voice was gone. 'Tell me.' The comfort of your command. 'I don't know,' I said.

A strange gappy tense silence and then, 'Are you going to work today?

'No.' I had Mondays off. And anyway – wouldn't they close the school, the railways, the world?

'Are you free for a coffee? In a few hours, I mean? Today?' You were always so formal. 'I could take some time out of work.'

I could have cried with relief. 'Where are you?'

'In the bunker this morning.' It was across London. Far far on the other north side.

'I just want to see you and comfort you. We could grab half an hour.'

Scalding tears. No thoughts. 'All right. Yes. I'll be there.'

'I'll text you the postcode. Message me when you're near and I'll tell you where to park.'

Thank god, I thought. Thank god for you.

I'd forgotten you'd said there was no signal in the bunker.

I drove in a fog of longing. All across London for such a long time, checking my phone, distracted in the November grey and rain. I should be going into college anyway – supporting my colleagues – I was clearly insane. People on the pavements and in the car, people with no emergencies, people with ordinary lives. I messaged you when the Satnav said I was close and you were very sharp very particular about where I was – and I said I could see the turning to the bunker and as I was pulling in to the gates looking at the soldiers holding weapons by the kiosks – you rang me – insisting down the phone – 'Don't approach the bunker – don't go into the compound, it's off limits – you won't be allowed to park – it's illegal, don't do it.' And I said, all right and turned the car around. 'There's another lane, just below turn in there, I'll be waiting.' It all seemed very John Buchan and hole-and-corner and I was amused by it. I don't know why. Nothing felt as if it were really happening to me anyway.

Parking – and you running towards me, so fit. I couldn't run to save my life. The sight of you – you looked like an immaculate advertisement for hyper-masculine casual wear – as if your clothes had come out of plastic wrappers, and not from any cupboard or drawer that I could possibly picture or understand, or from a costume department down a corridor of some film studio presided over by women whose lives were generously devoted to cataloguing and keeping them. But I'm straying from the point again. There you were, head to toe immaculate. 'You aren't in uniform,' I said.

'I changed,' you said, 'Uniform wouldn't go down well in the town.' I tried to imagine where this superman-like transformation could have taken place – perhaps in some changing room in the bunker but anyway. There you were. I couldn't imagine what you'd said to them, what excuse you'd found to get away. I was simply glad of it. 'Let's get back in the car. I'll guide you to coffee,' you said. Luke's desire to die had made real world details not only hard to comprehend but utterly unimportant like the waves on a faraway sea. Town centre in Northwood was ugly and damp. We parked in the sad municipal car park. You strode along towards the café – me breathless. You didn't move to touch or kiss me. I felt messy. You didn't say I'm so sorry or anything at all like that and I thought I am wrong to expect it – we are in the queue at Costa Coffee this is not the time or place. It was just you and me. Did you think that, Rob? Did you want to know? What time or what place would be right I was too confused to know. I do realise that in telling our story I am often very confused.

It took a long time to choose a sandwich and order our coffee. You really cared about what we had. 'You should eat,' you said. You seemed distracted and disturbed, I think because the sandwich you usually ordered was sold out – ill at ease. I put my head on your chest, your hand was on my back as we stood there and I shook and cried tearless perhaps for a second but you were embarrassed standing there I could tell. I felt nothing from you. It was a numb embrace but then I knew I was in shock. We sat down on plastic leather bucket armchairs, peeling cellophane from our sandwiches and exchanging sugar and you didn't say I'm so sorry. You asked me if the college would be in the clear. You told me a story about your father's funeral and your mother's grief, that she'd only be able to cry once everyone had left and it was a story I'd heard before and you told it word for word the same as if you weren't there then and weren't with me now – you held yourself away. Why funerals, I thought – why?

I think I must have looked at you in blurred mute enquiry with eyes still damp and smudged. Then you said, 'Here, take my handkerchief,' producing it from your pocket, ironed, folded, laundered, square. It was red with white dots. In *Gone with the Wind* Rhett gives Scarlett his handkerchief when she is crying and that's how the audience knows he truly loves her. I will leave it to you to acknowledge the banality of how much this meant to me, dearest Rob. I took it as a sign. I kept it. You'd given me your handkerchief, ironed, cotton and red spotted and you looked at me and held my hand and so it was all right. It had to be. I was so touched. No one had ever given me their handkerchief before. It smelled so clean. You apologised for telling me the story about your father a second time. You didn't ask me about Luke and I didn't tell you anything. It was as if he'd never existed at all. I decided you were awkward about emotion but that was all right. I decided to be comforted. I went to the loo and when I came back you told me how amazing I looked in my jeans. It seemed entirely irrelevant to me – more than that I'd had no idea. You never showed what you were thinking, you never showed attraction, everything everything was hidden.

You said that this public place was nowhere to be together. So we went back to where my car was parked in that north, north London tarmacked hole. We had a conversation with some old ladies who were short of change for the car park and you were very dashing and solicitous and then we sat in my car. You said there was a wood. I don't remember thinking clearly at all but I did want to be with you. I drove and you directed me and we parked in a sandy car park – deserted except for one other car and I took my coat from the boot and we plunged into the wood, looking for somewhere private to lie down and be together. It wasn't cold and the sky was clearing. You walked very rapidly, holding my hand. I trusted you so much that I remember thinking quite lucidly, good thing it was you I was with because this was potentially a very dangerous situation to be in with someone I'd only known fourteen weeks. I would never come here with a stranger but you were my love.

We passed someone walking their dog and I laughed. We lay down in the bracken, I spread my coat and we made love, awkwardly, with passion – I don't even know or remember just that it was very quickly done and I looked up at the sky – the clouds moving and I felt alive, as if you had given me the life force back. And utterly dazed. We didn't even take off our shoes. I wiped you with a leaf – fearful for a moment because there was a little blood from inside me. Blood on a sword, blood on a baby being born, all shocking but when you said you didn't mind my blood I felt comforted and you were warm. You were in and of me. I kissed you and you were still firm under my mouth. You made a pillow for my head and I felt free floating and quiet of spirit looking up at the sky. Then at you, the side of your cheek, your eyes. On your chest, in the crook of your arm. Close. We were happy. Or was that just me? My mind was open to the sky. Where was yours? Now I hit my head with my hands trying to know the truth.

All too soon you said it was time to go. I think I said something about how being with you in the wood was exciting and innocent in a babes-in-the-wood way while being deeply sexy too. I didn't say I felt skin close but completely detached. I didn't say I was free floating. It's always safer to put words to a thing – I find even if they are not exactly the right real true ones but the ones you wish were true. I don't remember what you said. Yes, perhaps. Yes, I think it was yes.

Once on the path – elated – you ran back for my glasses that I had left by the tree. 'I wish to be your hero,' you said, running back with them towards me like a boy in a race. 'I wish to serve you.' You remain the only person I have ever met who said, 'I wish'. Not I want or I need but I wish. Fairy story, courtly word. You did my bra up for me. You told me I was beautiful – you adored me. You hugged me from behind. I felt so alive but also distanced from myself as in a dream. You said:

'And you must keep the handkerchief as a token of my esteem.' And I gave you a stray daisy plucked from the side of the road. In the midst of death we are in life.

I drove home light-hearted. Part of me talking to you. Part of me talking to Luke. It was too strange for my mind.

You and I messaged but we did not speak again. Access was restricted. I told you I was going to the funeral – the family had said we were welcome. I thought it was important to go. I wanted you there and I didn't want you to have anything to do with it. 'This is quite a burden to put on a new relationship,' one of your messages said. I had such rising panic at that and tried to forestall it and to this day I don't know why it mattered.

Going back to college the next morning I decided to be brave like you. I'd missed the meeting on Monday because that was my home day where we'd been told to behave as normal and not talk about it unless we were asked but we were emailed too and when I arrived in the building and went into the room where all the tutors sat it was as if there were ice swathes between us: huge vast ice flows and dark water. We all avoided one another's eyes. And then holding the banisters tightly, I made my way up the stairs. The students' set faces showed how much they needed to be reassured and I reassured them that a terrible thing had happened but it was all right and we would go on with our work.

'Who'll go to the funeral with you?' asked Pip. He looked wan.

'My colleagues will be there.'

'Will you be all right?'

'Of course.' I was always all right. I always kept going. I didn't want or expect you to be there. I remember that. I accepted the gulf. There was a great deal of silence while Luke's soul hovered just above our heads as Shakespeare would say. One of those interim mornings you called me. 'I want to wish you all the best for the funeral today.' Formal you.

'It's tomorrow,' I said.

'Oh I'm so sorry. Well, for tomorrow then. Look I have to go – work.'

'Of course,' I said. You were slipping away over the rim of the world like Luke. Even then I must have known you weren't real.

The funeral was in a small grim church in North London and there were so many people. I felt like an intruder. The coffin was covered with Christmas roses in bright colours – they're really hellebores which is quite an appropriate name – at least the first part. The bright colours – were they right or wrong? Were they gaudy or life-enhancing? At least they weren't lilies – those and orchids always seem to me to be such evil flowers. Young people shouldn't have coffins. It was the wrong time of year for the wild white flowers which are my favourites – the ones I wanted to take for him – Maytime roses – but who the fuck cares what I wanted. I think I took white narcissus – nothing is seasonal any longer anyway. I held onto your handkerchief in a twisted ball in my pocket. I held onto it so hard. We sat in the cold of the church and I remembered what Luke had said about religion being a construct while I listened to the words about how much he was loved and how difficult it was to come to terms with such a death as this and I couldn't look at the family openly weeping and felt ashamed. I was in the row behind my colleagues and they seemed quiet and dignified. My thoughts were violent as if they would leap out of my head. I understood why the Victorians wore veils. Luke must have made a mistake I kept thinking. He wouldn't have wanted this. Pip had said, 'You know funerals are just for those left behind don't you, Mum – they're nothing to do with anything real?' So many people around me and they cried so much. As I came out of the church – hanging back so the important could approach the grave first – you messaged, 'I will be standing right behind you. You are constantly in my thoughts. Marriage is no longer for me but I want to build a lasting relationship with you. I send you all my love. Rob.' I wondered – stunned – why you were talking about marriage – why you were messaging me now. 'I am holding onto the handkerchief,' I typed with cold fingers, turning away from the crowd. No longer tucked into my coat pocket it was now twisted in my hands, was held against my eyes for all the tears that could not be shed, like some bizarre talisman of red and of white. I'm so angry now. So angry that he'd had to die and that you'd had any part of it at all.

I could not go to the reception – I felt it would be wrong.

But I left the flowers by the grave. Turned damp earth – all that was left of him.

The next day dawned with no choices in it. I was used to battling all the enemies of despair – and I told myself, why should this be any different, I must work, there was nothing else to do. Nothing left to do but get up and go to work. I think my sense of overwhelming bereavement embarrassed everybody – it certainly embarrassed me. It was too large. We were all stricken – why was I a special case. Pip stayed behind. It was not that I didn't care it was just his was a battle I could no longer fight.

On the way to the second day of teaching after this appalling ceremony, as I went up the tube stairs to the mouth of the station you sent me this message: 'I have decided I no longer wish to be in this relationship. I'm sorry. Goodbye.'

You immediately blocked me and your face disappeared from my screen.

Part Three

My knees buckled under me. I collapsed on the very dirty station stairs and a kind stranger helped me up. It was devastation, utter desolation. People feel embarrassed though and don't stay for long. When there was less trembling I couldn't decide whether to get on the tube and go home or on up the steep stairs to buy a cup of tea in Pret. It seemed disgustingly self-indulgent to buy myself a cup of tea. But that was what you were meant to have for shock. I wanted Pip. But there was my class waiting for me. I wanted to ask why you had gone away so suddenly and what I had done wrong. I didn't want anyone to see me. I stood stock still and paralysed. Then I called the college and said I had to go home – the walk to college was impossible. I succumbed. And you will not be told what happened next.

I woke in the morning and could barely move. Pain was all over my body and it was seized and stiff. I was hot and cold and dizzy. I'd thought I'd be able to go and work and see the students but I couldn't move at first, swinging my legs over the side of the bed and walking cramped across the room to dress.

'You need to go to the doctor, Mum,' messaged Pip from school. I obeyed – asked the doctor if I had flu or something worse and he asked me kindly what had been going on recently and I explained. He said he did not think I was ill but that my body was breaking down – he was very young – he prescribed tranquillisers and rest and wrote me a sick note for college. I felt ashamed. What was extraordinary was that I didn't think it was anything to do with my illness. I just didn't understand why I couldn't keep going. Since my diagnosis I had always kept going.

'Suicide is a legitimate cause of death. Like cancer or heart failure,' the doctor said. 'But it takes its toll. And you have had other stressors.' Medical language is hilarious, it really is. 'You must not blame yourself. In the end though,' he said. I wanted to wring his neck. In the end – what? 'You are in no fit state to work.'

'I won't get sick pay,' I said. 'It's zero hours. And I'll be letting everyone down.'

'Sometimes your health comes first,' said the doctor. I tried to imagine the race.

But if I couldn't go to work and I couldn't do anything at all, what was I supposed to do. I didn't get in to bed. That would be giving up. I curled up on the top of it with the animals and hid.

Pip came out of his room and looked at me. 'I'm sorry, Pip,' I said. 'Rob's left me and I can't—'

'It's not your fault, Ma,' he replied. 'I know you always do your best.'

I closed my eyes and gave in to the remembering. I thought about the dead – all those I'd loved who'd gone into the dark. They hovered around my bed. All the good angels while the bad ones had survived.

Pip sat beside me on the bed. 'I'm going to call Richard,' he said. 'We can't have two useless members of society.' And he put a blanket over me. I said nothing – thinking that if I'd been less distracted, Luke would never have died. If I'd challenged his father that day – if – if – but I never had the guts. I only ever ran. I only ever broke. I wasn't the girl you thought I was. And that was why you'd left. I couldn't reply to Pip because anything I said would have been pointless or wrong. You'd said I was selfish. I was a self who could not do right. Pip rocked me with his hand. 'Mum – I'm going to call Richard.' Still I couldn't speak. 'What Rob did was wrong,' he said. 'He shouldn't have left you. You are a good person.' But still I couldn't say anything at all. Words were useless. There is still the rope around the neck.

When he left the room I tried to rouse myself.

There were messages on my phone but none were from you.

'I'm coming to collect you in an hour – I'll take you to lunch.' Richard.

That was so like him. So often he didn't answer my messages – he didn't answer my calls. But now here he was. I was to be dealt with. I hated myself for having resentful thoughts. Resentment is not your friend. One of my doctors had said that. I put the shower on like a very old person and found my best dress.

It was a lovely restaurant: glamorous scrubbed tables – wrought iron – flowers, waiters dressed in long white aprons, very pretty and young. I remember thinking how very thoughtful of him to choose somewhere where there were so many flowers because I loved them so much. Even though I was naked and surreal in the place, I understood why he would choose it – in defiance of my failure to live as a real person. To show me what reality he could. Or perhaps it was just what he was used to and wanted.

He ordered me a glass of champagne. I couldn't help admiring him for that. 'Maddie – I'm going to say something you mightn't much like. Don't get angry.' He dreaded my anger. He'd said that once. Or perhaps it had been recently. Memory was fading. This would have made me sad if I'd had any feelings left at all. I too dreaded my anger – even though it was justified I think in some cases. I really think it was.

Richard had wiry hair and his skull was wider than mine. He didn't look like me at all. 'I'm sure you'd agree that things have been getting on top of you lately. What happened at college and Pip.'

'My student killed himself. He was in my care.' I tried so hard not to sound bitter. I try so hard, Mum. That was always what Pip said.

'Yes. I know. But you know – suicide is nobody's fault. It's a legitimate cause of death.' (If I heard that again, I'd scream.) 'And of course your scare with Pip. And then that soldier chap—' Scare. Scare with Pip. I'd found him in a heap on the floor. *An anxious fascination around control exists in both these texts.* Who had written that?

'Rob. His name is Rob.'

'Yes – Rob. Leaving.' You hadn't left. You'd vanished.

'And Pip – not being . . . Things have been . . .' Oh god – he was trailing off.

He was going to say it was all my fault. He was going to say I had done it wrong. He was going to say I wasn't fit – I knew that, Rob. That was what he was going to say. And I sat with my head down looking at the flowers on the table – they were in a jam jar – it was the year when everything was in jam jars – and I could feel nothing at all.

I managed to look up. 'Exactly. Pip has been struggling.'

I thought I sounded quite good when I said that – found some courage to continue. 'I can't get him a psychiatrist on the National Health. I keep trying.' CAMHS is a chasm was a favourite joke of Pip's and mine. I could have said, 'And you've got pots of money . . .' That's how one of my friends put it – I can't remember who. But I didn't say it – I didn't say it, Rob. You must always work hard and never rely on anyone, that's what you'd said, wasn't it? Be a radiator and not a drain. I only punish people when it's fair and right and right and fair. Your boys were alive and the one I'd meant to care for was dead.

'Well – what we were wondering . . .'

Who was we?

'We were wondering whether Pip—'

Was he going to lend me the money to help Pip with a private doctor. To salvage something? Was he going to help with the rent while I couldn't work? Was there something he was going to offer to do? Because for the life of me I had no more left.

We were interrupted by the waitress – oh, how pretty she was and young and blonde and very tall – bringing an exquisite salad of figs with pecorino, I think it was. And oranges.

'Look!' I heard myself saying – like a child. 'This is lovely.' And it was. Like the still lifes in the Prado I had seen when I was young.

'We were thinking – Amanda and I – that Pip could come and stay with us for a while. And when you're feeling better – we could all have Christmas together. It's time to be together as a family, Maddie. For Pip's sake – We know his father is away – and he did call me.'

Your darkest actions, nay, your privat'st thoughts/ Will come to light. Who'd said that? It had happened.

'How did your lunch go, Mum?' Asked Pip – as the little dog threw herself on me and the cat pretended unconcern. I didn't know how to tell him – couldn't remember how I'd thought it in the car.

'Did you know what he was going to say?'

'No.'

'Is he going to lend us some money till you get better? Dad can't—'

'No.'

'Is he going to help buy us a place to live so you won't have to keep paying rent? We'd be safe then and you could—'

'Don't be silly, Pip. He's not that rich. I don't know when we'll ever have a place of our own.' Why was I saying that? 'But we did talk about how Mummy is having a hard time and perhaps it would be best for you to go and stay with him for a while – till I'm better.'

We were in the hall I think. Not in the kitchen with the black windows.

'But you'll be alone, Mum. How could that be a good thing?'

I tried to walk past him. But he just stood there – in the way. 'Am I a burden to you, Mum?' He was looking at me but I looked past him over his shoulder because of the shame.

'How could you ask that? Never. You're the light of my life.' It was true. 'Come – let's get out of the hall.' I nudged past him as gently as I could and he spoke to my back.

'I don't want to go. You know that – don't you, Mum?'

'Yes. I think so.' I was walking in front of him now. It was very difficult to discern what I did and did not know. You had seen to that. But if Pip didn't see my face and I concentrated very hard on not crying it might be managed. 'Darling, the thing is that at the moment it is for the best. I can agree with Richard on that.' I tried to lilt with my voice

– lighthearted.

He began to follow me into the kitchen.

'I can cook for the freezer so there's stuff when you get back.'

'Yes.' In the freezer there was one popsicle from the previous tenant and a bizarre bowl of parsley sauce in a Fortnum and Mason pudding basin that I'd decided could live there.

At last I looked at him. 'And I'll clean your room. If you say I can – of course.'

'Yes, Mum. You can. But I think you should concentrate on getting better. So you can go back to work and see your students. You like that. And we can have nice chats like we used to.' His brown eyes were so forgiving.

'That will help get me better.' In the old days I would have painted his room.

'I think you should take Puppy,' I said. 'She'll cheer you up.'

'But what about—'

'I've already checked with Richard. He says it's all right.'

After that we watched reality TV because nobody could feel bad about themselves while that kind of disaster was going on. That's what we used to say. But all the people on the screen glided past and I couldn't understand what they were doing and saying. And then we went to bed.

'It won't be for very long, Mum,' said Pip, his bag in the hall, the dog looking bewildered at the end of her lead.

'Yes. And think of all the burgers he'll take you for.' I wasn't properly dressed. I'd forgotten to pack his toothbrush and he wouldn't have remembered either. But there was Homer and Plato tucked away in his bag.

The taxi Richard had sent was waiting. We continued standing there.

‘I’ll see you very soon.’ We didn’t look at each other and we didn’t embrace. He walked ahead of me down the garden path you had sprinted up so many times. And then we said goodbye.

The worst that could happen had happened. Pip had gone.

Richard sent me a message. ‘Pip received with thanks. He’s having Molly’s old room. Will keep you posted. Love you.’

Time went away – the days were so short anyway they weren’t even real days. I lay down and remembered Pip. What he’d said years ago – he must have been quite little – still at primary school. I could hear his voice in my head like a recording. ‘They’re teaching us this sing-song rhyme, Mum. “Love is something if you give it away, give it away, give it away, Love is something if you give it away, you’ll end up having more.”’ He had sung tunelessly and then broke off. And he had said, ‘It makes no sense to me if they are saying give it away, to have more – because the point is you need to be generous with love – they shouldn’t need to add that you’ll end up getting it back because then really you’re only doing it for yourself. They’re bribing you. Which makes love selfish and I don’t think religion or goodness is meant to be selfish. They shouldn’t use love like that, like a bargaining chip, but they do. Religion is all about being rewarded for being good at the end with everlasting life. It just gives up on the world – it’s so wrong. And anyway I don’t want to have everlasting life and live for ever. I mean, what’s the point? Why don’t we reward ourselves now by making the world better?’ I hadn’t said, because we’re all flawed and greedy and broken and the ones who are in charge are venal and brutal and power hungry, because that’s not what you can say to a child. It's like when you teach them to read, showing them pictures of farmyards that no longer exist presided over by plump and smiling farmers and their wives.

Then he'd said, 'All religious people want to do is dress up. Look at the Pope.' I'd laughed so much. And after a while so had he. Then another memory glided by of when he was about five, dressed in purple, taller than the other children, holding out a casket in the Nativity play and calling loudly, 'And Myrrh.' He had been so proud of his casket of Myrrh. I think I'd said something about how maybe the rhyme meant that everybody must give love and not hoard it. But he was unimpressed. I'd taught him about Agape and Eros and Philia and that pleased him. He'd always felt happier with ideas than people. And I had told him that art was important and he said, 'At least it's better than the consolations of capitalism.' I'd laughed and told him that should be the title of his first book.

But now Pip was different. Those were his ghosts. Now he said, 'You're a romantic, Mum. You believe that souls can merge and there will be a union, or if not that, personal redemption – but I know that the postmodern, post-truth late capitalist society has no call for that any longer. It has perfected loneliness.' I'd told him not to be so superior and tried to tickle him but that never worked. Lying there and thinking of Luke's grave I wondered how I could have tackled his mind, counterattacked, found the route through. If there was anything, any tiny thing I could have done. I'd never arranged the time to practise his essays.

I dozed and dreamed about the apple tree I'd planted in the walled garden in the country. It was called Discovery. There had been one crop and we picked it too early before we'd had to leave and that was the last garden.

Footsteps in the flat above woke me. There was a

message – for a wild moment I thought it was from you. It was Paula. She said she was coming to stay because I shouldn't be alone. At least someone had sense. 'The flat is messy.'

'I don't mind. I'll see you tomorrow. Wait for me – you won't do anything stupid?' I told her I would wait.

I couldn't stand the thinking. Being assaulted by memory. How I'd painted the walls in the country. How I'd found the perfect sky blue – the perfect pale pink. The blind at Pip's window was made of sea blue with little red boats sailing bravely in it – his chest of drawers was from eBay – dark wood it could have come from a ship – and his view was over the garden to the barn with the apple trees and olives that hadn't survived the first winter. But there were tangled home grown roses – I was so proud I had grown them myself. In the walled garden I had always dreamed of. All my life. But it had not been perfect – it had never been perfect – or had it got broken. When they laid Pip after he was born on my chest wrapped in swaddling clothes he had looked very worried. He hadn't breathed straight away and did not know what to make of the air.

'Don't worry, Pip,' were the first words I said to him. 'It's all right. It's a good life. You'll see.'

But now it was clear that I'd been wrong. It was a dirty tarnished life. In spite of everything I'd tried to do in it.

I had to get dressed properly for Paula and look almost as if I were real. And as soon as I saw her I was real more real made real the way other people make you.

'I'm glad I had the time to come,' she said. Her children were with her ex – the one who starved her of money while he had two houses.

We sat and we had wine. 'It can't hurt,' said Paula.

'Pip will come back – won't he?' I asked her. 'Luke and Rob won't. I understand that.'

'Of course. This is just for now.' And when I couldn't answer – 'Maddie – Pip will come back. I promise.' I'd always been so afraid someone would take him away. 'I can't believe he left you like that. Rob. And now at all times.'

Rob. 'It's understandable. All this death.' And there were all the things that were so very wrong with me that you'd found out – just as I had always been afraid you would.

'No, it's not. He said he truly loved you. You told me.' I couldn't say anything. 'Mind you – he did come on scary strong. And you never knew much about him.' Paula's practicality seemed like blasphemy. 'Those pictures you sent me of him were very dashing, I must say,' she added. Dashing. What a word.

'But I did know. His marriage, his boys, his job. All the pictures.'

'All things he told you. It's weird what's happened. This is more than you being bereaved. Let's google him.'

'I tried once but never found him. I think it's because he's in the army.'

'No one has no trace at all, Mads. That's odd.'

Dear Rob you must be laughing. It had never occurred to me to question you before.

Blackness at the windows and the flickering of the artificial electric wood burner. We googled Robert Benedict Fordham. Lt. Colonel. Nothing.

'It's because he works in Intelligence,' I said.

'How do you know?' said Paula. 'How do you know that

for sure?'

'I went to the bunker. Last time I saw him.' When – so trusting – I had taken your hand as you led me into the wood.

'When he wouldn't let you drive in? When he completely lost his shit when you told him that's what you were doing?'

'Why would he lie to me about it? Why would he say things that aren't true?'

'You read about it all the time, Mads. People do it to pick up women. A top secret job is impressive they think – or maybe because they're just mad – I don't know.'

'But it wasn't like that. He's honourable. He said he loved me.'

'Yes. What is it about that word?' We sat on the brown rented sofa where you'd 'taken' me the first time. Paula's eyes, pale and clouded.

'I'll try LinkedIn and Facebook.'

'What about Insta?' We searched and scrolled – two women with dyed hair who would never bear children again. 'I don't use social media – so—'

'Nothing. Nothing at all.'

'How do you know he was even in the army?'

'He sent me all those pictures.'

'Let's see.' I showed her. 'They're quite old. He could have left years ago.'

'That was active service. He sent me his citation.'

'With his name on it?'

'No. No name at the top. Just the citation. Which referred to him as Major Fordham. And now he's in Whitehall. Here are the pictures of him at his desk with his ID tag on.'

'Yes, but nothing connects him to the bunker but his say-so.' But you lived at the barracks at Camberley and why else would you have been there that day – in North London? I felt as if I were breaking our trust, Rob, just to show the pictures and messages to her.

'You're not allowed to take pictures of the bunker. But he sent me them from everywhere else. I felt—'

'Establishing his whereabouts. Don't you think that's odd? Who does that?'

'He was always sending me pictures.'

'How do you even know where he lived? Truly.' And then after a long silence, 'What a gambler.'

We could not speak for a while.

'Did you feel loved?'

'Yes. No. Sometimes. When he came to comfort me like an angel in my bed that time – before Luke – breathing into my hair.'

'Oh god, Maddie. Let's stop this now.'

Leaving Paula on the sofa bed – I had not cleaned Pip's room – I went to bed. I slept and dreamed of Pip ahead of me in the wood – not little Pip but tall fully grown Pip – holding himself so painfully. Of course I couldn't call or speak to him – I was afraid of what I might say or be unable to say.

I woke, drank water, dreamed again: Dracula, dark lord beside me behind me sucking my neck drowsy I was and stunned.

Four o'clock and cold sweat, no chance of sleeping again, I fetched the computer from the sofa where we'd left it and googled again sitting on the floor outside my room. I could not take you into my bedroom. I tried just the surname, the name of the mission you had been so proud of, and suddenly there it was – the picture innocently posted on Facebook by the organiser of the talk – you shaking hands in front of a clumsy whiteboard with the map pinned up in what looked like an ordinary public library – you in your blue linen jacket, the clothes, the leather briefcase, you as you'd been dressed when you'd said you'd ask me to marry you one day, ('Our time will come') your eyes expressionless, mouth in grim smile line and underneath the handshake the caption:

Stephen Merrell with Lt Colonel Jacob Fordham. Headline: *Operation Silver Falcon – A Fascinating Talk.*

You can scream all you want to I thought as I put my hand over my own mouth.

Your hand and bitten nails – Rob. I was looking at them in the picture. The organiser was smiling proudly, happily.

Rob did not exist.

Rob was a construct.

Rob was imaginary.

Rob did not exist.

Luke did not exist.

No landline, no address, no car reg., no face on WhatsApp, no nothing.

Screaming inside your head is far worse than screaming in real life I think.

Not that I've ever done that. Properly brought-up women don't.

I did not want to wake up Paula but when it was time I brought her a cup of tea on the sofa bed; I told her what I had found.

'Show me,' she said.

Together we looked at the picture. It actually made me frightened – Rob/Jacob like some graphic terrifying scene of violence – I flinched at it and had to look away. Is that what you wanted? To terrify someone inside their soul? And I did not know what I was supposed to call you in my head or whether anything in the world was true.

'Will you be all right, Maddie?' Paula said, as we said goodbye. Then, 'Stupid question. Forget I asked it. Call or text any time. I'm here.'

Because it was nearly Christmas, the days were dark and short and while I knew that the best way to beat a bad depression (suffering unto death) was to have a routine of tasks and purpose, exercise, work and 'things you enjoy' – as my first and most beloved doctor used to say – I knew there was no point in this at all because I didn't have to set an example to Pip or keep the show on the road, any road at all. There was no show anymore. I had failed. I did get up. But it was so hard. I was still very very frightened. And I couldn't change the sheets. I remembered changing the sheets with you and laughing about hospital corners. Sometimes I bit and gnawed on the flesh around my wrists to make sure I was still there and could still feel. Because it is the thoughts that torture – the endless repetitive insistent thoughts about how I had ruined everything because I was so stupid. I wanted to die. But I thought that if I killed myself, I would destroy Pip and I really couldn't do any more harm.

I tried to close the door on Pip's absent spirit, on Luke's ghost until Christmas and the resurrection and the life eternal, Amen. But I could not close it on yours.

'Good morning, Central Services.' I had not known I was going to make this call. I didn't plan it. My heart was knocking but the fear was moving now – moving in a silver anger – it was moving forward to pursue you.

'I'd like to make a complaint.'

'What might that be about, Madam?'

'It's about a serving officer.'

I was sitting in my car in what passed for a morning in England in December.

'What sort of complaint might that be, Madam?'

What was this – a department store in the fifties?

And then I couldn't speak. Just choking images of you. 'It's about a – it's a Lt. Colonel.' My voice trembled but was clear. 'He works in Whitehall and in the bunker. Conduct unbecoming to an officer.' I knew that was a phrase, even if it was from the nineteenth century.

'What sort of conduct might that be? Can you give me his name?'

'I'd like to speak to someone in charge, please.'

'If you give me his name, we will be able to proceed.'

I'm making this up because actually – I can't remember how the conversation went – it was nothing like as orderly as that. They said they'd had trouble finding you. Something about finding the right department. They said they'd call me back. Very quickly – stunningly fast – someone called back and then someone else and I told my story. How you had lied and used a false name and left me when my student had died.

There was a long pause down the phone from the authority figure in a uniform who was now connected to my destiny and yours.

'May I ask you a few questions, please, Mrs Vane?'

'Ms Vane. Of course.'

'Did this individual allow you to see any army documentation?'

'Apart from his citation – there was a report once. He showed me the second page – then put it in his briefcase. He left the briefcase behind at my flat and came back in a great hurry very upset. But I didn't look in it. I put it in the cupboard for him to come back and collect. He said it had important documents in it.'

'Probably just his lunch.' Did I imagine the Major said that?

'I didn't look anyway. Oh – and there was a picture of his ID tag.'

'Yes. We have that.' They'd asked me to send pictures to corroborate and I sent the ones you'd sent me when we first met, and our messages, our private messages so they could see what you had presented – how you had presented yourself to me – so open and clean. 'Did this individual take any money from you?'

'No.'

'Did this individual try to involve you in any illegal scheme?'

'No – but that's not the point. The point is he lied about who he was and behaved dishonourably.' I could have added and he's a member of the British Army and we see them at the Cenotaph and cry. But I didn't. There was no point saying he took my love and my imaginary future and my belief and my sanity. Gross misconduct in the court of humanity and ethics and – oh god. It was not revenge; it was justice. That's what I thought. I sounded mad – I knew it. Mad Maddie. 'What I'm trying to say is that he discredited the army. And that's why I am reporting him.' An officer and a gentleman would never lie to fuck a lady. There had been an officer in one of my books.

There should be a name for the crime you committed, Rob, but there isn't. No record of it – no concept of it – no mark made. Isn't that strange.

'Yes, I understand.' Said Major whoever it was.

'Please tell me you will investigate this.'

'I can assure you that we will. However, our protocols forbid my providing you with any further detail than that.'

This seemed peculiar to me.

'You promise you will look into it though?'

'I promise.'

But what good was a promise in this world.

More grey time passed.

'Good afternoon, is that Miss Vane?'

'Yes.'

'I am calling from — On behalf of — We thought you would like to know that we have identified the individual you reported and that steps have been taken.' There was no room to interject even if I'd been able to think fast enough. 'I'm sorry that there has been a delay in this matter. The individual concerned was not in our department. However, the army do not take lightly this behaviour towards a vulnerable woman.' It was as if he were reading his lines from a cue card.

A vulnerable woman. Would it have been all right if I hadn't been vulnerable? I found out afterwards that vulnerable does not even mean vulnerable, it means mentally ill or physically impaired.

'Could you tell me what you? – Have you?—'

'I'm afraid that's all we can tell you. No discernible crime has been committed. However, we apologise. The Major asked me to make this call on his behalf.'

'Can you tell me anything about his – about his true circumstances?'

'I'm afraid that's confidential.'

Mind reeling. 'I see. Thank you. Goodbye.' How could it be confidential? Had these people shared a bed with you? Made it with clean sheets – watched you dress in the morning – heard you brush your teeth – gripped your hand in passion – exchanged the stories of your lives? Did they know about the Afghanistan plug you always carried with you in case of emergencies – that you had Raynaud's disease in your hands – that you liked mushroom omelettes and sausages but hated curry? Did they know you? They had seen you in another life on the other side of the curtain on another island than mine. I was so angry I was so angry I was so angry.

I scrambled into the car and tumbled through the afternoon streets to the dim blustery park.

Battling the wind in an open part of the park – my phone began to ring and it was you. I had not expected ever to hear from you again and anger turned to fear. Like magic you returned from oblivion and the gulf of black. You called and called and called and all I did was stare at the screen with your name and your bright smiling picture and put the phone back in my pocket. Then the messages began. 'Maddie, please pick up. It's Rob. I need to speak to you.' 'Maddie. Maddie, please.' Over and over again. Then, 'I understand you do not wish to hear from me. I will not trouble you again.' Then five minutes later, 'Maddie, please I need to speak to you. I need to explain'. No no no no I was so afraid.

'He keeps messaging me—' I texted Paula.

'Who – Rob?'

'Yes.'

'Don't pick up.'

'No.'

'Block him.'

I knew I couldn't do that because you would never allow it.

'It's important please Maddie I need to speak to you *please please please please please*!'

I looked up around me and there was no one in the park. It was wide and rimmed only by the trees the walls and sky. It was very cold. The bracken was cut and the branches of the great old trees immovable against a white sky.

I was too frightened to hear your voice. I messaged. 'I can't talk to you.' I thought if I did that then maybe you would stop and go away.

'*Please*.'

Still no one close by. It wasn't as if you could appear out of the phone and hurt me but that was how it felt. 'Can we speak on the phone?' Your message said. 'It would be easier.' And another, 'I need to speak to you and explain.' And still another, 'I can call you tomorrow evening from the car.'

It was extraordinary. You were alive: you did things like go to work and drive your car and make calls from it. I ignored the messages. The phone began to ring again over and over. I put it on do not disturb. Another message.

'I'll call you at six-thirty tomorrow evening. Please pick up.' I'd always used to tease you about your precise use of time. I couldn't imagine how I could ever have been so confident in you.

'Please remember,' one message – and then the second, 'I've never stopped loving you.'

Of course I wouldn't answer – how could I? What good could it possibly do?

At six-thirty the next evening I was on my way back from tutoring after college, cold and standing at the bus stop on the bridge over the railway away from the crowd who were filing on to the bus, each in their own world. I was on high alert, my heartbeat violent. When the phone moved in my hand once again I felt a terrible resisting terror.

'Hello.' It had become inevitable.

'Thank you for talking to me.' Your voice was cool. But it was your voice. That's all I could experience. I could hardly believe it – thinking less about the fact that all begging and entreaty had been abandoned.

'It's all right.' I still find it hard to countenance or explain how frightened hearing you speak made me feel.

'Maddie – before we continue I need to know that you have stopped your complaints to the army.' The voice of authority had returned.

'It was just one call.' I knew in my mind that this was the only reason you had contacted me, but it was a distant knowledge like a boom on the horizon. I was being managed because I had done a bad thing. Damage control. 'I—'

'It was a terrible thing to do. Can you see that – how humiliating it was for me? What you did? Yesterday I was summoned into this office, to stand in front of this person I didn't even know – I had no idea why – and told that a complaint had been lodged against me. Your name was not given. Only when the accusations were read out . . . I realised. It was you.' (A beat; the full count of theatrical three I'd say.) 'Thirty years in the army, a perfect record, about to retire. And now this.'

There was a reason – I'd had a very good one – and I knew I had to tell you what it was. But I couldn't think of it at all. I couldn't recall the facts of the matter – the matter of the matter – the loss. You said, 'What gave you the right?'

It took ages to remember, although of course I had no rights because I was not married. 'You lied to me. You gave me a false name.'

'What do you mean a false name? Why would I do that?

Rob's a nickname. I've always been called it. I did nothing wrong. Nothing.' Your voice was patient and neutral and then became slow, low, explaining: 'You felt terrible – because I'd ended things, I understand that, but imagine if the situation had been reversed and you left me – would I complain to your boss at the college?' As you spoke the hurt in your voice mounted, accelerated and intensified; you were the innocent and maligned accused making his case. I was muffled and confused in my mind. 'You must see that public and private are separate. Separate places entirely.' (One was a bed chamber and the other was the real world of the court.) 'I know you're upset. I understand that. But tell me you do see that?' You insisted. You had always been so good at that. You spoke to me as if I were a small child. And I was humiliated: entirely.

My mind was a board you were writing on. Paralysing my mind was your special talent. Crystallised inside this same mind of mine was a new thought: I had behaved like a mad woman. That was what you were evenly explaining to me.

Expressions such as 'toyed with my affections' and 'wooed under false pretences' were not going to cut it. You don't say you want to marry a person and then leave them by the side of the road and not be who you say you are but then here you were, explaining that this was entirely all right. All all right in fact. Clearly, I had been a fool. I should never have been allowed to be a parent, that was also clear: I failed to understand the simplest of things. 'Yes.' Accountability was a vengeful fiction and certainly not for this world. It was probable you were right and I was wrong. Highly probable, in fact. I said, 'What's going to happen?'

'I don't know. I'm hoping not disciplinary action – something on my record. I'm hoping that.' And in the feeling silence I began to hope it too. That you at least could be unblemished. The long quiet silence lengthened.

Then you spoke and you were tender. 'How are you? Is it – has it been very hard?'

I nodded blindly. 'Yes.' Turning away from the other people in the bus queue I bowed my head.

'I'm sorry.' Horrible pause. 'I'm sorry I left you the way I did.'

I could say nothing.

'I just couldn't handle your grief,' you said. 'It was too much for me. After everything I'd been through in the army. We'd only just got started—' Silver tongues and coral graves. 'I haven't been well myself – mentally, I mean. You're not the only one who's lost someone they had the charge of . . . And I've missed you and haven't known how to get in touch. There are no winners here.' I felt a wave of sorrow for you, my soldier, and shame for myself. I didn't know whose side I was meant to be on. We had been on the same side – against the world – or was that me and Pip? Pip had refused to meet you. Pip had gone away. And now what was it – who was I loyal to? I felt alone, with only your condemnation remaining. Is that what you did with the men, Rob? They feared disappointing you because you loved them so much? Is this how it worked?

'Please don't say any more. I'm sorry I did what I did. Really.' I just wanted to disappear.

The rain had begun to come down needle fine and I could sense another bus coming. I wanted to end the conversation but was unable to sever the connection, trembling and weak as I had become.

'That's all right. As long as you promise not to do it again.' Very gentle, again. Almost a hint of a smile in your voice.

I nodded in the falling rain and humiliated and sorrowful tears. 'Are you crying?'

'Mmm.' Your voice was painful to me when it was warm. 'Yes. Yes I am.'

'Dry your eyes. I have an idea for you.' What could this idea possibly be?

But of course it was always in the plan, wasn't it, Rob/Jacob?

'I think we should meet.'

On the bus I decided to write you a letter which I would give you when that time came.

I would start on it when I was home. Forgive us our trespasses as we forgive those who trespass against us. My father. My father as he slept. The Bible. Shakespeare. All are punished. That was the prince – he said that. It was so hard to curb the racing thoughts. They had been slow for a long time and now they were moving, it was moving again, my mind. I never had known what to do when I had no one to inhabit it.

'*Dearest*—' No. Not *dearest*. '*Dear Rob.*' Or was it Jacob? *Dear Jacob*.

No. That word still had nothing do with you. Or us. *Dear Rob*.

Dear Rob

You said and wrote so many things to me about your feelings when we were together and I want you to know how much that all meant to me. I'm deeply sorry for causing such disruption to your life in the army. The loss of my student has skewed my compass and the hand on the tiller, as you used to describe it, has been violent to others – in this case you – in a way I regret. Forgive me.

Maddie

I felt the words had some sort of dignity. I hoped that was the case.

We – you – arranged to meet in town in the week before Christmas. I skip over the long phone call where we made this plan. Your honeyed words. I spoke to you from a glowing bed, all the other lights in the flat turned off.

I suggested the National Gallery to look at the pictures and have coffee. I wanted to go to a public place. This felt very important.

You kept messaging me on my way there – saying you'd been delayed – persuading me to meet you – not in the café – but outside in the darkness of Trafalgar Square, between the lions and the steps. I walked past you twice, you said. You were wearing a baseball cap which was strange – I'd never seen you in one before – a small bag from Brora dangling from your hand. You must have been doing your Christmas shopping. I looked at you and thought: Is this ordinary brown-haired man the one who made all those things happen in my soul? You tried to kiss my cheek but I kept space between us. I tried to talk to you in the road about how you'd hurt my feelings – I'm not sure why. I hadn't done lovely make-up; I did not wear lovely clothes. I was not going to try and impress you and add to the charade. You took me to an ugly pub. Black inside and out. No views. Water on the tables, old men and drunks and tourists, a big news screen you kept half an eye on while I tried to decide what to have to drink. I was ready to bolt.

'I used to come here ages ago,' you said, very calm. 'With work. It's changed.' We were strangers.

Then you looked at me.

'Open the bag,' you said. 'Happy Christmas.' In it wrapped in tissue paper, an exquisite pair of cashmere gloves, pink and blue, my favourite colours. They were perfect.

'For me? Why?' I know this is going to sound ridiculous

but no man I'd known had ever given me such a perfect present.

'Because.' You took off your cap. 'Look. It's me. Remember?'

Now you looked like Rob and not some indeterminate unimportant stranger. I felt very hot, sweat in my scalp. 'I don't like it here,' I said.

'I'll take you somewhere better.' I could see you thinking and calculating like a robot in a sci-fi film. 'Ah. I know where.'

I hurried to darken my eyes and stain my mouth with make-up in the urine-smelling cubicle and we went to an expensive hotel bar with velvet and fairy lights and gazed at each other. I tried to tell you what you had done wrong and you tried to tell me that what I had done was worse and it was utterly pointless; you were like someone in a visor or a suit of invisibility and then you said, 'What you don't realise is how much I've loved you all this time. Seriously.' Seriously was one of your words. I'd forgotten. (*'Be careful, Mum,'* said Pip.) But I was moved and could not speak and looked down, embarrassed because nothing before or since had ever equalled the radiant attention you could bathe me in when you chose.

'I wrote you a letter,' I said. I tried to give it to you.

'No. Read it to me instead,' you said. 'I love hearing your clever voice.' And read it to you I did. 'Now put it away. We don't need it anymore.'

'All is forgiven. It's terrible what happened to you,' you said. 'Luke.'

I was astonished you remembered his name. 'Can we not talk about him? I—' I trembled on the precipice about him. You knew that.

'All right. But I promise to stand by you from now on. Please forgive me for being afraid.'

'It's all right – it's not normal – for the beginning of a

relationship – it's true what you said.'

You reached for my hand over the table.

'Your mouth looks gorgeous,' you said. 'Can I kiss you outside? Then I have to go.'

'Oh but . . .'

'It's a work thing. I wasn't sure you'd have that much time to give me. I didn't want to be presumptuous about it. I'm sorry.' And I felt I could make no objection to anything you did – ever – ever again – and you went off to the loo.

The bill came and I paid it. *('Why would you pay the bill, Mum?'* sang Pip.)

You were back and we were threading through the tables, your hand on the small of my back.

In the very cold courtyard, 'We will meet again. After Christmas. If that's all right with you.'

Revellers surrounded us, tripping into us, invisible. 'Will you be away the whole time?'

'At my mum's. Yes. But after that . . . I've decided to leave the army earlier than the summer. April I think. There will be more time for us. Between job interviews.'

'Ah.'

Mine eyes dazzled. And you were gone.

Paula called to check on me. As soon as she heard my voice she said, 'You've taken him back, haven't you?'

'He explained. It was a misunderstanding. A nickname.'

'Really? Just think about it, Maddie. Why would he want you after what you did to him? That was a very big deal – reporting him. Did he say why?'

This one was very difficult. 'I don't know. He says he loves me.'

'Oh well, that's all right then.'

'It's—'

'But how can you trust him? Really trust him, Maddie?'

There was so much cotton wool in my mind. 'The strange thing is I don't think I do.'

'What are you doing with him then?'

'I don't know. It just feels inevitable somehow.' Like shaking a locked box.

'You sound weird. I should come up and see you. I've got the kids coming though – we'll have to put a date in the diary.'

'Of course I'm weird. I feel bereaved – and . . . there is so much pointless time.'

'Maddie – I just wish you'd walk away.'

'But then I'd have nothing, would I? Nothing at all.'

I went to Richard's house for Christmas and Pip and I gave each other presents. Richard had paid for Pip's. It was beautifully wrapped. It was surreal. We were left alone for a little while they were cooking but I didn't think he wanted to talk to me. I was afraid to ask him how he was. 'I like your new shoes,' I said.

'Thanks. Richard let me choose them.' I was not sure if this was a criticism. 'Are you feeling better?' he asked as if he hardly knew me at all and I was an aunt visiting for the feast.

'Will you be ready to come home soon?' I wanted to say. Or was it – 'Richard – can Pip come home soon?' Or should it have been, 'I'd like to bring Pip home soon.' None of these things could I say. We lapsed into silence until Richard and Amanda returned and I felt sorry for them because they seemed so ill at ease and were trying so hard. We all knew this and we all pretended it was all right and lovely – that everything was grand. And I went back to the flat alone. They offered their spare room for a few days – but I felt I couldn't impose. It was all like white icing – we didn't talk about anything.

‘Have you seen your friends?’ asked Richard.

‘I’ve been keeping busy,’ I replied.

‘You seem better rested,’ he said. ‘A bit more lively.’ ‘Look lively’ was a family joke between us. He didn’t know I was nourishing my secret again.

On New Year’s Eve – improbably – I was at a party. Old friends in their stylish house in Maida Vale. You messaged me all through it, encouraged me to dance, told me it was all right to be happy for a few seconds if I could. ‘I am watching the fireworks on TV,’ you said. ‘The boys have gone to bed. (Your happy healthy children.) Sending all my love.’

‘Happy New Year.’

‘Happy New Year to you too. I miss you so much.’ It was not your actual voice but I imagined it – the one where you admired and loved me – not where I’d done something wrong.

‘Pip’s not here with me.’

‘Why not?’ You didn’t seem to remember I’d told you about Pip going to Richard’s.

‘Because I—’

‘You’re all right now. Go and get him,’ you said. ‘Go and get him tomorrow. It’s a New Year.’

I obeyed you and went to collect Pip.

‘How is this going to go?’ I said in the car.

‘Why are you asking me?’ He looked bigger and older and cleaner.

It was very beautiful the way New Year’s Day sometimes decides to be.

‘Did you have a lovely time?’

‘What are you talking about, Mum? It was weird. Everything was shiny all the time. I missed you. And then you visited for Christmas which was even fucking weirder.' Pip rarely swore.

'Nice things to eat?'

'I'm not five years old, Ma. Yes – there were nice things to eat.'

'I see.'

'Can we go and get hot chocolate and have a walk in the park on the way home? Even though it's stuffed with annoying bobble-hatted rich people?'

'We can.' The dog – having thrown herself on me with cries of joy – settled herself on Pip's knee and groaned. 'There's no Christmas tree.'

'I don't mind.'

That night we sat on the rented sofas looking at the black windows to the garden, now invisible.

'Shall we watch something? Take our minds off things?'

'I like horror.'

'So do I. But proper horror.'

'Not me. I like the shlock stuff.'

'Pip, I've never seen you watch horror in my life.'

'You can do anything on a phone, Mum.'

'Well you're not meant to be doing that. You're meant to be chatting to your friends and torturing yourself with social media, aren't you?'

'The thing is, Mum, I haven't got any friends. Plus you can't control me. I read articles and educate myself on my phone too.'

'Phones are evil.'

'Tell that to yourself when you don't look up from yours when I speak to you.'

'Shall we stop rowing?'

'I thought we were having a conversation.'

'All right.'

We sat with our bowls of ice cream on the sofa. He liked marshmallows in his but I preferred straight chocolate.

'So. What shall we watch?' This had still not been resolved. 'How about one of those three-part genre dramas where bad things happen but it's all all right in the end?'

'Only if it's really properly bad.'

'All right.'

We found one. We were an example of the consumer finding tailored content.

We watched for a while in silence. Women were having a difficult time with unfaithful husbands and there was a lake with a body in it.

We began to discuss the women's clothes and kitchens. We laughed so much we were nearly sick.

I messaged you that Pip was home. 'Home is where the heart is,' you said.

Pip, me and Pip, Pip and I made French toast in the morning.

'You're not all right yet, are you, Mum?'

'Not completely all right. But I'm trying very hard.'

'So am I,' said Pip.

'Do you think that maybe—'

'I'm better off there for now – with Richard?' I couldn't make out his tone – his intention. I didn't want to embarrass him. There had always been clarity between us but he had become part of the fog.

'Do you really think that?'

'I don't know, Mum. I'm a child.' I frequently forgot this – for long periods at a time. He knew that. He made a little sigh. 'No. I don't. I want to stay with you.'

'What about school?'

'I promised Richard I'd go. He said if I didn't, he'd

come here and get me – and nobody wants that.'

'Yes, but Pip—'

'Like you said, Ma – sometimes we have to do things we don't want to do.'

'I'm going back to work.'

'Good. They need you.'

'What I mean is, I can't make you go – I can't. You know that.'

'Well you'll have to trust me then – won't you.' And he went away.

I had imagined such a life for Pip. Glory.

January and we were reunited – the stranger and I. 'I know there is a sexy girl hidden under there – I just can't find her.'

We never spoke what had happened – the rift between us – you had forgiven me for what I'd done and I was thankful.

When we made love – I tried to dress it with those words – we were more separate than ever. But I did not want to add any more complaints to the army. Sometimes we were together I felt and believed. Sometimes. But at others you would pull my hair. Very hard. I did not know why – because it hurt and you didn't listen when I asked you to stop. 'God you're gorgeous,' you would say. But I felt dirty. Once you put your hands around my neck and pressed your thumbs tightly until I cried out. It was horrible. I felt so ashamed. You set your alarm early in the morning so there would be time for more. Leaving at five-thirty – your quick hurried step, your clothes laid out tidily, your handkerchief, your socks tucked into your shoes. 'Don't get up – I'll call you later.' And I would get up anyway – it felt more dignified.

'This is like Napoleon and Josephine,' I tried to laugh once. I didn't want you to see how sad as I was. Because then you wouldn't come back. Yet I was confused and wanted you to explain. 'Are you sure this isn't all about sex? For you? You and me?'

'Trust you to say that,' you said. 'You should have more faith in yourself Butterfly. More faith in us.'

I began to recall, vaguely, fondly, sadly – with some detachment – our early days in September when you'd asked me if I'd still be with you in November because you wanted to book tickets to concerts with me. You'd given me the dates. I had never heard about these concerts since and I wondered what had happened. I began to buy tickets of my own, cinema matinees to coincide with the few afternoons we spent together which unaccountably you'd cancel at the last minute because of a meeting with a general, or a drive to Cambridge or having to be in the bunker early or some such thing. These imperatives were unquestionable and they made me so sad. When you stayed over it was still sneaking in late because of Pip. But now you rarely stayed – surprising me with calls and demands to see me for a couple of hours. You had abandoned the idea of meeting him – as if it didn't matter any longer and we'd never discussed it. Instead we always seemed to be in my car after a snatched drink, kissing and other things I don't like to remember but which are always starkly in my mind and I thought I don't want to be in the car doing these things but somehow it seemed inevitable in the way everything between us always did, orchestrated and preordained and timed. You were such a stickler for time. I did not feel desirable any longer – I did not feel desire – I did not feel.

My strange depleted class continued. I made cakes and gave them to my students. We couldn't talk about Luke. We couldn't not talk about him. But it was not the way I'd expected. 'Luke would have loved this' – said one of the girls when we got to the end of *A Farewell to Arms*. Would he have agreed that Catherine was the true hero. Another thing I would never know.

'I thought we'd meet somewhere different and special for a change,' you said. Had you read my mind? 'Shall we go back to the pub off the King's Road where we had our first date?'

'Ooh, yes.'

'I can't do a slap-up dinner but we could have a bite.'

'Sounds lovely.'

'I'll meet you there after college. Do you remember where it was?' Of course I remembered – what did you take me for? I grew up in London. When Pip was in his pushchair we used to look at the gargoyles on top of the red-brick buildings off Sloane Square. You know nothing about me – the tiny remaining part of me was shouting. Nothing. Six-thirtyish?'

'Yes. I'd love to see your face at the station,' I said – I don't know why I said that when it was not what I felt – but I did. Some obscure challenge. It frightened me that I had begun to lie. 'But the pub is good too.' Perhaps because we always met in a crowd, away from the station, away from public gaze and I worried about it. Truth or dare, Rob. And it was sad that we were even thinking of meeting there – it really was.

I still had butterflies getting ready in the hideous college loo – but they were more like dragonflies or wasps now – the feeling of constant alert and fear – not hope – never that anymore. (Any longer, I'd say to my students – Pip used to tease me about it. Never any more. Any more is wrong.)

Before I was even on the tube you messaged me, 'I'm

here early. Just as well – it's packed. And so loud. Can't get served.'

This seemed odd on a Monday. 'Really?'

'What can I get you to drink?'

You sent emojis of wine glasses. 'Yes, please'.

'Usual colour?'

'Yes.'

'I'm at the bar. It's heaving. I'll keep you posted if I get a table.'

'All right. Fast as I can.' ('*Look at you, jumping to attention,*' said Pip.)

Emerging from the underground I began to walk – frightened of something down the King's Road – frightened of being late, frightened of being wrong, frightened frightened frightened – oh what could it be – then I was truly tipped up tripped up, scared:

'Boo!'

You were behind me, reaching to grab my elbow, dressed in your immaculate suit and raincoat. For a second I had no idea who you were. I was going to meet Rob and you didn't look like him. Not at all. You were a total stranger. I always forgot how small you were and you looked so ordinary and middle-aged, your face arranged into bland lines.

Yes, really truly I was frightened. I said, 'I thought you were at the pub.'

'I know. I wanted to surprise you. Because you said you'd love to see my face at the station.'

This wasn't the station – it was the road. ('He described exactly where he was in those texts – didn't he Mum? In the pub,' said Pip when I got home. 'And you imagined it. Because that's what you do.')

'I'm confused.' And I was so weary and just wanted to rest.

'Don't be. It was just a little trick. Just a little game. I'm sorry. I wanted to make you happy,' you said. 'That's all I've ever wanted for you, sexy girl.'

In the pub – which looked so much more vulgar and less sedate than it had before – you took hold of my arm and traced over the veins of my wrist with your finger the words, 'I love you'.

I withdrew my arm.

'So how did you get the nickname Rob?'

'Say again?' You always said that, never 'what?' or 'pardon' or 'eh'.

Exaggerated gentlemanly expression, another example that you were there to serve.

'I just wondered.'

'Oh – it was from when I joined the army. I was so idealistic about everything, they used to call me Robin – for Robin Hood. It kind of stuck. Everyone has a nickname in the army.'

'Ah.'

You went and got the drinks. I must stand up for myself – I must. You were back.

'So the name?'

'And I always felt that Jacob was a bit too – biblical. You know – because my Mum was very – religious. Strict and all that.'

'I didn't know that.' You'd never mentioned that, Rob – I could have sworn.

'Well – ' You leant closer. 'And Jake is an awful shortening. Sounds coarse. So – you know . . . there it is.'

'Does everyone call you Rob? Even your friends?'

'I told you – I don't really have any friends. I'm a private person. People tend to disappoint me. It's to do with morals – you know. There was the odd couple from when I was married. Don't see them anymore. And in my job it's colleagues more than anything. And the men.'

The men.

All doing what you said, you who were so much smaller than they were. You – who they called sir.

'What about your brother and sister?'

'I told you I don't really talk to my brother. (Had you told me? Yes, I think so. Back in those heady first days.) You know how much I disapprove of him for cheating on his wife. They only found out because he was pulled over for drunk driving. And my sister – well she's good with my mum – does much more than me, there every day, but we've never really got along. I think they resent me. Because we have a different father.'

I knew it wasn't meant to be a good thing to be involved with someone who was on bad terms with his family. But when I looked at my own I knew that this wasn't a fair standard to hold to you at all.

'You just don't get it, do you? I love you so much.'

You said that I could choose whether to walk back to the station along the back streets where you imagined 'taking me' in one of the basement areas, or along the King's Road, public and bright. I chose the King's Road – I thought it would be fun to walk together and look in the windows. It was also because part of me did not want to be alone with you in the dark. Felt it held danger. Because of this you were silent and would not touch me or kiss me goodbye at the station. 'No kissing today,' you said. 'That's it.'

Spring did not come for a very long time.

It was always dark outside. Outside the English room, outside the windows of the bus, outside the flat. Pip avoided me. He knew Rob was back but did not speak about him. He had not honoured his promise and he did not go to school. He stayed in his dusty room. Every two weeks I'd take a broom and sweep it out – and bag it up – like a stable – while he waited in the living room with patient sadness.

I was always tired, pulling myself up the stairs to the English room with both hands on the handrail, trudging home, waiting for your message, waiting for your call, staring into space, curling up in the embryo position, waiting life out, trying to look pretty for you when you came. I didn't want you to go away and I knew that meant I couldn't do anything wrong. The worst thing about that was that I never knew when it would come – the icy-cool reply to something I said or wanted or felt that was wrong.

You started to grow a beard. This inspired a sort of terror in me I could not understand. 'It will be softer for you,' you said. You sent me selfies as it grew over your face. You looked even more like a stranger – your eyes more prominent and glassy and glossy – the line of your mouth hidden. In one there was a modern knotted orange pine door behind you – the light was different than the one in your mother's house. I couldn't fathom it. I didn't know where you were. You had a job interview, you said. I was dying to hear how it went. A text came, 'Hi Mike, Thank you for a great meeting. I think I left my gloves in your office. Would you kindly return them to 23 Glasscourt House, Tindall Close, Guildford, GU35 EAU. Many thanks, Jacob.'

Many thanks, Jacob. I hated people who said *many thanks*. I knew the gloves. They were leather, like rapist's gloves, I used to tease you. But where was this place in Guildford? And who was the person who lived there?

Heart thudding again. I texted rapidly, 'Rob – I think you sent me this text by mistake.'

Quick as a flash, 'Thanks, Butterfly. Silly me.' As if it

were ordinary, as if it were all all right.

'I thought you lived at barracks – what is this address?'

'Oh that's one of my mates. Easier. Post is rubbish at barracks.'

I thought you didn't have any mates. And I thought everyone called you Rob.

'Who's Mike?'

'Told you. Job interview. Thanks again, gorgeous. Got a meeting now. Message you later.'

These were lies. I knew these were lies. I knew. I was angry again – shaking with it. I couldn't breathe. I had to grasp it while I was there – let it take me away and leave you behind.

'It's been nice knowing you,' I messaged weakly. Why I was bothering with sarcasm, I have no idea. It was like poking you with a stick.

Silence. Your favourite weapon. You didn't care.

Two hours later, '?'

'This feels wrong.'

'What does?'

'That message.'

Rapidly – the phone rang. 'If you don't trust me and insist on being paranoid like this I really don't see how we can continue.' Your voice held so much venom. You despised me. I despised me.

Heart knocking again.

'I'm sorry.'

'It's just not good enough, Maddie.'

'I'm sorry I—'

'Every little thing.'

'Talk to you later? My fault. Not feeling good.'

'Fine.' You were gone with an instant click. Your silence lasted for days. A roaring silence.

Half term and you were with the boys. It was a raw February. I asked for your address at your mum's. Repeatedly, I asked. You gave it to me after some resistance. Cat mouse, mouse cat. I decided to try and distract myself and took Pip to the National Gallery to look at the Impressionists and their endless summers of water sky and trees. I bought postcards of the dancers that Degas gave the world, stretching their limbs and working so hard. I wrote on one card but sent three (I had to have them weighed at the post office), 'London is empty without you. I love you and I'm sorry for my strangeness. Hoping you are having some rest and fun with the boys. Love, Maddie.'

Despatched to the Yorkshire countryside to the household I never saw in the village I didn't know in the county you would never take me to.

Unusually you called me. 'I'm worried about you,' you said. 'That you might be feeling unwell.'

'I'm missing you,' I said. 'You're missing in action.'

You didn't laugh but I pictured a grim smile.

There are theories that say that love is never shared it always occurs parallel and someone is present at your loving and you might be present at theirs but that is all. 'I have been going out a bit,' I said.

'Good.' You didn't ask me where. Usually you liked to know.

'What have you been doing?'

'Making endless cups of tea for my mum. Swimming with the boys. Kicking a ball about. They have homework too. Rory has A levels coming up – I told you.

Mocks when he gets back. He's sweating over *Othello*.

'I know *Othello*. I could help . . .'

'No need, Butterfly. You have your own students to look after.'

'Yes.'

'Look I've got to go, freezing out here. I'll message you later.'

That was good of you – it really was.

Two days passed.

'The post is bad in Yorkshire,' I messaged.

'How do you mean?'

'I sent you something.' I remembered the cards you had sent me in the early days. So proper and controlled, the green pen. How I had smiled at their quaintness and formality. How much of an innocent you'd seemed. How above you, you'd placed me. How had it come to this from that? Luke had breathed then, been somewhere alive.

'Oh really? Maybe it got lost. My mum has this big curtain thing for the drafts. I'll check.'

I didn't know your mum's first name but I googled your surname and the town and went on the census. I had become more cunning to myself and more obsessed with the puzzle. There was an Ivy Fordham in the town you mentioned, and even near the road you stipulated on Google Maps but the address listed was in a street around the corner to the one I'd written to. Why would you give me an address close by? Why not her address? Had she moved? And what about the address in Camberley – what was that – why was I so afraid of it? All I had to do was get in the car and go there but I couldn't. Who would open the door? Frozen, I couldn't move.

I took Pip to see more paintings – but he had a fear of the crowds and we had to leave. We stood outside the Tate

Gallery and contemplated the river, the statue of the man with a dolphin behind our heads, the signifier of a classical past dwindling in time. 'We could make popcorn when we got home,' I said. 'That might cheer you up.' When he was little and we were married there'd been Sunday lunches with friends and bread and butter pudding and laughing. Now crowds of strangers – I understood why he was afraid.

In the car in the dwindling light, your message:

'Coming back tonight. See you in our place at seven?'

'Sure. Yes. Of course. Why not? I'll be there.' Any one of those phrases could have been one of the phrases I used.

And now we come to the dirtiest parts of the story. There's no other word for it really. It is the only word that will do.

We had a drink at the place; it was spring cold; you had forgotten your wallet; you patted your pockets with surprise at their emptiness, reaching for it. You were so theatrical I almost laughed. I didn't mind paying for the drinks – you'd never let me usually – why didn't you just say.

'Have you eaten?' I was hungry.

'I got them to do me a boiled egg at barracks. Skipped the hot meal. Just hard boiled – nothing fancy.' I knew this was a lie. It was so elaborate. 'But you go ahead – don't let me stop you.' I didn't want to eat after all. You were taut, distracted, still waiting to hear about your job. 'I really think they're starting to mess me around now,' you said, sounding so angry.

'No. It's just the civilian world – don't worry. Everything takes ages – everything takes too long.' I felt my job was to reassure and calm you, but I also felt that this job was surplus to requirements, that it was a game we played. You didn't really care what I thought.

'You'd know more about it than me, Butterfly. Thank you for explaining. I'm sorry I'm distracted. A lot on my plate. They're working me to the last minute – the army.'

'What about taking some time off – in between jobs?' I didn't dare say we could go away somewhere. I simply meant for you.

Quick breath – 'No.' Short, vehement passionate. 'Let's go,' you said. 'They're closing up now. I'll kiss you goodbye in the car.'

There'd been no room in the car park. I'd parked outside the pub, on the road, close to the pub tables where we'd had our first kiss.

You climbed in beside me.

Dark but light enough in streetlight and pub lights to show your face all covered over with beard. The windows were misty, streaked with rain. We kissed and it was passionate – we knew each other's hunger by then. And you said, 'I have to have you now' and we were fucking on the back seat and I could hear the voices of two men on the other side of the window and I couldn't believe this was me. I didn't dare think even that they could see us. Just the other side of the glass. It was a stone's throw from the table where we'd talked about Hemingway. Just the throw of a stone. How quickly you left when it was over, after a rueful laugh and a, 'I can't believe we just did that —' I couldn't believe it either. Incubus.

And after that – open season.

We planned – I planned – a day at the sea that never happened because you had work. And so instead we went to Starbucks in Wimbledon – ending up upstairs where there were slits for windows and I made a remark about it being brutalist architecture's version of those windows knights fired bows and arrows from and you didn't answer and I sang to you a love song from *Guys and Dolls* which I had cried in front of that weekend in the car on the way to our pub and you told me how beautiful my voice was and I gave you a blow job in the car with people walking by and my dog's towel over the window for imaginary privacy and there was no time for the pub because you had to beat the traffic – meetings to tie up, you said – and I asked you to keep in touch more because I never knew the plan and you called me when you got there – I forget where it was you were going and you told me how much you loved me and I couldn't understand why I felt so bad. You sprinting away from my car to yours. The vision revolves in my mind. Your journeys: Cambridge, the barracks, Yorkshire, the bunker, Whitehall, me. There was never anything in your car. Not one piece of incriminating evidence, it was just an old beige Volvo and there was never anything in it, not of yours, not of the boys, not one tiny little thing.

'What happened to the sports car you picked me up in – for our first date?'

'Ah. The end of my marriage fit-of-pique car? I sold it.'

It had always seemed like a woman's car to me. And I wondered why you hadn't told me. I told you everything.

My mind was a torment to me; my soul a wounded animal. It ran on you, round and round you. And Luke – Luke's face, Luke's words, Luke's life, Luke's death. Whenever I wasn't teaching, I lay down and looked into my phone or played our conversations in my head, while at night I dreamed of sea monsters and swarming cliffs and falling. I tried to remember lovely things like Pip and I swimming in the water in Turkey and the memories of his childhood but they were torture too because they had gone.

I looked and looked and looked through all the past I'd shared with you.

I found a number for a private detective; it was easy. I spoke to him on the phone. 'Am I being paranoid? Or is there something wrong?' I said, to another strange man who wasn't you. It can often be necessary to ask a man whether you are having the right feeling I think.

'Have you got his reg number?' He said. 'For the car. That would help start things off. But I can tell you for free, in ninety-nine percent of these cases, your suspicions are bang on. A basic check will cost you three thousand pounds. If you want him followed or photographs it will cost you more.' I didn't have the money to play that game. 'Are you still seeing this person?' he asked. 'If you are – I'd be very careful. These individuals are not like you and me.'

Paula called. 'It's your birthday soon. I thought I could come up and we'd go to Pizza Express.'

'That's really kind but I want to be with Rob,' I said.

Not only did I want to be with you, Rob, but I had an exact idea of what I wanted to happen. I wanted you to have dinner with me, Richard and Amanda. I don't why I chose them but I wanted to have dinner in a restaurant like a real couple with a real life. Do you remember, Rob? You said that you were shy and wary of meeting my family. You wondered whether it was really the right time what with work and leaving the army and all the pressures. I insisted. 'Even if you just come for a drink.'

'I hate social situations,' you said. 'I—'

'Please. It's my birthday.'

'Of course, Butterfly' – you said. 'Anything for you.'

It was arranged that we would go to an Italian restaurant on the Fulham Road.

You would come to college and collect me at six o'clock. We had had parents evening and one of my students had given me a bottle of champagne. I was exhausted and enervated, waiting in the English room with my colleague, putting the tables back in their places.

'I don't know where I am,' you messaged. 'I'm lost.'

'Where are you?'

'Just down from the station.'

'Keep going, take your first right and walk along a little.'

'Hasn't he got Google Maps?' said my colleague. 'He's in the bloody army.'

'I really am so lost,' you messaged again.

I called you. I was terrified you'd give up and go away and not come and collect me at all after all. Your voice was genuinely panic stricken and I couldn't understand why. I tried to explain the way calmly. Then I waited on tenterhooks for the worlds to collide.

'I'm here. Look out of the window.'

And you stood, the square and its cold trees behind you, the students leaving on the pavement, the darkness, your head tilted, looking up.

'You look beautiful,' I said.

'So do you.'

'I can't believe what I'm hearing,' said my colleague. 'What is this, Romeo and Fucking Juliet?''

'I'm coming down.' It was hard not to run and fall down those slippery old stairs.

Outside it was cold after the heated building and you were like a distressed small child. 'Where are we?' you kept saying. 'I don't know this place.'

'We could walk to the restaurant, but we're a bit late.'

You kept glancing around as if looking for snipers – it was the strangest thing.

'Let's get a taxi,' I said. 'No sense panicking.'

'I can't – I don't . . .' You didn't hold the door open – you lowered your head.

In the taxi you said, 'I can only stay for a drink, I'm afraid. Not dinner.'

'Oh.'

'I have a very early meeting and have to get back.'

'All right.'

'I'm disappointed too,' you said, but without your usual conviction. It was as if the ink that made the drawing of you was fading and damp – seeping away onto the sugar paper.

When we got out of the taxi again, you seemed almost to shake with fear.

'It's just here,' I said.

'Very fancy,' you replied. It wasn't. It was a trattoria and I can't even remember if there were tablecloths and it was in a smart part of town – but fancy it was not.

Richard and Amanda were waiting, awkward, sitting down.

'We haven't ordered anything yet,' Richard said, standing up in greeting.

They were looking deliberately casual; Amanda without her customary lean and expensive dazzle and Richard without a tie. You, Rob, were in your lovely suit, but you were held inside yourself, subdued. I was in my prettiest teaching dress which immediately looked shabby compared to everyone else in the room; my hands were dry and scuffed and my nails looked unkempt, bluntly cut.

'What'll it be?' said Richard. 'Champagne? Bottle of wine? Cocktail?

'What's your wish, birthday girl?'

'Ooh, I don't know.' It felt grotesque. What had I been thinking? I looked at the menu because I was afraid to look anywhere else.

'I'll just have a glass of water,' you said. 'I can't stay long.'

That was an actual pain to me, Rob – like a shard of glass.

We ordered some wine. Richard said, 'Glad to have a chance to finally meet you.'

'Yes. Likewise.'

'Maddie tells me you've had a long career in the army.'

'That's right.'

It was like an interview between two people who already disliked each other intensely. Amanda and I watched. Behind the men, the people were blurred, the waiters' presence an embarrassment.

'Admirable – to serve your country.'

'Thank you. I've been proud to serve.' You seemed visibly to flinch then.

'Getting out now?'

'Yes. The company I'll be working for have offered me a great opportunity.'

'What are they called?'

You said the name – one of those ones with weird phonetic spellings, and surprising me, Amanda smiled over to Richard, relieved, 'Oh, that's the company Toby works for. Got a few branches, haven't they?'

'Yes. This one's in Bristol,' you said. Bristol again. Bristol.

'He'll have to move,' I added pointlessly.

Rob sipped his water.

Richard said, 'Mads tells me you live in the barracks at the moment. Unusual.' You said nothing.

'Rob's boys are at school near Bradford-on-Avon. Bristol will be quite good for that,' I said. No one acknowledged this or looked at me.

'Did you meet Laurence Fairburn? At this new place? He's the chap I know there.'

'No,' you said evenly. 'Another department, probably.' I was beginning to be furious with Richard, trying to catch his eye, wanting him to stop. But he didn't look at me.

'What is it you'll be doing for them?'

You uttered some phrases I didn't understand. I never understand the jobs men do. Richard nodded.

'Look, I'm sorry to cut this short,' you said. 'But I'd love to give Maddie her present. I've got a train to catch.'

'So sorry. Yes of course. Then we'll order.' Richard motioned to the waiter to bring the menus and you opened your briefcase to produce a bag from Jo Malone.

Inside was a beautiful velvety body cream and a card that read, 'To my darling Maddie, Wishing you the happiest of birthdays. Thank you for the times you have given me. All my love, R. PS You make the best sausage sandwiches in the world.'

'Thank you so much,' I said, reaching out to take your hand over the table. Awkwardly we brushed fingers and you stood up.

'I really must go,' you said.

'I'll walk you out.'

'There's no need.'

'Yes. Yes there is.'

On your heels I was, like a dog. Outside on the pavement, you kept saying, 'Where are we? I don't know where we are.'

'The station is that way.' I pointed – clumsy. 'You can

bus it. Or taxi. You won't be late.'

'All right. You'd better go back in now.'

'I'm sorry. I'm sorry he spoke to you like that.'

'If he weren't your brother, I'd say he fancied you and was possessive but it can't be that.'

'He's just protective that's all.'

'Strange family, yours,' you replied. And then, refusing to hug or kiss me – angry I knew it – you got into the taxi and were gone.

'I didn't know they let you have a beard in the army,' said Richard when I sat back down. 'Let's order.' We all pretended to look at the menu and then Richard said, looking up, 'Just one question. Didn't this Rob turn out not to be Rob at all? This is the same chap isn't it?'

'Don't do this, Richard,' said Amanda. 'Not now.'

I blushed. Richard has always been able to make me blush. 'He explained it was a misunderstanding.'

'And now it's all tickety-boo then? So tickety-boo that he turns up to your birthday dinner, drinks a glass of water and buggers off home? And that's meant to be A-OK?'

'Richard!' Said Amanda again. 'You're upsetting Maddie.'

'Just one more question before we move on with our tedious civilian lives,' said Richard. 'What's Rob for?'

As spring flowered you began to tell me about all the things that were wrong with me. I wasn't responsive enough in bed. I was too needy, too moody. I began to get increasingly disturbed – upset because I didn't understand why I couldn't see you at the weekends, why you were always with your boys or working on your MA. I could come to Bradford-on-Avon, I suggested – not to meet them – they who were not ready for my corrupting presence – but we could chat on the journey – you could see them – then we could meet up later. Stay somewhere. Drive back to London together. No. Furious childhood cartoon-like frown. 'We could make plans,' I said. 'When we met you said you wanted to take me to concerts and movies. You said . . '

'I can't believe you're doing this. I'm too busy. You know that. Why should I wrap myself in knots because my girlfriend says she wants more time?' My girlfriend. That sounded so strange. What confused me was these cruel disputes would only happen by text, after which you would vanish and would be unreachable. You'd threaten me with ending things, you'd threaten me, accuse me, rage at me, assassinate me. But when you saw me, you'd continue to – in your words – 'worship' me. To tell me that when the army was over we'd have more time. I didn't know what to do. I felt I was truly going mad.

You came to stay for two whole nights. We listened to music sharing your headphones and walking home in the early summer night, city streets I'd known from childhood – looking up at the moon. It was unreal and very beautiful – it filled the whole sky – and I thought, Now. Now we are together. A soaring gleaming glimpse and you were gone.

There is blackness after that. I deliberately did not think about what the messages you sent might mean. I thought about it all the time. You sent me a picture of the menu from your Passing Out dinner. You in some sort of cummerbund. I thought of Cambridge – the boys from my past whose families had country houses and gardens and horses and the best and most beautiful of things and I'd hoped and expected one day I would too. 'Such a shame they don't allow guests,' you said. You told me you had handed in your army kit and surrendered your credentials. 'Did you keep anything?'

'I kept my jacket. The heavy one. The one I've had for years.' I didn't believe you. I didn't believe anything you said. But of course I believed you wholly. I had to. My mind running round the rat trap – I was the silver ball in the maze game you were tilting with your hands.

'Have you started flat hunting?'

'There's no need. They're putting me up in Bristol for a while.' You always gave the impression of arrangements that whole institutions and corporations made just for you.

I put my head down and concentrated on the students and their exams. Redrafting with them, rewriting them, editing them. 'Your students always write so well,' said my colleague. 'So cleanly. How?' How? I don't know. Sharp precise persuasive incisive concise analytic true. Are you picking up the irony here Rob? Or did that never exist in your lying mind?

Richard called.

'How's Pip?'

'He still doesn't go to school,' I said. 'But he seems a bit better. He reads all the time – when I'm out of the house. Educates himself. When I'm gone.'

'It's not really good enough though, is it?' he said. No it wasn't. Not at all.

Now I remember our endgame.

It seemed you had moved away and were not in barracks any longer but I couldn't understand when this had happened and where in fact you did live. Sometimes at your mum's, you said. That I couldn't understand – she was half the country away from your new job. You said they paid for a motel near the new office – also that there was a bunker under that building like the one in the army because it was needed. Which was why you didn't always get my messages. I tried to imagine this bunker. You said that because you were busy starting a new job you would not message very much. I was absorbed with my class exams and all the others and I loved the drenching light in the English room even though it was too hot.

I was excited when at last we made a date to meet and wanted so much to celebrate the end of term and your job and have dinner in Bristol and stay the night.

I messaged, 'Shall I find somewhere special?'

'Money is tight. You're always so impractical.' I was angry that the notion of celebrating was so foreign to you but I felt in a defeated caged way you were right – I couldn't pay. You had already decided where we would meet. 'Book the coach – it's cheaper,' you said. 'I'll send you the address.' I stared at the timetable on my phone feeling again the surge of horrible pointless anger. I had a summer job interview in London early the morning after and could not imagine how I would make it back in time. But you wouldn't move the day. I felt it was the only day and otherwise you would go away. I didn't want to go and yet I thought I longed to see you. You accused me of being disorganised because only at the last minute did I make the booking. I was very confused all the time. You told me to walk to the place from the coach station. You couldn't meet me from the coach because you had to go back to the hotel from work and get changed, so you could 'look good for you'. That's what you said.

For once I was there first – despite the confusion of the coach. A builder whistled at me as I ran across the road.

The BrewDog Pub is on the banks of some stagnant looking water. It was full of men. There was no table – I found a stool and a high counter. I was trembling. You arrived – pristine – one shirt button undone. I'd never seen that infinitesimal adjustment before and I knew you were thinking about it and wondering about how you looked. You barely tried to conceal your anger that I had got an Uber from the station.

'I sent you a map,' you said.

'I have a good sense of direction but I've never been much good with maps,' I said. 'And the roundabout and the one way system – I was confused – I didn't know which way I was going.' You left my words unanswered such was your distaste.

But I could hear them in my mind, 'You're always confused,' you said. The men would have found their way – not been found wanting. I thought a great deal about the men.

It was loud. I couldn't talk. We couldn't talk. I didn't want to talk. There was nothing to say.

'You look beautiful,' you said – peremptory – as if you didn't like me at all. And as I watched you standing at the bar, head tilted up, the way you had on our very first date, I knew this was the last dance.

We had supper across the dirty road in a dirty noodle place. 'I have lunch here,' you said. It was empty. The food was bad. They didn't have a licence. I had pictured a nice dinner to celebrate the end of my term, your new job. Nice meant expensive to you. Nice meant me taking advantage. Nice had made you angry. In the middle of noodles you disappeared to the loo. Though I was used to it I was afraid. I couldn't eat looking at the gelatinous syrupy liquid with the dead meat lying in it so quietly. I waited for you for a very long time.

'You haven't finished,' you said, coming back.

'I've had enough, thank you,' I said. But no reward was forthcoming for the perfection of my manners. I always taught Pip how important manners were.

We walked down the road in the wind, silent. It was early. 'Would you like to go for a drink somewhere?' I said.

'No. Let's just go to the hotel,' you said. You were angry I wanted to take an Uber because the hotel was out of town, instead of the bus. How I knew you were angry was the pressed set mouth, the silence.

'It's been a long journey already,' I said. 'And I'm a bit cold.' I wore only a white shirt and jeans. The shirt was a little transparent, the broderie anglaise I had so carefully ironed seemed to mock me and I had an obscure sense of shame. Bristol was colder than London, which had had a heatwave; the air was sharp and the seagulls were screaming.

'There is such a thing as the weather forecast,' you said. 'You could have looked at it.'

In the taxi, which I flagged without your permission, 'So will you be based here for a while?'

'I told you. Yes.'

'Always in the hotel? I don't see—'

No wonder you were so callous, so dismissive, watching me struggle so stupidly with your obvious lies.

'I'll find somewhere to live. I just haven't had time.'

I said nothing – staring blank and blind out of the window at the ring road and the flat featureless land. It had been carved up for infrastructure. I wanted it to look the way it had a hundred years ago, the way it had looked in the books I'd read. You took my hand. 'What are you doing for the next twenty years?' you said. Turning my head to look at you I felt a gut fall, a womb pain, and realised I had no idea what I was looking at. It was something other. Something evil.

'I've always meant everything for the best,' I said.

You didn't blink.

In the motel room a strange sour bottle of Prosecco from the mini bar tried to warm me.

I sat on the chair, you on the bed.

'Let's listen to some music,' you said, playing instinctively a song Pip and I loved, sharing the headphones. 'All the young soldiers who listened to this,' you said.

'Yes. And all the young girls.' Such a petty rebellion you didn't even acknowledge it.

I had come to need the passionate impersonal love we made – the hungry darkness – and you slept like an innocent babe.

Wide awake – something burrowing in my brain – I went to the tiny bathroom. I looked at your spartan leather washbag, your expensive aftershave.

I went over to the dressing table, bolted against the wall, in the dim light from the bathroom. Your wallet was lying there. Glancing over at your sleeping form, I opened it: no receipts, not one slip of paper, no cash, just the one card: J M Fordham. Even your middle name was not true, had been a lie, it was not Benedict. It was not Rob's wallet and you were not Rob and this room was not ours and you were not mine. I did not know who was writing the story I was in but I knew I would never see you again.

Five o'clock in the morning. I sat on the bed fully dressed beside you looking at you as you opened your eyes. 'Now the roles are reversed,' you said, calm as a corpse. Again I knew you were intensely angry. 'Don't forget your sleep mask.' I had left the black silk slippery thing in the bed on the pillow. Impulsively I put it over your eyes. This is not me, I remember thinking. I can't believe this is me doing this.

You didn't budge but stiffened. I pretended to tease you with it and laugh, pretended it was a game.

I can't remember what I said, what questions I asked that you evaded. I just remember leaving. Your body stiff with rage. Mine burning with it. It made me feel free.

The coach was late getting in to London.

I was late for two appointments.

I left my wallet on the bus.

Confusion subsumed me. You sent me horrible messages about my incompetence – how careless and stupid I was to leave and lose things. How I couldn't organise anything. I was angry. I said that I had minded terribly that you had not met me from the coach the evening before. It was such a pathetic fact to pin my disavowal of you on. You said how tired you were of my constant spoiled and selfish demands. These messages hit my phone as I was driving back from the bus station where I'd tried and failed to find my wallet – the end of the line. I was texting and crying and driving – and I thought I should pull the car over but I didn't care if I crashed. Another message, my eyes on the rear view mirror, my eyes on the screen, my glance at the road, 'You expect too much of me. You always have. You are so weak.'

Pleading and crying – 'No Rob – I'm sorry'.

More messages: 'Selfish. Spoiled. Demanding.'

'No.' I wrote – 'No.' 'No.' 'No.' But you had decided.

I pulled the car over at a service station on the A3. Hyperventilating like the idiot I knew I was. I undid my seatbelt.

'You are not fair to me. I love you. Please.'

I could see, *'Typing . . .'* It was a long message. I begged it was one of forgiveness. Then it sprang, bright onto the screen: 'You have never understood or supported my transition from the army. You have never cared. I've tried to be understanding of you but you are impossible. I can't afford to keep driving to see you and you cannot afford to come to me. Goodbye.'

Frantic I messaged – 'Is this really the end?'

And you said, 'If you like you can message me, I will always answer.' I closed my eyes – there was a chance then that if – and opened them again – and your picture had gone.

You'd left me – vanishing from my screen – vanishing from my breathing world like something created from mist. I knew it was final. It was such a shock because we were in the middle of an argument, in the middle of the conflict that had come to define my life and clearly had very little to do with yours and you exited with words so inadequate it would have been laughable if there had been any laughter left. All your imaginary spaces – the ones I'd believed in: the barracks, the boys' school, Whitehall, the bunker, the new office, your mum's house in Yorkshire – they all vanished too. All I had was the messages, the handkerchief, the gloves and the cards and the depth of the most terrible and appalling shame that I had colluded in your rape of my mind and my body, my spirit, my soul and my dreams. I had traded all of it – all of myself – for the promises and the prison you made me. I was left broken with a broken child. Another child was dead. But it was the shame. I can recover from any pain. But it was the shame. You despised me. I had disappointed you. And I could tell no one. *They aren't people. They're the enemy.*

My students' cards that year. There had been a few but I think this was the loveliest: 'You are the kindest most wonderful teacher I have ever had. I shall never forget the time you spent marking my essays and helping me. Thank you for being a second mother to me. All our chats.' Who was I? If I was that person in the English room, who gave beauty and grace and common sense and warmth and discipline and guidance, how could I be her – the one you hated so much? The one so despicable and weak and ridden with sickness? What would my student have thought if she had known about me pinned under you in the back of the car – how you stilled yourself within me – raising yourself on your elbows to look – calculating – out of the windows, raising and rearing your head like a lizard over its prey stopping eating and feeding for a second to make sure you wouldn't be disturbed, briefly wary – and so coolly so calmly on your guard when you heard voices outside the car. You were fucking me in the car parked at the pavement with only mist and glass between us and the pavement – the pavement outside the pub where you had wooed me with such devoted clumsy boyish grace. Not even in the car park away from the garden. In plain sight you held me underneath you and I waited as still and silent as a mouse. And how – how could I – how could that – that person – that trapped person be me? I hadn't said no, I hadn't said no – not once I had spellbound done what I was told. And how could that dark devil be you?

I tell you no more about the suffering. I don't want you to crow over it. I tell you no more.

Time passed as is its habit. First the summer when I swelled like a balloon. No nineteenth-century wasting away for me. You'd left me with a horrific pregnancy of bile. I trawled the internet to find an explanation for why I couldn't move. Pip would come and look at me and we took the dog for walks and went to the sea but I was so tired.

We didn't talk about you. We talked about his future and I promised him he would have one. We bought some colouring books and did some colouring in. Adrenal fatigue, cortisol, exhaustion, abusive relationships, coercive control. The dark triad. Sociopath, psychopath, narcissist. Which was it – take your pick – why the fuck did it matter? I ate and drank and slept and all the world around me was parched and beautiful and not at all real. I looked at the sky and it wasn't there, the leaves, my favourite flowers, they didn't exist and I didn't understand them. I pretended to the world but in my head I talked to you.

Pretending became my one occupation. I who had always been so painfully honest. We went on holiday with Richard and Amanda. It was so kind of them. And I pretended I was on holiday with Richard and Amanda and said things that people on holiday say and performed actions that people on holiday perform. They did not discuss you with me. We never spoke of what had happened. I knew they thought badly of me for being involved with you when Pip had been suffering so. So did I – Rob, so did I.

I just wanted to know. Had you left the army years before? All the uniform pictures were taken long before we met. Had you simply had a desk job? Had you ever been in the bunker? Was it an invention – your longing to be a secret spy, your strange childhood fantasy projected onto unwitting me? Was it an army Whitehall desk job? Where did you live – who did you live with? Were any of your constant journeys real? Was I the only one you flattered and fucked and tortured? Into whose mind you pried and preyed? I could not have been the only prize. This was the hardest conclusion to reach because it had felt so absolutely personal what happened between you and me. Your email address had a date two years before you met me. Were there others? Who were they – were they still alive, were they wounded or perhaps they had not been found wanting and you were with one of them happily. No that wasn't right you would never be happy you would always torment that's what you did. You gave your torment to other people and then you went on your way in your perfect clean clothes smelling of flowers with your perfect haircut and your perfect rueful simple expression, advertising your purity and your purpose and your values and your honour and your dependability to whoever would listen. I wanted to rip the mask of flesh off your face I wanted to claw your skin. How had you manufactured the light of understanding in your eyes in the first picture – how had you looked at me so luminously and then thickened your eyes to opaque after that – why why why why why why?

August and I drove to Camberley. I drove to the block of flats – the address you had so stupidly sent me. Unless it had been a dare – but I don't think it was. I had looked up online this place on one of my blank Christmas evenings when we were still nominally together and then forgotten it, in one of my sustained efforts of will to be true to you and forget everything you didn't want me to know or think about..

I trawled for the messages. I knew I shouldn't keep your messages but I did. I didn't read them because it would have made me too frightened to revisit the mind I was in when you'd sent them.

If it would make me a madwoman to drive to these flats in search of the ghost of you then mad I would have to be. Women are always afraid of being thought mad – even worse – thinking it of themselves. Does it make me mad to doubt him? Does it make me mad to do this? Does it make me mad to think that? Oh my dear god no I mustn't be mad. What did I expect to find after my journey? I found nothing but the modern block from Google Maps and couldn't park outside – the way I had imagined gliding into a space and looking up at the bricks and windows – this wasn't the movies. I drove round and round hammering with fear. The building I circled was more prosaic, more ugly even than it had been in the picture but simply and only a low-built façade, unremarkable – no doorbell with a name, no clues. I could have rung the bells, all of them, I could have knocked and hammered, I could have screamed your false name. But I knew you were long gone. Somewhere in the West Country was where you were now. I was sick – dry water into the gutter – before I got back into the car, sick at my own intention and at the fact that your feet had been there once, I knew it, and your hand touched that doorbell that I had gazed at with my straining eyes.

I drove home thinking thinking thinking. You must have lived there. And you did not want me to go there. Either because it was your hole and you kept it private or because there was someone else there. It's strange that until that moment I'd never considered that you were married still, even with all the preposterous limits on your time and the bizarre story of the tree surgeon and the baby – perhaps because the lie was so great and so grotesque and you had told it to me in bed on one of our early happy days that I couldn't countenance its truth. I just could not. I preferred to swallow it. Thank god I hadn't swallowed your sperm.

Time insistently passed and I insistently went on living. Sometimes I was all right but mostly I was out of my mind. You were in it. I imagined you in quiet white oblivion – I tried not to think about where you were, who you were and who you were with, what you were doing and who you were torturing. I tried to relinquish wanting to know the truth. But I could not hide in the plays and books with my students because it was the holidays. It was just me and Pip and the dusty garden and I was mad. I went back to Google and to read all those books that I wouldn't wish on anyone to have to read. Everything you'd done and the actual words you'd said to me were in the books. In these clumsy horrible poorly written books. The banality horrified me. I'd thought you were so unique. That we were. I began to understand what you had done to me: Idealise, Devalue, Discard. The books said it wasn't my fault. But that could not help me – I knew it was. I had invited you in. My shattered life. My last lost innocence. I wanted you to say it – I wanted to hear it from you. I wanted you to admit I wanted you to tell me the damned fucking truth. And I never wanted to see you again. You who haunted me and tunnelled into my brain.

On results day I went into college. The trees in the square were weighty and overblown, waiting for change. The students had done better than ever. I wondered – still wonder – what Luke's results would have been. We did not say this – the head and I. We sat and looked at one another – in her small viewless room.

'How's Pip?' she said. It was a jolt. She'd never asked after him before. I always felt she viewed him as my weakness, my excuse for being late, for not coming in to college, his unhappiness a mark against me. At that moment I did not know if she was being kind or manipulating. I didn't have any sensibility remaining. But she brought Pip into the room with us – Pip who was always left at home, folded in a box like the handkerchief – like the wads of paper with scribbles and typing on them that defined our lives. Direct questions in small rooms are very frightening I find.

'He's doing his best,' I replied, tears I didn't want immediately standing in my eyes. She made some gesture – perhaps looking at her screen. It felt misty in the room.

'As you know, we don't offer scholarships – but I know of another college that does. It's small like ours – small classes – good people. Write to the principal. Mention my name. They might be able to help. I don't doubt he's gifted. I don't doubt it at all.' (*Don't doubt me, you'd said.*). But this might be good – could it be good news? I couldn't wait to tell Pip.

I brought him a cinnamon bun home to celebrate.

'I'll never pass the exam,' he said.

'Of course you will,' I replied. 'You're much cleverer than me.'

The world was empty without you but it was starting to be clean.

And on to another September. This September. The year curled like a shaving from a block of wood. On the way to college – on the bus. Glancing at my phone, I saw a new email: 'I think of you often.' That was all it said.

Three months. It had been three months. Three months in our year of for ever. My heartbeat as fast as a rabbit's – fast with terror – and I had to check that this wasn't an old email that I'd missed – but no you'd sent it right now a second ago while I was on the bus – you existed in time while I was on the bus with strangers and the moving trees – when I thought you had shut all operations down – and why was I so frightened when it was only words and you were nowhere near – but the extraordinary thing was how frightened I was. I did nothing, gazing out of the window as the bus passed a butchers with its whole carcasses and smaller slabs of meat pierced by hooks and hanging in the window. 'I miss you, Butterfly.' Pause. 'And I am so, so sorry.' I did not reply. At least I'd learned that much from you. I began to cry silently like a fool. 'You're everything to me,' you wrote. 'I'm so so sorry.'

I did not answer you.

'He's messaged me,' I texted Paula after Pip had gone to bed.

'This changes nothing, Maddie. Don't answer him.'

But my mind would not stop racing, running, cavorting, spinning, hurdling, sliding away. What if I met you again – what if I forced you – made you tell me the truth. The gauntlet was down – I felt it. Instinct knew it was a call to arms – nothing more or less. I think this is why all of this happened because I had wanted to be getting better – I had wanted to recover and be a proper person and a proper mother and a proper teacher again but you wouldn't let me do that. I knew you weren't really sorry. That could never be. But still I wasn't angry. It was just that same thought – the one I'd had so long: I just want to know.

I waited another hour. It was all I could manage.

'Why are you writing to me?' I wrote.

'I miss you Butterfly. Truly.' This was not the reason, I knew. Narcissists are easily bored and come back for more attention. All the books say so. It's called hoovering – a ridiculously inappropriate term. My turn to say truly but I'd never thought you would come back. Not once. I had believed in my insignificance – there you had succeeded. To you it was only three months – to me it had been purgatory.

And there was more. You returned to my WhatsApp – the glowing eyes, the straight nose, the cap. 'I've been so troubled. It was all my fault.' I'd forgotten how you liked to use that word. Truly. I wondered at your clumsiness. The world had changed for me. You had not changed. Enclosed under the ice of your insanity. You thought this would work. It wouldn't work. I had read all the books.

'It's over,' I wrote.

'I know there's no chance for me now with you. But I've been doing so much thinking. I ask only for a chance to explain. Would you give me that? Please?'

'That won't be necessary,' I messaged. This time I knew I was waving the handkerchief. I knew it would stir you, neat black bull. You couldn't bear not to matter – not to influence, persuade, flatter, deny, destroy. I put my phone on the bedside table quite calm, contemplating in my mind – Bonnard's tree. I didn't feel a thing. When I picked up my phone again, I noticed all my shaking had stopped. My hand was steady.

'I can't stop thinking about you.' You'd left more words out there on the open screen with callous unconcern. 'That I was too hasty. What we've lost. I know you'll never forgive me. I just want to explain.' What had you lost? Your reputation – or so you told me – and I'd lost – almost everything. You wanted another bite of me. 'We could meet. I'm in London often. I'm in London tomorrow.'

Even knowledge could not be worth the ordeal of meeting you. I took a deep breath and wrote, 'No.'

After that nothing. No. Could it be as simple as that?

It was hard to sleep and the next day my legs were weak going to work but there was nothing more from you. You couldn't hurt me – that's what I kept telling myself. Once inside the college building I felt safer – at first shaking when I opened my books and wrote upon the board. But as I walked through the day excitement filled me and a pure release I mistrusted but adored. I had said No. You could not – would not – vanquish me. I could be free.

It was a beautiful afternoon as I stepped out into the square. I bought buns for Pip on the way home. There was a welcome feeling in the flat and I tidied and swept the floor and made a fuss of the animals and crossing the terrace took off my shoes to walk on the grass, being careful not to step on the anthill and the thistles, narrowing my eyes to look up at the slanting light.

As it grew cooler I began to feel a vague sense of unease. Why had you let it be so simple? It wasn't like you. I felt and feared that there would be more. And Pip was late. I started to make spaghetti bolognese – his favourite. Restless I felt and driven by a peculiar energy. He must have gone to the park after school. Perhaps he had made a friend. I messaged, 'Where are you?' Pip was quick to answer messages and I thought immediately of the gangs outside the school and the warnings and the knives. Mothers always think of things like that I heard your voice say. Of course he was safe. It was broad daylight.

I turned my silent setting off and began to pace – unease returning. And then a sound and message. 'I'll be home soon.' This was unlike Pip who always told me exactly where he was. I began to feel sick. 'Where are you?' I messaged again. No answer. I didn't know what to do. 'How much longer will you be?' Still nothing. 'Pip! This is important. You're scaring me.' But it seemed Pip did not care about that. I called and it went straight to message so I waited on the sofa clutching Puppy.

I heard Pip's key in the lock as the sun was setting, drenching our glass-eyed room with orange heat and light. I was sweating.

'Oh my god – Pip – where were you?'

He lifted his chin to look at me with a strange wary look and said, 'I met Rob.'

'You did what?'

'I met Rob,' he said again.

'That's a really bad joke.' I replied.

'It's not,' said Pip – calm, defiant. 'It's what happened.'

You remember it – don't you Rob – everything you said and did.

I stared at him. He said nothing further. 'What are you talking about? I don't understand. Are you telling me the truth?'

'Didn't you always tell me the truth was what we owed to ourselves, Ma?' He said this with unexpected challenge.

I could barely breathe. 'Just tell me what happened.'

'He was waiting for me outside school. On the other side of the road. He stands so straight, doesn't he?'

I said nothing. Just stared at him.

'He seemed to recognise me. Crossed over and was very polite. He asked me my name and introduced himself. We shook hands. He was really nice. Looked me right in the eye. Not strange – not how I'd imagined him at all. At first, I said I couldn't talk to him – because of how he'd treated you – and he just said he wanted to know if I was OK because the last year must have been hard on me.'

'What are you talking about?'

'He said it had been hard on him too. That what had happened had been a lot. That you were a lot.' I just stood there staring at him. 'He said we both knew you were a lot but we both loved you. And he wanted to see you again but you wouldn't speak to him.'

I felt I was suffocating. 'This was all outside the school gates?'

'No, we went to the park. He bought me an ice cream.'

'He bought you a fucking ice cream? You know he's a complete lunatic, don't you? That he nearly destroyed me?'

Pip surveyed me. 'Mum. There are two sides to every story aren't there? Another of your teachings.'

'But you remember – when Luke—?'

Pip continued to stare at me as if he wasn't Pip. There was a horrible pause.

'All you cared about was Luke, Mum. I was nearly dying if you remember. Your actual child.'

Some obscure part of me watching this knew that the more I argued with him the worse it would be but I couldn't stop. 'He's a liar.'

'He told me he'd always wanted to meet me – he'd heard how clever I was – he wanted me to meet his boys, and you didn't—'

'This is what he does, Pip. He flatters. He lies.'

'You left me out – you only wanted to be with him.'

'You didn't want to have anything to do with him!'

'You haven't had a great track record since you left Dad. You could have tried harder to persuade me.'

I was drowning. 'I know you're angry with me – I know you being so low must have been partly that – but please, Pip – don't take his side.'

'That's a really babyish thing to say, Mum.'

We were still standing opposite one another – Pip and I.

I remembered after what seemed a long time looking at him that it was you I was dealing with – not Pip.

'What did he want?'

'I don't know. Nothing. He wants us to meet – all three

of us. He said it could be a new start for us all.' Fight or flight is a lie, Rob. I couldn't move.

Pip turned and walked away.

I went back into the garden and sat on the wall. It was quite cold. I knew I was angry because I was no longer afraid. I was filled with rage so perfect and pure that I no longer thought in thoughts only images. The anger streamed from my gut and into every blood vessel of my body as I saw Pip in the incubator they put him in on the first night of his life. I saw him holding my hand as he struggled to walk. The look of concentration on his face as he held the pencil when he was learning to write. I saw him kneeling down to hug our puppy when we'd gone to choose her. I saw myself looking through the bars of the school gates at his sorrowful back; I saw myself bundling him into the car the night we left his father. All the battles I'd fought for him. I saw him next to me on the sofa with his tub of ice cream, so tall and grown looking at me with his kind eyes and I choked with rage. I could barely breathe with it. Pip was the one true thing. He was the only thing that mattered and you were not going to hurt him. My breath was ragged. Now there was only one word. Enough.

We ate dinner in silence and I tried to control my shaking body so Pip would not know about the anger. All the time I was thinking how I would do it – how I would catch you and corner you and hurt you so you would never be able to come back – not ever again. I remembered the little Swiss Army knife still in the cutlery drawer.

Pip went to have a bath and I went back into the garden and messaged you.

'I hear you saw Pip today.'

You answered straightaway. 'Yes!' Heart emoji. As if it was all perfectly normal. 'What a wonderful young man.' The shaking came back. It was my whole body shuddering. I could barely hold the phone to read the words. Then another ping – it was a selfie of you both. I tasted bile. Pip looked ill at ease but not unhappy and was trying to smile. You looked different. Even after three months. Your mouth pressed together in a thin line.

'Yes. I think so.'

'I know you worry about him a lot. If you like – I could help. I'm good with young men.' Calm came over me. Of course. The men.

Without hesitation I typed, 'Why don't we meet first? Just us. Could be awkward with Pip straight off.'

'Seriously?'

'Yes. I was hasty earlier. Surprised to hear from you.'

A celebration emoji. Then a butterfly. 'I can never stop thinking about you.'

'How about a picnic?' I'd need time to plan it. It had to be somewhere out of the way. 'We'd be by ourselves. Talk.'

'Great.' It was a pantomime conversation where you pretended to be the ardent suitor and I the flustered object of desire. It was a parody. It had always been a parody and a part of me had always known.

The place in the wood was arranged. You weren't suspicious. Do you understand the circularity of it now, Rob? *Wisdom comes at the end. Remember it.* I'd had time to choose it – you said I could choose anywhere I liked because you were so sorry and you wanted everything to be all right with us. I remember some part of my mind thinking perhaps the quarry in Bristol had bored you after all. And also why weren't you seeing your boys – but all these things felt remote. I'd looked at my map. I have a real old-fashioned paper map of England and I consulted it carefully to find this particular wood. You'd think I'd be afraid of woods but I knew it was the only place. I had been there long ago with Pip. We'd got lost in the dark on an overambitious walk but we had been merry. It would be familiar – and it would be private – it would be wild. I'd have to go there before we met – to pick the exact spot. I who never prepared for anything would survey the ground. You would never expect that of me. I would not leave it to chance. Planning is everything. *They aren't people. They're the enemy.* It was for Pip – you understand. I did not tell him where I was going. He would not have liked it at all.

I was there first and I waited in the car. It was surprisingly easy to get out once I saw your car passing mine, drawing up carefully almost out of sight. I wasn't even frightened. You walked towards me from the bend in the road.

'Maddie?' You looked so small. Neatly turned out as ever. I wondered what I'd ever seen in you – I choose that expression carefully – and I began to tremble. You strode towards me all confidence and bravado in exactly the same way as when we'd first met. But I had supplied the grace – you were only brutal. We stood opposite one another, on our marks in the green English lane, the leaves dry gold and waiting to turn. *And song and friends and ever you with smiling and familiar eyes, you but faithful, you, but true.* If they ever scoop out the contents of my head and weigh my brain the only thing they will find is quotes.

'So good of you to meet me again,' you said. I'd forgotten – the old-fashioned speech, the lilting cadence – as if you'd taught yourself to be a person from reading books. Or was that me? I knew I was meant to respond but I was completely blank except for the feeling of falling.

'Hello,' I said – smiled, shielded my eyes from the imaginary slanting sun – pretending – it was low but not blinding me – holding my hand against my forehead like a visor.

'We should get out of the road,' you said, putting your hand out to take my elbow and guide me. Of course that would be what you would do – take charge.

I stepped back. 'I don't think anyone comes here much, but yes.'

'Same car, I see,' you said. It hadn't been that long – what did you expect? Or perhaps you changed your car all the time.

'Yes.' Without glancing at you I knew you would be scanning the terrain, the stunted horizon, the entries and escapes. 'I'll get the picnic.' It was in the wicker basket with the leather buckle, remnant-relic of Pip's childhood, its shape awkward and unwieldy. All the other mothers had had plastic ones with zips, ready waiting always, wiped clean, stored away. Inside the picnic basket along with the drinks, bread, cheese and strawberries was Pip's pen knife, wrapped in your handkerchief.

'Let me help you.'

'It's all right.' I didn't want you anywhere near me, anywhere near the basket, anywhere near the car.

'You didn't bring Puppy.' I'd forgotten you knew the nickname of my dog – that you ever knew her at all. She loved you. She loved everybody.

'She'd only have got in the way.' Turning again to face you.

'Everythin' all right? You seem on edge.' Your voice, expression – frank, open, boyish. Your eyes intent. Your eyes.

'No – I'm fine. Really.' There was no harm in you thinking me flustered after all. 'It's just odd, isn't it? – so much to say and here we are with a picnic. Doesn't feel real.'

More coolly, 'It was your idea.'

‘I know.’ Straining to smile again.

‘You look beautiful by the way.’ Of course, of course you’d say that. You’d always say that. But I knew I had no beauty left. ‘You said you knew a spot.’ You must have felt quite confident, or desperate perhaps, something I’d never considered, because it had always been you who had chosen the places where we met.

‘Yes. I’ll take you.’

You were behind me now and so I called over my shoulder, blindly and as if it were all all right, ‘It’s not far.’ Light slanted through the trees and it could have been celestial but it was sad. It was lonely and quiet and I felt cold. I could not stop shaking. My legs were watery – above the knees where the strength was.

‘Seems a shame to be going into the dark on such a beautiful day.’

‘I thought you liked the woods,’ I said. And still the thumping of my heart, the hammering. I remembered what had happened, that fatal day. I knew you were remembering it too.

I found the clearing. I could see directly to the line of the wide open field on the other side, where the wood ended, but not the road and the car we had come from and left behind. There was not even a lonely plane in the sky, not a cloud, not a bird. Just a strange quiet. I spread the rug. You watched me.

‘I brought the beer you like.’ You sat quietly, your back against the ridges of the old and sturdy tree.

‘Why are we here?’ you said. ‘I mean – really?’

You didn’t smile. I knelt down on the rug – opposite you. My body didn’t feel a thing.

‘I don’t know what to call you.’

‘Call me what you’ve always called me. Nothing’s changed.’

‘All right.’ And after a little pause, ‘Rob.’ Rob wasn’t

there any longer – he had been our own peculiar creation. 'It's because—' I hesitated. 'You said you wanted to explain.'

And with all your old directness, 'Do you want to know if I still love you?'

'No.'

'Because I do by the way. I always will.' I wondered vaguely how long you would persist with this and still it wakened a shadow of all the old make-believe.

'It's because I want to know why. I don't understand. I need to be clear.'

You nodded, curt. (Did I really think you'd tell me anything? Did I ever really think you'd allow me the dignity of an explanation?)

You said, 'Why I've come back? Because I want you. I've always wanted – everything you are. You have no idea of – how I—' It would be a sob story. I couldn't bear it.

'And what about the others?' My heart rammed itself against my ribs.

'There were never any others. There was only ever you.'

I wanted to cry with rage. I wanted the Furies to come and pluck out your eyes.

People don't make up false names and go on the internet and lie and lie and lie only once do they? It must be compulsive – there had to be others – to maintain the high. On the rug was the picnic basket, between us. I moved it so that it was behind me then carefully opened it and pretended my eyes weren't blind. There were the little paper plates left over from some birthday of Pip's – ready to be watered by my tears: the napkins, the things I'd bought, lying there. They were so banal. I felt for the knife concealed. You watched me – taking it all in. I didn't want you to think I had concealed it, concealed anything. You hated that – you needed your victims to be open like mussels when they come out of the pan.

'Are you hungry yet?' I asked.

'No.' You said it with the same vehemence and determination that I'd always found so charming. It was a discovery you were delighted to share with me.

I didn't know how to sit, how to arrange my body. So I stayed kneeling opposite you and you shifted to the same forward movement and we were mirrored.

'You're shaking,' you said, with a little delicate frown. 'Perhaps this wasn't such a good idea.'

'It's just—' I said.

'Maddie, look at me.' I couldn't. You dropped your voice. 'Please.' I knew I had to look at you. 'I'm so sorry. Really. I'm so sorry. Doubt everything about me but never how much I've loved you.' I kept looking. Sorry for how angry I was that day – the things I messaged. It was wrong of me.' This was peculiar. You never usually referred to the past. 'I couldn't be what you needed. I've seen too much death. Everywhere I go there has been tragedy,' you said. 'But I never wanted it for you. I was no good for you.' How I wanted to scream then.

'Please – there's no need.'

'Our time together was beautiful,' you said. Oh, the deep velvet eyes. Had you forgotten your vicious cruelty, the callous reckless violent way you left me – twice – the horrible things you'd said? Your crazy action with Pip? 'I've had a lonely life,' you said. 'I simply wanted – to be loved. But you were too fragile for me. I couldn't carry you.' This was a lie that was partially true. Here you paused for me to say something.

'I know.' This too was a lie that was partially true. It was hard to say without nausea. I couldn't stand it. I couldn't stand the talking: trite phrase after trite phrase – the same disgusting mess and mass of murdered words.

'Where did you really live?'

'Barracks. I told you.' Blank eyes.

'Were you married?'

'No.' You didn't flinch but I knew – just as I always had – that you were angry.

Your denials did their work though. Although they did not achieve your intended objective. My anger too was building. I began to inhabit my body. 'Let's have a drink.'

Rueful smile. 'Good idea.' I turned to the basket. I checked again for the position of the knife. I'd packed your beer in a cool jacket and pale pink rose cordial disguised as wine for me because I didn't want to be even a little drunk for this final scene. 'Tradition,' you said. 'Mmm'. We clinked metal and glass together and I wondered if I had started to dream. 'So tell me. How's Pip?'

'Pip's all right. He enjoyed meeting you.' I forced those words.

'I'm sorry if I – I thought maybe he could get through to you more than I could.'

I said nothing for a little minute – trying to breathe. Then again – 'Please could I have some answers now?

Your eyes began to blacken and darken. 'Why? Why should it matter?'

'I have to know, Rob. If there's ever to be a chance for us. I have to know.'

You kept staring. 'How strange this is,' you said. And it was true the world was tilting. The wood was real – the woods were the only thing that had ever been real.

'I bet you've never told anyone how clever you are,' I said – without very much conviction.

'Trying to flatter me? Clever girl.' And there it was – the flash out of your eyes of exactly where we truly were.

Not all that clever, it seemed.

I expected the tears you would often use but they didn't fall.

'I was afraid you wouldn't love me if you knew everything about me.'

'I don't believe you.' I think that made you more angry. We were both shaking – leaning closer.

And then you said it. 'You need to know nothing. You are nothing. I did it because I could. You stupid bitch.'

And you lunged at me. The sound that came out of me was not a sound I knew any human could make. My arms went out. My hands on you – pushing your stomach and chest. And the sound I made. I cannot describe. Nor the sound of your head against the tree – I'll never forget that sound or how it happened – how I could have had the strength – and how immediate the silence that followed and how leaning over you I saw no wound just your white face. And you were so quiet. I was afraid to touch you. I watched you for quite a long time before scrabbling for the knife, loosening it from the handkerchief. I had been going to wait for you to fall asleep – that was what I'd planned. But here you were utterly in my power – still breathing your eyes closed.

Lying against that wise old tree you seemed a boy asleep – a boy again. I stared at you – wondered at your eyelashes so long on your cheek almost as I had when we first met – and quivering – felt the anger leave my body – felt so much sorrow. Pip's face sleeping lay beside yours on the floor of the wood, while Pip's pen knife was gripped in my hand. I closed my other hand around it for better purchase. I had you. I had means, motive and opportunity. Now was the moment to execute you properly – to have what no court of law would ever give me. What right had you to life, to harm and crush the souls of others because it gave you satisfaction? I will have satisfaction – that's what revengers think.

There is a time to live and a time to die they had said at Luke's funeral – what a cliché it was but somebody had wanted those words. You had killed my soul and taken everything. And what other souls had you murdered – were murdering, right now, yesterday, tomorrow, for all time? These thoughts weren't conscious, they reverberated in my mind, in the walls of it and tissues of my body. I looked at you fallen and very peaceful. And I missed you and began to be afraid. I had not expected to mourn or grieve or miss you. It was the most extraordinary thing. I couldn't do it. I am not a killer. I am not the creature who leaves another to die. That is you. That is what you do. I sat down at your feet and waited. The strange trance came.

When I came to myself and you were not there – I was very frightened. The wood was full of life and I did not know where you were. There was confusion. I was imprisoned in it but after breathing I could see quite clearly out and what the right thing was to do – tell the police what I had done – that I'd killed you and you were dead and gone.

A wood pigeon whirled up out of the darkening trees into the light at the top of the trees into the light of the sky. I heard these loud sounds compete with my thrumming ears, eyes fixed on retracing the path we had taken, longing for the silver clean gleam of the car and above it the darkened sky.

I went to the police station all clear in my mind like a glass ball.

You know the rest of it. I began with it. I've been waiting at Paula's – in her son's room with the Union Jack flag on the wall and the insistent streetlights outside – waiting for you to come back. You always come back. I saw you in that glass ball and I began to write to you in my head. You who have no name. You who loved your lies.

I have been writing this with eyes open not moving for a time that has not told me itself. In that time the police called and spoke to Paula and they confirmed that no trace of you, nor of the car I had described, nor anyone answering your description in the vicinity had been found and I am not surprised. Such a resourceful fox. How could you be found if you were never real.

'You were confused, Maddie – you were in shock – and that's all,' said Paula. 'I'm just so grateful you're all right.'

I looked at her and from somewhere I said, 'Yes.'

Richard came to pick me up from Paula's – my dog dancing beside him – and for once it felt as if there were no judgement nor defiance nor apology nor confession. 'I'm just so happy to see you,' he said. 'Paula has told me some of the things. I'd had no idea.'

In the car he settled me – securing the seat belt, covering me with a blanket and putting Puppy on my lap. 'I've had a long talk with Pip,' he said not looking at me. 'He feels a fool.'

I gazed out of the window at the empty featureless land. 'He mustn't. I should never have terrified him.'

'It wasn't your fault, Maddie,' he said. 'I was too hard on you. It was all . . . I'm so sorry. We will talk about it when you're better. We will make things right. Things will be better.'

He pulled the car blanket higher over me and Puppy. I clutched her tighter and fell asleep.

I cannot say it is over. You are always with me and I have tried to write you – Rob/Jacob because I wish that you – the real living you – whoever you are – had not ever touched my life and washed it in blood and shame because I made a vain and foolish decision one summer afternoon.

In some moods on some days between the nightmares it is all right – not knowing. A knowledge as firm and complete as an apple. I hold on to the real. I hold on to all that is alive and good before the next nightmare – the next terror breaks. If this is ever read – if my mind is ever read – whoever reads it remember – in this veiled, lying labyrinthine life – please – hold on to the one true thing you know.

Epilogue

PIP and I stand together on the corner of High Street Kensington and a narrow cul-de-sac, a bookshop on the corner. It is drizzling. I turn and look over my shoulder, scanning the people walking behind just to make sure none of them are you. I do this everywhere – it's as instinctive as breathing. On the streets – walking in the park I'm afraid – if any jogger comes running towards me, that it is you – come to kill me. More than once I have been certain. Because the one thing about you is that you always come back. I do not tell anyone this. I tell myself it will pass. You would never take the risk.

'I'm glad we bought this before the interview,' Pip is saying – holding a book of poetry firm in his hand. 'Thank you, Mum.'

I smile. 'It'll give you something to talk about too. Remember how nice they are. How much you liked them. Do you want me to come in with you?'

'No. It was good you were there for the exam but not this time. I can do it.'

'All right. Message me when you're finished. It's going to be great.'

He stands so tall so pale and so determined with his

thoughtful eyes. 'See you in a minute, Mum.'

'I'll be waiting.'

I watch him walk away – the ghost of you behind me.

Acknowledgments

I am forever grateful for the continued support of the Royal Literary Fund, Clare Conville and Laurence and Stacey Mutkin. To my colleagues at The Authors' Collective, I am proud to be publishing with you. My thanks, as always, are due to Catherine Farmer, Louie Fooks and Isabel Lloyd. This book would not have been possible without you, or my two sons Edward and Thomas.

The poem 'Invictus' was written by William Ernest Henley (1849-1903).

About the Author

Melissa Jones was born in London and educated at Westminster and Oxford. She worked in film and TV before becoming a writer. She lives in East Sussex and has two children. This is her fourth novel.

For more about her work, visit melissajoneswriter.com

Also by Melissa Jones

Cold in Earth

Sick at Heart

The Hidden Heart of Emily Hudson

www.ingramcontent.com/pod-product-compliance
Ingram Content Group UK Ltd.
Pitfield, Milton Keynes, MK11 3LW, UK
UKHW042047150326
469009UK00003B/2705

9 781068 527326